Bello:
hidden talent rediscovered

Bello is a digital-only imprint of Pan Macmillan,
established to breathe new life into previously published,
classic books.

At Bello we believe in the timeless power of the imagination,
of a good story, narrative and entertainment, and we want to
use digital technology to ensure that many more readers
can enjoy these books into the future.

We publish in ebook and print-on-demand formats
to bring these wonderful books to new audiences.

www.panmacmillan.co.uk/bello

Richmal Crompton

Richmal Crompton (1890–1969) is best known for her thirty-eight books featuring William Brown, which were published between 1922 and 1970. Born in Lancashire, Crompton won a scholarship to Royal Holloway in London, where she trained as a schoolteacher, graduating in 1914, before turning to writing full-time. Alongside the *William* novels, Crompton wrote forty-one novels for adults, as well as nine collections of short stories.

Richmal Crompton

STEFFAN GREEN

First published 1940 by Macmillan

This edition published 2015 by Bello
an imprint of Pan Macmillan
20 New Wharf Road, London N1 9RR
Basingstoke and Oxford
Associated companies throughout the world

www.panmacmillan.co.uk/bello

ISBN 978-1-5098-1033-8 EPUB
ISBN 978-1-5098-1031-4 HB
ISBN 978-1-5098-1032-1 PB

A CIP catalogue record for this book is available from the British Library.

Typeset by Ellipsis Digital Limited, Glasgow

Chapter One

THE road wound down the hill, swerved sharply, and dived into a wood. Obviously it wasn't a high road any longer. She must have gone wrong at the fork. She stopped and wondered whether to turn and go back. A few moments ago she had been intent on getting to Dorrie's as quickly as possible, and now quite suddenly it didn't seem to matter whether she got to Dorrie's or not. In any case Dorrie wasn't expecting her. She might even be away from home. When she came to think of it, she usually was away at this time of the year. She'd set out on a crazy impulse, thinking that Dorrie would be able to help her, knowing at the bottom of her heart that no one in the whole world would be able to help her. Dorrie, solid, matter-of-fact, conscientious, conventional . . . no, she wouldn't understand.

She had dreamed of Dorrie last night and, awaking from an uneasy unrefreshing sleep, had decided to go to her and ask her advice. Good old Dorrie . . . so kind, so dependable, so good-hearted. . . . And off she'd started, compelled by that mysterious force that had made her for the last few weeks like a marionette dancing at the end of invisible strings. "Go to Dorrie," the strings had said, and she'd gone obediently, driving blindly along the roads, hardly knowing what she was doing. It was a wonder she hadn't had an accident. She remembered someone's shouting at her as she went through a small country town. Perhaps she had had an accident. Perhaps she'd killed someone on the road. She wouldn't have known if she had done. . . .

It was a warm day, but little gusts of shivering swept through her body, making her teeth chatter. Her nerves had been going to pieces for some time, of course. . . . Well, what was she to do now? She waited for some command from the mechanical force that had ordered her doings for the past few weeks, but none came. She glanced at the clock on the dashboard. Half-past three. . . . She must do something. She wondered if she had had any lunch. She couldn't remember. No, she was almost sure she hadn't. She dropped her hands from the steering wheel and looked about her. Trunks of silver birches rose like shining slender pillars from a golden floor of bracken. Here and there in the tangled undergrowth a bramble leaf showed vivid red. A stream rippled in a winding course through the wood, disappeared under the road, and reappeared on the other side. It had rained in the night, and the stream was full. It burbled noisily and exuberantly, impatient of its narrow bed. The sound of it broke the heavy silence with an effect of incongruous impertinent gaiety. A sense of unreality invaded her, as if she and the wood were part of a dream. . . . She took herself in hand, tightening her lips and trying to control the spasms of trembling that shook her from head to foot. Pull yourself together, she admonished herself sternly. You're letting your nerves get the better of you. You know where that leads. You've seen it in other people. You've always said that there's a point at which they can tackle it themselves, and, once they let it get beyond that point, they're done for. Well, you can tackle it yourself at this point, and if you don't you know where it will lead you. . . . It's with not sleeping properly, she excused herself, but almost simultaneously brushed the excuse aside. Nonsense! Get some stronger stuff. . . . It's with yesterday, she excused herself further, and had no answer to that but a sharp, Don't, Don't. . . .

She started up the engine and looked round again. No use going to Dorrie's in this state, even if Dorrie were at home. She'd been mad even to think of it. But she felt oddly reluctant to go back to the empty flat, with so many of Harvey's things about, things that he hadn't taken with him and that she hadn't had the heart to turn out. Still, there was nothing else to do. She couldn't wander about the countryside all night. She would just go to the end of the wood. She remembered the fascination that woods had had for her when she was a child. She always wanted to "get to the other side." And the "other side"—the country one reached through a wood—had always seemed in some way quite different from the country one had left behind, endued with some magical quality she could never explain.

The road curved sharply, now this way, now that. It had probably been a path through the wood at first, winding among the trees, then a track along which the pack-ponies went. Then they'd widened it bit by bit. Even now it was barely wide enough for two cars to pass each other. It described a wide sweep around a beech tree whose branches hung right across the road, forming a golden tunnel.

The wood came to an abrupt end, and the lane wound between low hedges with fields on either side. She stopped the car again, loath to go on. There had been a curious element of protection in the shade of the wood. It was as if, emerging into the open country, she was once more at the mercy of life and its cruelty. She could still hear the rippling of the little stream behind her. Muted by the distance, it seemed to hold a note of tender melancholy beneath its gaiety.

Better turn now and go back. But the road just here was too narrow for turning. She'd go on till it widened or till she came to a field gate. A church tower over a cluster of trees proclaimed a village a mile or so ahead. She went on slowly. The nervous energy that had sustained her all day seemed to be ebbing, and a leaden weariness pressed down on her. Then, at a sudden bend in the road, she came upon the village – a square green, with a few shops and houses set round it, and in the middle a chestnut tree, its massive trunk encircled by a wooden seat. A narrow road ran round the three sides of the green, then rejoined the main road. She could turn by driving round the green. The first side consisted of a post office that was also a general shop, a small butcher's, and a blacksmith's. The second . . . A wave of faintness swept over her and she stopped the car. What a fool she was not to have had some lunch on the way! She noticed mechanically and with faint relief that she had drawn up outside a cottage on which hung a sign "To Let." Her stopping there could arouse no curiosity even in this out-of-the-way place. She would stay till the faintness passed, then go home as quickly as she could. She bent her head down, and the mist of faintness gradually cleared. Raising her head, her eyes caught the words Pear Tree Cottages No. 1 on the small green gate. Next was another cottage with Pear Tree Cottages No. 2 on the gate. Probably they had once been a small row of cottages – now divided into two. Long, low, of mellowed red brick. Fifteenth century, she guessed. A narrow garden in front was enclosed by a green painted fence. The other cottage was occupied. Curtains of spotted muslin hung at the window. Beyond it, also overlooking the green, was a small compact Georgian house that seemed to hold itself aloof in conscious superiority. It had Nottingham lace curtains, a fern at each window, and the name Eastnor carved in Gothic letters on the gate.

Suddenly she saw a girl standing at an upstairs window of the other cottage, watching her. She couldn't stay here much longer, of course, but she still felt reluctant to go. The quiet serenity of the wood seemed to brood over the little place. She wondered vaguely what it was called. She would look at the post office on her way back. She ought to stop somewhere and get something to eat, too, though at the thought of food a feeling of nausea came over her. . . .

She had switched on the ignition and was just putting her finger to the starting-button, when the girl who had been watching her from the upstairs window opened the front door and came down to the gate. She was young and sophisticated-looking, her dark hair done in the fashionable bunch of curls on the top of her head, her lips coloured an unconvincing almost defiant shade of scarlet. She wore a grey sweater and a pair of navy-blue slacks, which she hitched up about her thin figure as she came down to the gate.

"I'm afraid the key's at the agent's in Beverton," she said, "but he left one with us in case people came to look over it."

She spoke curtly and without smiling.

"The key?" said Lettice vaguely. Then, "Oh, I see. . . . The house. No, I wasn't——"

"You might as well look round," said the girl, still in that curt,

4

business-like way. "There's nothing wrong with it. Not like ours. Ours was in the foulest mess you ever saw when we took it."

"Thanks so much," said Lettice, "but I was only—"

Then she stopped.

At first she couldn't think why she wanted to stay, for a few minutes at any rate, with this somewhat abrupt young woman. Then she realised. This woman – didn't know. It was so long since she had talked to a woman without seeing gloating pity in her eyes, hearing it in the tone of her voice. The more sympathetic they were, the more they gloated. Even Dorrie, trusted old friend as she was, would all unconsciously have gloated. It seemed to restore a little of her self-respect to be with someone who didn't know.

"I'll get the key," the young woman was saying. "It won't take a minute."

She disappeared into the cottage and reappeared a moment afterwards carrying an old-fashioned key and smoking a cigarette.

"The garden's a bit run to seed," she said, "but the house is quite shipshape. It's only been empty a few weeks. A dear old soul called Mrs. Kipps lived here. She only left because her daughter's husband died and she went to live with her. . . . She kept everything as clean as a new pin. Why is a new pin supposed to be cleaner than a new anything else?"

"I don't know," said Lettice.

She opened the door of her car and stepped out onto the road.

"My name's Lydia Morrice," said the girl. "My husband and I have only been here two months. We nearly moved to this cottage after Mrs. Kipps left, but, when it came to the point, it was too much fag. And we'd sweated blood getting our own to rights. It seemed sort of mean to leave it just when we'd made it almost habitable."

She opened the garden gate, and Lettice entered the garden.

"The real gardens are at the back, of course," went on the girl. "The garden *is* in a bit of a mess, as I told you, but that makes it all the more interesting, don't you think? I mean, a garden can't get filthy like a house, if it's neglected. Gosh! you should have seen ours. *Thick* with dirt!"

She turned the key in the lock, and Lettice followed her into a little hall. At the end a narrow staircase with slender balusters ran abruptly out of sight, and a door opened from it on either side of the front door.

"Dining-room . . . Parlour or lounge or whatever you like to call it. Blessedly simple, these old cottages. Kitchen just there by the staircase. The old dame adored her kitchen. It's quite up to date. Electric light. These small windows make the room a bit dark, of course, but one gets used to that. I wanted to have a bay thrown out, but Philip – that's my husband – foamed at the mouth when I suggested the idea. He said it would take away its character. You can do what you like at the back apparently, as long as you keep the front as God made it. As a matter of fact the man who originally converted them (I always imagine him in a Salvation Army hat) built out a room at the back into the garden with a bay that gets quite a lot of sun. I use it for the nursery."

"You've got a baby?" said Lettice, without much interest.

"Yes, worse luck!" said the girl. "It's a ghastly bore."

The two front rooms were small, with low ceilings, lattice windows, and basket fire-grates. The walls were distempered cream, and there were deep window seats in the thickness of the walls.

"They were built to last till Doomsday, of course," said the girl. "I find that rather helpful. I mean, when you think of all the people who've lived in it and all the dramas it must have witnessed, one feels it's silly to worry if the milk turns sour or the fishmonger doesn't come round. New houses are apt to fuss with one when things go wrong, but old ones make one feel a fool for worrying. . . . I hope that's not whimsical. I hate whimsey."

Lettice smiled. It was the first time she had smiled for a long time.

"No," she said, "I think it's quite sensible."

The kitchen was stone-floored and very tiny. Gas stove, dresser, and sink took up nearly all the room.

The walls were painted blue, and a church calendar, depicting

Abraham on the point of sacrificing Isaac, under the sardonic gaze of a ram who bore a striking likeness to Mr. Gladstone, still hung between dresser and doorway.

"The old dame who had it before you" (Lettice made a quick disclaimer, but the girl went on as though she hadn't noticed) "adored her kitchen. She pottered about here all day. She seemed to be always making jam and pastry. She made it just for the sake of making it. I believe that she buried it in the garden at night to get rid of it so that she could start making a fresh lot the next morning. She's the only person I've ever known who kept the right things in the right tins. You know, sugar and salt and tea. . . . Here's the "built-on" room.

The "built-on" room was not much larger than the other rooms, but the bay window made it lighter. It had a parquet floor and a low brick fireplace.

"The old dame hardly ever used this room. She didn't like the parquet. She said it was new-fangled. Besides, she said there was nothing to see. She liked to sit in the front and watch the green. . . . That's the garden – what there is of it."

Lettice stood in the bay window and looked down the tangled neglected garden. A rickety wooden fence divided it from the next-door garden and was itself divided in the middle by the trunk of a tall tree that stood between the gardens and overshadowed them both. At the bottom a small wooden gate stood open onto a narrow lane. A sudden gust of wind sent a shower of russet leaves floating down through the air.

"That's the pear tree," said the girl. "They say it's wonderful in spring. It's the biggest for miles round. I like the way they've given us half each, don't you? Now come and see the upstairs."

"No, really," said Lettice. "It's not fair to put you to all this trouble when I'm not——"

But the girl was already half-way up the stairs.

"You can't see the sky through the windows in the bedrooms unless you're lying in bed," she said. "I wouldn't get used to it at first. I rather like it now."

They came downstairs to the little gate a few minutes later, and the girl immediately opened the gate of the other cottage.

"You must have tea before you go," she said. "I was just going to make it."

Lettice hesitated. The prospect of the long drive home oppressed her as if it had been some tremendous undertaking needing more energy than she had in her to summon. She was glad to postpone it and to stay a little longer with this girl, to whom she was an ordinary casual passer-by – not an object of contemptuous pity.

"Thanks . . ." she said vaguely.

The room into which her hostess led her was furnished with unstained wood. Doors and skirting board, too, were unstained.

"We sweated blood getting the paint off the doors," the girl was saying. "And we had to get through inches of dirt before we reached the paint. Miss Pendleton, the old bird who had it before us, lived all her life in it, but the concern her money was in had failed and she lived here for years on about a loaf a week. Never went out. Took to drink at the end, though I don't know how she found the money to buy it, and never touched the place by the look of it. It was simply filthy. Then she crocked up, and they took her off in an ambulance to a cousin's a few miles away. They didn't think she'd live, but she's a tough old guy, and they say she's getting over it now. Sit down. I'll bring in the tea in half a sec. The brat's still asleep. . . ."

Lettice leant back in her chair, fighting the stupor of exhaustion that was stealing over her. All she wanted to do was to sleep . . . if only there weren't the waking up. Despite the weariness of her long nights, she dreaded sleeping, because of the sick realisation that waking brought with it. Sometimes she would look round instinctively for Harvey, and then – knowledge would engulf her in wave upon black wave. It was unbearable to have to face it afresh each morning. Sometimes by night she had almost steeled herself to it, but when morning came sleep had washed the memory of it away and it was all to do again. . . .

The girl entered with a tray, which she set down on the little round table in front of the window seat.

"Housekeeping's not too bad here," she said. "Tradesmen come out from Beverton, and you can get eggs and butter from Crewe Farm."

Lettice said nothing. The memory of Harvey's face had suddenly become cruelly vivid – the laughing creases at the corners of his grey eyes, the faint smile that lurked always in the curves of his well-formed mouth, the cleft in his chin. She fought for self-control, biting her lips to keep them steady, but, despite all her efforts, tears began to course down her cheeks. She covered her face with her hands.

The girl stared at her.

"I'm sorry," said Lettice in a choking voice. "It's – nerves, I suppose. . . . I had no lunch."

"What time did you have breakfast?" said the girl in a matter-of-fact voice.

"I don't think I had any," said Lettice.

The girl handed her a cup of tea.

"Have a rock cake. They ought to be sustaining enough if heaviness counts for anything. I made them myself. . . ."

"I've just divorced my husband," said Lettice unsteadily. She had herself in hand now and was wiping the tears away with quick furtive dabs of her handkerchief. "I got the decree nisi yesterday. I had to stand in the witness-box and tell them all the foul things he'd ever done to me. Things I'd kept from my best friends. I didn't want to, but my solicitor made me. He didn't want the judge to think it was one isolated case. They're always afraid of – collusion, they call it."

The girl nodded.

"I know. . . . Did you love him?"

"Terribly. I still do. There doesn't seem enough of me left to go on living now he's gone. I can't believe he'll never come back. I was so sure that he loved me – in spite of everything. When I found that he didn't, I felt as if I'd been killed. I wish I had been killed. The worst of everything is to have to go on living."

"Why did you divorce him, then?"

"I had to. He said he wasn't coming back to me in any case."

9

She spoke in a low jerky voice, twisting her handkerchief between her fingers. "He'd always had – affairs. He said that they didn't mean anything, and I know that in a way they didn't. I didn't know that this was – different. I didn't know about this at all till it had been going on for months. Every one else knew, of course. I disliked the woman, and I thought that Harvey disliked her. I used to make fun of her. I could do a rather good imitation of her, and I was terribly gratified when my friends laughed at it. I didn't know the cream of the joke, of course. I used to imitate her to Harvey, too, and he used to laugh. I supposed it amused him as much as the others to think that I didn't know. ... You see, he was the only man in the world for me, and I thought that I was the only woman in the world for him. I couldn't believe it when he told me. He'd have been quite content to let things go on as they were, but she said she'd leave him if he didn't get me to divorce him and marry her. Someone had probably repeated things I'd said about her and she wanted to get her own back. She's little enough for that. I suppose she loves Harvey, too. And I suppose that Harvey must love her more than he loves me. She's the most foul-minded woman I've ever come across, and I think Harvey likes that. Some men do. ... I'm a bit of a prude and I suppose he was tired of it. I've lain awake night after night trying to understand, but it wouldn't make things any easier even if I did understand." She looked down absently at her handkerchief and spread it out, showing a jagged tear. "There! And one of my best. ... Harvey gave them me. ..."

The girl stared into the distance.

"I wonder if I'd care as much as that if Philip left me. I suppose I should. It's – frightening in a way to think how little we've changed down the ages. We're as ready as ever we were to make fools of ourselves over a man."

"I didn't really believe it till yesterday," said Lettice. "It seemed one of the things that couldn't happen. Right up to the last minute I expected Harvey to come and say he wouldn't go on with it. Isn't it funny to think that hundreds of women get divorces every day, and yet I can't really believe that any other woman's ever gone through what I've gone through?"

"I know," said the girl. "You feel like that when you have a baby. I just couldn't believe that for every one of the millions of people in the world someone had gone through the hoop like me."

"You've got something to show for it, with a baby."

"Not much," said the girl. "Wait till you see it!" She was silent for a moment, then said, "Why did you set off on the loose like this alone? You ought to have got a friend to come with you. They'd have seen you had some lunch, anyway."

Lettice's lips tightened into a bitter line.

"My friends have been marvellous," she said. "They've rallied round me from the very beginning. They've adored every minute of it. It's given them something to talk about and made them ten years younger. They all came to the Law Courts yesterday, and they all came round to see me last night. They don't want to miss a second of it. It's a free entertainment. Even those who are really sorry for me gloat over it. They'll be wild to find I've escaped them today. The ones who've lost their own husbands are tickled to death that I've lost mine, too, and the ones who still have them despise me for not being able to keep mine."

"Yes . . . we are rather like that, aren't we?" said the girl slowly. "I got quite a kick out of it while you were telling me. Not as much as if I knew you well, of course. . . . Come and see the rest of the house."

Lettice rose.

"Thanks," she said. "I feel a little better now. I don't know whether it's the tea or the rock cakes or telling you. . . . I'm a fool, of course. I was loving meeting someone who didn't know about it, and now I've spoilt it all." She paused at a mirror on the wall. "God! Don't I look awful?"

"How old are you?" said the girl.

"Thirty-eight."

"I'd have put you down at forty-five."

"Before this happened I was supposed to look young for my age. Harvey used to say—"

She stopped. Again that vivid picture of Harvey flashed into her mind. He and Olga would be celebrating his freedom today. She saw him laughing across a table, holding up a glass of champagne. . . .

"Don't!" said the girl sharply. "You look fifty at least now."

The tension of Lettice's features relaxed into a faint unwilling smile.

"I'm sorry. I must try not to think about things."

"Gardening's supposed to be good for that," said the girl, leading the way down the passage to the "built-on" room.

The walls were covered with gay nursery pictures, and a playing-pen stood in the middle of the floor on a brightly coloured rug. A small wooden table and chair were painted light blue, with stencils of yellow chickens.

"Loathly, isn't it?" said the girl. "I feel sick whenever I come into it. It reminds me of those foul women's twopennies. Coy articles on preparing for the little stranger. Why it had to pick on me of all people I can't think. I've always loathed brats. The first thing I said when Philip proposed was, no brats, and he agreed. It shows how little you can trust science. . . . It's literally shattered my life."

"How?" said Lettice.

"Well, I always vowed never to live in the country for one thing. I hate the country. Philip and I had a flat in Chelsea and adored it, and I've had to come to this Godforsaken place that bores me to tears all because of the wretched brat."

"But why need you have come here?" persisted Lettice.

The girl took a cigarette from a box on the mantelpiece.

"Oh, well," she said vaguely as she lit it, "brats need country air, don't you think?"

She opened the door, and Lettice followed her into the garden, where a pram stood under the pear tree. The girl was passing it without looking, but Lettice stopped and peeped under the hood. The loveliest baby she had ever seen slept there.

"She's beautiful," she said.

The girl shrugged.

"Twelve months old and not a gleam of intelligence," she said, "not one solitary gleam."

"What's she called?"

"Matilda. I thought it time Matilda had a come-back. I really wanted Jemima – Jemima's come-back is long overdue – but my courage failed me and I called her Matilda. I'll call the next Jemima."

Lettice threw her a surprised glance.

"The next? I thought you didn't like them."

"I don't," said the girl promptly. "I hate them. But if you have two they can look after each other and you can forget they're there. . . . I mean, all chance of peace or happiness or comfort is gone from life, so you may as well do the thing in style. Look," she pointed to a row of small wooden crosses against the fence. "That's where the old fool buried her cats when they died. There were ten cats in the house when they took her away. It gives me the creeps to think of it."

"I must go now," said Lettice. "You've been so kind. . . ."

"I haven't," said the girl, and added, "You're taking the cottage, aren't you?"

"No," said Lettice firmly. "You see, I hadn't come to look at it. I'd just lost my way and was turning by going round the green. I'd suddenly made up my mind to go and see an old school friend. I haven't seen her for wars and I thought she might understand——"

"She wouldn't have done," said the girl. "Old school friends never do. One never meets an old school friend without wondering what on earth one saw in her at school. And no doubt the old school friend wonders the same about oneself. I suppose that actually school friendships are based on hating the same mistress or liking the same sort of pudding or having desks next to each other or both keeping tame mice."

"I think she'd have disapproved," said Lettice. "She has a very high moral standard, and she wouldn't like being 'mixed up' in it. . . . Anyway, I'd just stopped the car for a rest, and was wondering what the village was called – What is it called, by the way?"

"Steffan Green. Philip will tell you about it. He's inclined to be archaeological. Steffan is supposed to be a corruption of Stefn, which is Anglo-Saxon for the prow of a ship, and in prehistoric days evidently this place was under the sea – one still finds tiny shells in the stones – and legend has it that once the prow of a ship was dug up here. All very uninteresting, I consider. But you will take the cottage, won't you?"

"I don't want a cottage."

"Why not?" persisted the girl. "Just for a year. You'd get away from all the gaping busybodies. You could get back your poise."

"Have I lost it so terribly?"

"You've got a knocked-about sort of look. The sort your friends will gloat over. They'll say, 'Poor' – what's your name?"

"Lettice Helston."

" 'Poor Lettice! It's absolutely broken her up.' They'll flock round to comfort you and keep you company. . . . Wouldn't you rather disappear for a year and then reappear – calm and mistress of the situation?"

Lettice smiled crookedly.

"You seem determined that I should take it."

"I am determined," said the girl calmly. "I made up my mind you should take it as soon as I saw you from the upstairs window. I knew you hadn't come to see it, but I was determined you should see it, and I was determined you should take it. It all fits in so beautifully. You *are* going to take it, you know."

"But why were you determined I should take it?" said Lettice. She felt vaguely flattered. "Did you think you'd like me?"

"Oh no, it wasn't that," said the girl. "It was that you looked quiet. I've been scared to death of someone noisy taking it. Brats need such heaps of sleep."

Chapter Two

LETTICE stood at the window, looking down unseeingly at the straggling little garden. A thick white mist enshrouded it, completely hiding the further end. Through it came the muffled sounds of the outer world, the hooting of a car in the distance, the twittering of birds, a sudden snatch of song. Drops of moisture hung from every leaf and twig. A deep hush seemed to pervade everything, as if the whole world were asleep beneath the grey blanket of the mist.

She turned from the window with a sharp sigh. What a fool she'd been to come here! She'd wanted to get away from her friends, with their insistent clamorous sympathy, their never-ending chatter, and already she was homesick for them, longing for the warm solace of their company, the ceaseless trivial activities that she had shared with them. She hadn't realised till she took the plunge how entirely these had filled her life – pottering about the shops, going to theatres and pictures, playing bridge, popping in and out of their houses for tea, cocktails, or dinner. She'd only moved here yesterday, but already the long days stretched before her, terrifying in their emptiness and futility.

She took up Harvey's photograph from the table at her side, and again everything faded into that sharp racking heartache, that bitter torment of regret. She hadn't meant to bring it with her. She'd meant to burn it. "If I hadn't got that to remind me of him every minute," she had said, "it might be easier to forget." She'd put off burning it till she'd finished packing, then she'd put it off till she got here. . . . And now she knew that she was going to keep it, though even to look at it sent that shaft of unbearable agony through her heart.

"I don't want to forget him," she said stubbornly. "I'd rather remember, however much it hurts. It would be like dying to forget. . . ."

Besides, even if she destroyed the photograph, almost everything she had reminded her of him . . . the little Sheraton commode that they had bought together, the Queen Anne kneehole desk at which he used to write his letters, the lustres he had taken a childish delight in tinkling. . . .

She possessed hardly any jewelry that he hadn't given her. He had always been lavishly generous. He had a lordly conquering-male manner that she used to laugh at but that secretly she adored. She had learnt early enough not to rely on him too much, but nothing ever annoyed him or put him out. His inexhaustible vitality and power of enjoyment made him a delightful companion. He – she shrugged her shoulders impatiently. Couldn't she think of something else even for a moment? She slipped his photograph upside down into a drawer and glanced round the room. Her furniture seemed strange and unfamiliar in its new surroundings. The smallness of the room made it look unnaturally big and just a little menacing. It seemed to wear a slightly aggrieved air as if it resented being uprooted from its comfortable London flat.

"I know," she said aloud. "I'm sorry. I feel like that, too. I – don't know why I came."

She didn't know why she'd come. Looking back, it seemed to her that she'd come for no other reason than that the woman next door wanted a quiet neighbour for her baby. Certainly she'd gone straight to the agent, taken the cottage, and moved in as quickly as she could arrange it. It had seemed at the time a way of escape, but now that she'd come she knew that there was no way of escape. She had only spent one night here (the vans had arrived yesterday) and already she was bored and depressed. She could hear Harriet moving about downstairs, putting things to rights. Harriet – the housemaid she had had at her London flat – had offered to come for a week to "settle her in," but had made it quite clear that she did not intend to stay. "No, madam," she had said. "I'll see you settled, then I'll look for another job. I've never fancied the country."

Lettice was rather relieved than otherwise. Just as her friends' excessive sympathy jarred on her, so Harriet's lack of sympathy jarred. Harriet had never liked Harvey. She was one of the few people who had failed to succumb to his charm. Right up to the end he had never relaxed his efforts to break down her defences. Harriet was middle-aged and plain, but Harvey couldn't endure to have anyone about him who didn't adore him, and Harriet's thinly veiled dislike had been a perpetual challenge to him. Every other servant they'd had had adored him. . . . When Lettice told Harriet about the divorce she had set her lips grimly. "I'm not surprised, madam," she had said, and Lettice felt that she despised her for having put up with it so long, for having shut her eyes. . . .

She'd have to get someone locally. Probably no London servant would be willing to come out so far. Steffan Green was three miles from Beverton, and the 'bus only went there once in the half-hour. She was completely cut off from the world. Despair seized her afresh.

"Why on earth did I do it?" she said helplessly.

A sudden burst of whistling came from outside. She went to the window again and saw through the mist the young man next door at work chopping up a packing-case with a hatchet. He was tall and elegantly slender, with fair hair and a long, thin handsome face. He wore wide green corduroy trousers and an orange pullover. A strand of fair hair fell over his forehead as he worked.

Lettice went slowly downstairs. Harriet, still in her print dress, was sweeping the hall.

"Let me do that," said Lettice.

"No, thank you, madam," said Harriet. "There's nothing you can do."

Her manner was aloof and vaguely reproachful. Lettice felt that she had lost "face" irretrievably in her eyes by coming here.

("Are you aware, madam," Harriet had said that morning with a face grimmer than even Harvey's vagaries had ever made it, "that there's only one w.c.?")

"I'm sure you're tired," said Lettice. "I've done nothing."

"There's very little to do, madam," said Harriet, still with a look of suffering patience. "The place is little more than a workman's cottage."

"I suppose it is," said Lettice, trying not to sound apologetic. "I'm afraid that you're going to find it a long week, Harriet."

"I'm prepared to do my duty, madam," said Harriet.

Lettice knew that when she got back to London and met Mary, the cook, a perverted sense of loyalty would make her describe the place as if it were a country mansion.

There was a knock at the front door, and Lettice opened it, to find the young man on the doorstep, his arm full of pieces of wood. He grinned at her.

"I bet you never thought of firewood," he said as he stepped into the hall. "Where can I put it?"

Harriet turned an icy stare on him, met his grin, and visibly melted.

"Through here in the kitchen, sir," she said. "That's very kind of you."

Lettice looked with interest at the young man whose charm succeeded where Harvey's had failed.

He came back from the kitchen still grinning and wiping his hands on his trousers.

"Lydia told me to bring you back for tea," he said. He cocked an eye at Harriet. "You'll be glad to be rid of her for an hour or so, won't you?"

Lettice gasped and waited for Harriet to put this daring young man in his place. Even her oldest friends had never presumed to take liberties with Harriet. But Harriet was smiling, showing the back gold tooth that Lettice saw on an average once a year.

"Well, to tell the truth, sir," she said, "I can get on better by myself."

"Grand!" said the young man.

He took the fur coat that hung in the hall and held it out for Lettice.

"Come on."

She went with him down the path to the road and in at the other gate. The door was ajar. He pushed it open.

"I loathe removals, don't you?" he said. "I think of hell as one long removal. Sandwiches on packing-cases and nails everywhere and the clothes brush lost."

"Harriet's done it nearly all," smiled Lettice. "I think we've even got the clothes brush."

"How devastatingly efficient!" he said. "It turns one's blood cold."

He threw open the sitting-room door.

"Come in here. Lydia's just sticking safety pins into the brat. Its entire surface is punctured by now."

"Matilda?" said Lettice. "She's a lovely baby."

The young man looked affronted.

"She's no right to be," he said. "She's been consistently neglected since birth. She's quite definitely an unwanted child."

Lydia came in with a tray of tea things. She wore a bright yellow sweater with the navy-blue slacks and a cigarette drooped between her reddened lips.

"Take this, you great hulking idle brute," she said, giving the tray into her husband's hands, "and put it down somewhere." She turned to Lettice. "You poor pet! Isn't it foul! Aren't you half dead?"

"I haven't done anything but moon about," said Lettice. "I've got the perfect maid. She's only to look at a roomful of furniture and it sorts itself out."

"How marvellous!" sighed Lydia wistfully.

"It isn't. I've had her for three years and I'm as scared of her as I was the first day she came. She's not going to stay. That's my sole comfort. She says she's never fancied the country."

"Good for her!" said Lydia, sitting down on the window seat. "Do pour out, Philip. I told you Philip was on a paper, didn't I? He's working at night just now, so I've got him on my hands all day. It's an awful bore. I only married a newspaper man because I thought you didn't see much of them. I'd decided on a newspaper man or a sailor, but I couldn't find a sailor, so I had to marry Philip."

Philip grinned as he poured out the tea. His skin was smooth and close-textured like a child's, and his fair untidy hair emphasised the impression of boyishness. He had a pleasant finely moulded mouth and smiling blue eyes, and he managed his tall spare body with an easy grace.

"Don't forget to fix up about March," Lydia was saying. She turned to Lettice. "We want to go away in March."

"Where?" said Lettice, taking a cup of tea from Philip.

"South of France, I think. Philip and I and a girl friend for Philip and a boy friend for me. We always do it that way. It relieves the monotony of married life. We married because there's a certain convenience in the marriage state, but we allow each other perfect freedom." She put her cup down suddenly and sat, tense and motionless. "I thought I heard ... I hope that old wretch hasn't come."

"What old wretch?" asked Lettice.

"Miss Pendleton. The old wretch who used to live here. She came and stood at the back gate for over an hour yesterday muttering away to herself. I went down to her and found she was furious because we'd taken down what she called her 'arbour.' "

"A rustic erection of indescribably hideous design," put in Philip. "You know, an archway of trellis encircling a so-called seat that could never accommodate itself to any conceivable position of the human form."

"She wanted to know what we'd done with it," said Lydia. "As a matter of fact we'd used it for firewood. I was as rude to her as I could be. The damned *cheek* of it! When we've bought the house and got a jolly rotten bargain at that. She ought to be ashamed to come near it."

"She'd lived all her life here," said Philip, "and I believe she's not quite right in her head. And she drinks."

"Filthy old creature!" said Lydia, flicking her cigarette ash into her saucer. "I told you we had to scrape the dirt off the woodwork, didn't I?"

"I say, are you sure you locked the gate?" said her husband.

"I think so. . . ."

"I'll go and make sure."

"We'll come with you. Come along, Mrs. Helston. I want to show you my one and only chrysanthemum. I forgot to point it out the other day, and you'd never notice it otherwise."

They went out of the sitting-room into the little nursery. Matilda sat on a rug in a wooden pen playing with bricks. Plump dimpled legs emerged from a clean pair of rompers. The fair silky hair was brushed into loose curls. As they entered she raised her round rosy face from the bricks and fixed them with a solemn blue gaze. Then she smiled suddenly, showing small white teeth, and said:

"Dad – dad – dad."

The young man looked embarrassed.

"Don't know who taught it that," he muttered. "I never did."

They opened the french window and went outside. A breeze had arisen and partly dispelled the mist. Snatches of it floated across the garden like fleeting ghosts. The young man vanished in the direction of the gate.

Lydia pulled up the collar of her sweater and shuddered.

"The country's so crude," she said. "One can ignore the elements in town. In the country they hit one in the face."

The young man rejoined them, appearing suddenly and unexpectedly out of a strand of mist.

"It's locked all right," he said.

"And she's not there?" said Lydia anxiously.

"No, she's not there."

"Let's go in, then. This stuff gets right inside you. I'll show you my chrysanthemum another time. I'm sure it's not looking its best even if I could find it."

"I ought to go back now," said Lettice. "Thanks for the tea."

"Time I shoved the brat into bed," said Lydia. "Perhaps the mist will have cleared by the time I've finished and we can go across for a booze. We always go to the 'Fox and Grapes' for a drink when I've shoved the brat into bed. Even if we don't particularly want the drink we always go, because we love to see Mrs. Webb watching us through her lace curtains and looking shocked. She thinks we're abandoned and we love her thinking we're abandoned. We had great fun sun-bathing in the back garden for her benefit in the summer. She sat there with her eyes glued to the window watching us and being shocked. She even wrote to the vicar about us. He showed us the letter. . . . Well, I'll away to the brat."

Just as Lettice reached the front door Harriet opened it.

"There's a lady to see you, madam," she said, in her usual expressionless tone. "She's in the sitting-room writing a note."

"Oh," said Lettice, taken aback.

Callers. She'd forgotten that people called in the country. She shrank in sudden panic from the thought. She'd come here to be alone. She hadn't reckoned on having to know people. The young couple next door somehow didn't count. They seemed to go with the house. . . . She stood for a moment in the hall, summoning her courage, then opened the door.

A woman who was sitting at the writing-desk turned round as she entered. She wore a rather shabby raincoat and shapeless felt hat placed carelessly on fair greying hair. Her face was pale, her eyes a deep cornflower blue, and a long jagged scar ran across her colourless lips.

"Forgive me for coming now," she said, rising. A certain delicacy of build only just redeemed the tall untidy figure from angularity. "It isn't really a call. I've only just come to see if there's anything I can do. My name's Fanshaw. My husband's the vicar."

"Oh – it's kind of you," said Lettice. "Do sit down."

Mrs. Fanshaw sat down and there was a short silence. Meeting the curiously direct gaze of the cornflower blue eyes, Lettice moved hers uneasily away.

"What about tea?" said Mrs. Fanshaw suddenly.

"Won't you come to the vicarage or may I send some over?"

"Thanks. I've just had it next door with the Morrices."

The scarred lips parted in a faint smile.

"They're delightful, aren't they? Actually, though I don't believe they wanted the child originally, they've worshipped it ever since it arrived, but they still pretend even to each other to be bored by it. . . . They spend their time vainly fighting an ineradicable streak of respectability. It's a losing battle. I tell them that he'll end up as a churchwarden and she as secretary of the Women's Institute."

Lettice took a box from the writing-desk and handed it to her. "Have a cigarette?"

When she came in she'd hoped that the woman would not stay, but now – she didn't know why – she found herself anxious to detain her.

"Thank you," said the visitor, taking one. She had thin hands with long nervous fingers. "This is too much – knowing where the cigarettes are on the day of a move. I feel that I've insulted you by coming to ask if I could help."

"Oh, that's Harriet," said Lettice, giving her a light. "I'm not a bit like that. I'm muddle-headed and muzzy-minded."

The visitor smiled at her quizzically through her cigarette smoke.

"I don't suppose you are." The smile died away, and the blue eyes rested on her with that oddly disconcerting directness. "Do you think you'll like Steffan Green?"

"I don't know," said Lettice and added, "Do you?"

"I love it," said Mrs. Fanshaw, "but, then, my roots are here – my family, I mean."

"Have you children?" asked Lettice.

She was interested in her visitor, despite herself – interested and faintly resentful. The woman was untidy and badly dressed. There was no reason for the influence she seemed to exert so effortlessly.

The lips curved again into a smile that was ironic but without bitterness.

"I have a daughter. She's one of the practical jokes that life has played on me. Has life played any practical jokes on you?"

Lettice looked away, with tight lips and narrowed eyes.

"Yes."

"Oh, life's not always kind," said her visitor, "but you can't deny it a sense of humour. . . . However, I won't inflict the story of my life on you at our first meeting. I'll tell you some other time."

"Please tell me now . . ." said Lettice.

She couldn't think why she wanted to know more about this woman, but she did. Perhaps it was because she wanted, in her turn, to tell her about Harvey. . . .

The visitor threw her again that faintly amused glance.

"Very well. You shall be the wedding guest. You've asked for it, remember. It's a long story, and it's all ancient history by now, of course, but I was one of the leaders of what was called the Woman's Movement, when you were at school, I suppose. I couldn't endure the sort of life my parents offered me – living at home and doing the flowers and making my own dresses and being Little Lady Bountiful in the village and waiting for a nice young man to fall in love with me. I wanted freedom and a career, and I fought for them. I felt that I wasn't only fighting for myself. I was fighting for all the women who were to come after me. I put matches in pillar-boxes and chained myself to railings and went to prison. . . ." She paused for a moment, gazing meditatively into the distance, then went on, "I hated doing it. I was always literally sick before the – demonstration, as they called it, but I felt I was doing it for posterity. Well, we got the vote and I took a doctor's degree and then I married and had a daughter, and I thought, she shall enjoy everything that I fought for. She shall have freedom and a career. And the amusing part is that she didn't want it. All she wanted in life was what I'd fought against. She wanted to live at home and potter about the house and do the flowers and help in the parish, and she's tremendously interested in nice young men. It's funny to think that I killed my mother because I wanted to save my children from that fate. My mother literally died of shock when I went to prison and was in headlines in the papers. . . . And really all for nothing. . . . It would have broken my heart if I hadn't cultivated a sense of proportion."

"I wish I could cultivate one," said Lettice. "Tell me how it's done."

"Reading the Old Testament partly," said Mrs. Fanshaw unexpectedly.

Lettice looked at her. She was an odd woman. One never knew when she was serious.

"No one can ever read the Old Testament right through without acquiring a certain sense of proportion," went on the visitor. "Montaigne helps, too. There are lots of authors who give one a sense of proportion. I've concentrated on them. . . ."

"I believe an aunt of mine was mixed up in it," said Lettice vaguely. "I remember my father's being very shocked. But I never knew what it was all about."

Mrs. Fanshaw crushed the stub of her cigarette into an ash-tray. Her lips still wore their almost imperceptible smile.

"It was all rather futile. We were fanatics. We thought that the vote would bring the millennium and it didn't. Except for a few women doctors and M.P.'s we're pretty much as we were. And I've come to the conclusion that we're all right as we were. . . . Life's very funny. I never thought in those days that I'd end up as a country parson's wife. Have I bored you terribly?"

"No," said Lettice slowly. "I think you've helped me. Made me feel a little more – detached."

She wanted to tell this strange woman about Harvey, but already she was rising and drawing on thick woollen gloves.

"Things are never as bad as they seem to be when you're right up against them," she said. "You've got to get away and look at them from a distance with other things round them before you can see them in the right perspective. On the whole, life treats us better than we deserve. It's certainly treated me better. Sylvia – that's my daughter – is a darling. She's gone away on a visit in Egypt with some friends now and I'm missing her terribly. I'm realising that she was mother and nurse and maid to me combined. By the way, your maid says that she's not staying. What are you doing about getting another?"

"I don't know," said Lettice. "I suppose there's a registry office somewhere."

"Why not try Mrs. Skelton," said the visitor, "just as a stop-gap till you get someone else? She lives at Crewe Cottages. I'm going to see her now. An old friend of mine is taking a cottage here, and I'm engaging Mrs. Skelton's daughter as her maid. . . . I haven't seen the old friend since the days when we used to chain ourselves to railings side by side, but she's done more than most of us. She's a novelist with quite a fair public. Her heroines are gentle helpless little women – stupid but appealing – the sort we meant to wipe off the face of the earth. . . . Shall we go now or are you too tired?"

"No, I'd like to," said Lettice. "I'll get my coat. I wonder what the weather's like."

She went into the hall and opened the front door. The mist had turned to a grey drizzle.

"I don't mind getting wet," said Mrs. Fanshaw, "but you'd better take an umbrella."

They stepped out together into the gentle downpour.

"I'm sorry the mist has gone," said Mrs. Fanshaw. "It makes things so mysterious. A sense of mystery is one of the things the world lacks these days."

As they passed Eastnor, Lettice caught sight of a plump round face watching from behind the shelter of the discreet Nottingham lace curtains.

"That's where the Webbs live," went on Mrs. Fanshaw. "Mother and devoted son. He works in a bank at Beverton. I suppose you've not met them yet?"

"No," said Lettice, "I've only met you and the Morrices."

They crossed the green and went down a narrow lane between deep hedgerows. Mrs. Fanshaw walked upright, holding her face to the rain as if to the sunshine. Lettice cowered under her umbrella. They passed a small square house covered in ivy standing back from the road behind a broken-down fence. There was a rather dilapidated notice on the gate, "The Moorings."

"The Turnberrys live there," said Mrs. Fanshaw. "Another mother and son. I'm afraid there's not much society here. Just you and the Morrices and the Webbs and the Turnberrys and us. There are the Ferrings up at the Castle, but we don't see much of them. It's going to be dull for you, I'm afraid."

"I don't mind," said Lettice, carefully skirting a puddle. "I didn't come here for society." She was silent for a few moments, then added, "Now that I'm here, I don't know why I did come. I came on a sort of impulse."

"I'm a great believer in impulse," said Mrs. Fanshaw.

Lettice wondered if she ever laughed. One couldn't imagine her without that faint smile, but one couldn't somehow imagine her laughing. . . .

"Here we are," she said.

A low straggling group of cottages stood by the roadside, the thatched roofs overhanging the tiny windows.

"Mrs. Skelton lives in the end one," said Mrs. Fanshaw. "I think she'll be in."

A girl of about seventeen answered the door. She was slender and a little below average height, with china-blue eyes, a dazzlingly fair complexion, and ash-blonde hair, Carefully massed in curls round her head. She wore a red woollen dress and high-heeled shoes.

"Is your mother in, Ivy?" said Mrs. Fanshaw.

"Yes, Mrs. Fanshaw," said Ivy. "Come in, Mrs. Fanshaw."

She had a sing-song childish voice and a shy awkward manner. Despite her high-heeled shoes and elaborate curls, one saw a little girl sucking the corner of her pinafore.

"Mum!" she called.

They stepped down into a tiny kitchen – snug and warm and rather dark, with a red fringed table-cloth and an old-fashioned rocking chair in front of a roaring coal fire. Lettice went to the fire, and, drawing off her gloves, held out her hands to it. The mist seemed to have penetrated her very bones.

At Ivy's call a large powerfully built woman came in by the other door. She wore a sacking apron over a long full skirt of ancient design, a cardigan, and a man's cap attached to her hair by a long skewer-like pin, which she took out and rammed home again at frequent intervals and for no apparent reason. Her strongly marked features and good-natured expression gave her the look of a pantomime dame.

"Good afternoon, mum," she said, wiping her hands on her apron and smiling broadly. "Nasty day, ain't it?"

Mrs. Fanshaw's faint answering smile seemed to take the place of both greeting and comment on the weather.

"This is Mrs. Helston," she said. "She's taken one of Pear Tree Cottages and she wonders if you can spare her any time till she gets a maid."

Mrs. Skelton turned upon Lettice a roguish grin that suggested the opening of a comic song and said:

"Well, you're lucky, mum, as it happens. A lady in Beverton what I've been doin' for's give me up. Goin' to do for herself. I can let you have from nine till two reg'lar bar Saturday when I go to the Castle. I could come along of an evenin' and cook your supper, too. Ninepence an hour without meals 'cept for a cup of tea an' bread an' cheese at eleven."

The smile broadened as she ended, and Lettice almost expected an outburst of applause from some invisible audience.

"That sounds all right, doesn't it?" said Mrs. Fanshaw, "and I'm sure Mrs. Helston will give you lunch."

"Yes," said Lettice, shrinkingly facing a Harrietless existence. She looked doubtfully from the man's cap, skewered at a fantastic angle on the large unadorned head, to the massive boots that protruded from the flowing skirts. "Yes," she repeated. "That'll be quite all right."

"And now about Ivy," said Mrs. Fanshaw, turning to the girl who stood by her mother watching them shyly. "Miss Lennare is coming next Saturday. You'll be able to start then?"

"Yes, Mrs. Fanshaw. Thank you, Mrs. Fanshaw," said Ivy, in her sing-song childish voice.

The mother turned her large good-humoured smile upon them.

"Time our Ivy learnt how to keep a house, I tell her," she said, " 'gainst the time when she'll have one of her own. I'd have liked her to go to that Mrs. Morrice to learn look after a baby, too. . . ."

The girl nuzzled against her mother's stalwart shoulders like a young colt, blushing and giggling.

"Oh, mum!" she said. "Don't be so awful."

Mrs. Fanshaw smiled at them.

"George'll make a good husband," she said.

"He's worryin' me to let them get wed now," said Mrs. Skelton, "but I say, wait a bit. Don't try to make a woman of 'er before 'er time. Once the babies start comin' there's not much peace. . . ."

"Oh, mum, don't," giggled Ivy, her cheeks a glowing pink, her eyes bright with laughter. She butted the rocklike shoulders with her small golden head. "Don't be so *awful*."

Mrs. Fanshaw's faint smile enveloped them both like a benediction.

"You'll start on Monday, then, Mrs. Skelton, and I'll see you again before Miss Lennare comes, Ivy. . . ."

"Ivy's her tenth," she said as they walked back down the lane. "All the others have scattered – gone into service or abroad. George Harker lives at the next cottage and works at Crewe Farm. He's a nice lad. He's worshipped Ivy since she was a little girl."

They had reached the green now, and Mrs. Fanshaw pointed across it to a small house with a thatched roof and green shutters next to the "Fox and Grapes."

"That's Honeysuckle Cottage – the one that Clare's taken," she said. "She really *is* called Clare Lennare. With a name like that, of course, she had to write. No one could have resisted it. She's very conscientious about her backgrounds. If she's writing a novel about Florence she must go to Florence to write it. She's going to write a novel about the country now, so she's coming to live here. Oddly enough, the method has the effect of making her backgrounds peculiarly unconvincing. They always read as if she'd got them out of guide-books. . . . I'm glad Ivy needn't go away from home. She's a weak little thing. Her mother's spoilt her. . . . Well—"

They had reached Pear Tree Cottages again. The rain had stopped falling, but still swung in pearl-like drops from the hedgerows, and dripped from the trees in the fitful gusts of wind with a sound like the pattering of tiny feet.

"Won't you come in?" said Lettice.

She felt reluctant to part from this new acquaintance. The smile that was hardly a smile at all was strangely consoling and reassuring.

"Thanks so much, but my husband—"

She stopped. Mrs. Morrice had suddenly appeared at her front door. She looked tense and angry and a little frightened.

"I thought I heard your voice," she said to Mrs. Fanshaw. "That old devil's here again and I can't get her to go away. Philip's just gone off to town or he'd——"

"I'll come," said Mrs. Fanshaw quietly.

She went round to the back of the house. Lettice followed uncertainly.

She could see a stooping figure in a tattered black cloak leaning over the gate at the bottom of the garden. Wisps of grey hair escaped the rusty black bonnet and fell about the witch-like emaciated face. The skin – grey as cobwebs – was a network of tiny wrinkles deeply ingrained with dirt. The small mouth was sunken and puckered, the nose a sharp curve, the small brown eyes alive with malice.

As soon as she saw Mrs. Fanshaw she turned suddenly and went off down the lane, her cloak floating out behind her. At the bend she turned and seemed to shake a claw-like fist in their direction. They could hear her voice – thin, cracked, malevolent – though no words reached them. Then she vanished round the bend.

"What a horrible old creature!" said Lettice with a shudder.

Lydia gave a little shaken laugh.

"She gets my goat. . . . Philip said that he'd go to the police if she came again. She makes me feel as if spiders had been crawling over me."

"I'll go and see her tomorrow," said Mrs. Fanshaw. "I'll talk to her cousin. She mustn't be allowed to go out alone."

A child's cry, sleepy, imperious, came from the house.

"That's the brat. I must fly."

"I must, too," said Mrs. Fanshaw. She turned to Lettice. "Come to tea on Wednesday, will you?" adding, while Lettice was still hunting for an excuse, "I'll expect you about four."

Before Lettice had thought of one she had gone.

Lettice went slowly indoors. The memory of the old woman seemed to hang about her like something tangibly evil. Gradually it faded and instead came the memory of Mrs. Fanshaw. How understanding and sympathetic she'd been about Harvey! Then she realised suddenly and with something of a shock that she hadn't even told her about him.

Chapter Three

MRS. FANSHAW came downstairs, pinning a brooch onto the front of her dress as she did so. She generally finished dressing on the way downstairs. She had got into the habit in the days when she had been so busy – first as a leader of the Woman's Suffrage Movement and then as a doctor in the East End of London – that the days were never long enough for all she had to do in them. Now her days were quiet and leisurely – but she still finished dressing on the way downstairs. It was one of the things Sylvia teased her about. . . .

There was a letter from Sylvia on the chest in the hall. She took it up and went into her husband's study. He was sitting at his desk by the window – a tall thin man with sparse grey hair, rather high cheek-bones, and a long sensitive mouth. He looked up as she entered and smiled at her. An eloquent preacher, he was in ordinary intercourse, even in his own home, shy and inarticulate.

"It's from Sylvia," she said, sitting down and opening the letter. "Shall I read it to you?"

He nodded.

"MY DARLINGEST MUMMY [she read],
I'm having a marvellous time and the Milners are being adorable to me. I'm enjoying every minute of every day. Cairo's a thrilling place and we're staying at Shepheard's which is a thrill all to itself. The first day we got here we went up to the Citadel and got a simply wonderful view of the town – a sort of sea of domes and minarets right down beneath us.

We went to see the Pyramids the next day. Mr. Milner says it's all spoilt for him now by the electric tramways and motor roads that go to the foot of the Great Pyramid and by the crowds of photographers and people selling faked antiquities, but I thought it was all tremendous. Even Mr. Milner really enjoyed it because he could quote Herodotus by the yard and he likes doing that. There was a British Israelite there who kept telling us about the measurements and when the end of the world was coming. He said we were on something called the Low Passage now and started quoting Daniel about the thousand and three hundred and five and thirty days, but it was all terribly confusing and he couldn't get people to listen to him. The Sphinx had just that sneering sort of look that the camels have. I don't like riding on them much. They don't seem even to try to be comfortable. Bob's got a most ridiculous snap of me on one.

Yesterday we went by train to Helwan and then on to Wady Hof on donkeys and picnicked there. Bob and I found a tiny maidenhair fern growing among the rocks and somehow it made me feel homesick. We're going to Luxor next week. Bob says that the Valley of the Tombs is so wonderful that it's terrifying.

I'm having a lovely time but I'm homesick for you quite a lot. Take care of your darling selves. I'm sure you're wearing all the wrong things without me to look after you, Mummy. Do anyway, sweetest, wear the right skirts of your costumes with the right coats. And *don't* go on wearing that awful navy-blue hat even in the rain. You'd better not buy anything new till I'm at home to help you.

Kiss Daddy for me on his bald patch, and heaps of kisses to you and tons of love to you both.

Your own
SYLVIA

P.S. – Give my love to the Ferring girls. I'm afraid they'll miss me. Be specially nice to Lavvy."

Her husband sat watching her as she read. The scar on her lips twitched once or twice as they curved into a smile. He remembered his anger and irritation when he first heard the story of that scar – how she had gone on hunger-strike in prison in her suffragette days and a wardress had forced her mouth open with a broken saucer, cutting deep into the lip. His anger had been for the wardress, his irritation for her. It had seemed so stupid, so perverse. He always tried to keep his thoughts away from that part of her life. He couldn't endure to think of her having been man-handled, dragged about. . . .

She folded up the letter and sat for a moment gazing dreamily in front of her. She was thinking of Sylvia, with her rosy good-tempered face, her radiating happiness, her childish humility, her deep unquestioning affection . . . and realising afresh that she loved her far more than she could have loved the earnest intellectual daughter of her dreams.

"What are you thinking of?" said her husband.

"I was thinking how much wiser Providence is than oneself."

"Providence?"

She smiled.

"Yes – I suppose I mean God."

She had been brought up in a strict Evangelical household, threatened with the pains of hell and the anger of God for the most trivial misdemeanours. When first she met her husband she had been passing through a short unhappy period of atheism. She had recovered her faith – a deeper, richer faith than the one she had lost – before she realised that she loved him. To him religion was the one reality in life. He tried to surrender to it every part of him – even the very human love he bore his wife. Sometimes he was faintly troubled for her, distrusting her quick keen intelligence, her independent judgment, her fearless honesty. She would never stifle doubts if they arose, and his soul's salvation would be a bleak and barren triumph to him without hers.

She crossed the room and, bending down, kissed the place at his temple where the greying hair had receded.

"That's the one Sylvia sent you," she said. "And that's one from myself."

Without speaking he put up a hand, took hers and pressed it to his lips. She perched on the arm of his chair, leaving her hand in his.

"She's made me feel guilty," she went on. "Look at me. Do I look as if I'd flung my clothes on anyway?"

He raised his eyes to her.

"You look very beautiful," he said.

"Oh, I know you think so," she said. "That's what's so bad for me. It means that I don't take any pains over my appearance, and I ought to. By the way, you're coming to my tea-party this afternoon, aren't you?"

"I have to go over to Blake's Farm," he said. "The old man's worse. . . . Who's coming to your party?"

"Mrs. Helston. The new tenant of Pear Tree Cottage."

"What's she like?" he said. "She wasn't at church on Sunday, was she?"

"No. She's lovely. Very pale with those deep violet eyes one so seldom sees."

"I didn't mean to look at."

"No, I suppose you didn't. I don't really know. . . . She seems tired and hurt and bewildered. Lydia said she'd just divorced her husband. . . . Oh, Lydia's decided to have Matilda christened. I met her in the village this morning. She said, 'I'm not religious myself, but I mean the brat to be, and I'm going to start by taking it to church regularly when it's five years old.' She said that it would be less trouble. She didn't explain how."

He smiled.

"Good!" he said quietly. "I'll call and see her."

"I think you'd better not," said his wife. "Let me make all the arrangements. She might jib at it even now."

"All right," he said, obviously relieved. "I'll leave it all to you."

"I'm to be a godparent, I gather. I don't know who the others are. Philip suggested Miss Pendleton but Lydia wasn't amused."

"She's not been bothering them again, has she?" he asked anxiously.

"No, I went to see her this morning. She's promised me to keep away from the cottage."

He opened Sylvia's letter and re-read it slowly.

"I suppose the Ferring girls will miss her. . . ."

She sighed.

"I'm afraid they will. I'll try to get up to the Castle some time this week and see how they're going on." She drew a finger lightly over his forehead. "So you won't come to my party?"

"Can't," he corrected her. "You know I'm no good at tea-parties."

"No, you're not," she admitted. "You've no small talk. That's one of the reasons why I married you."

He smiled.

"Who else is coming?"

"Lydia can't come. She says she's got to take the brat out. . . . Mrs. Webb and Mrs. Turnberry. I wanted Mrs. Helston to meet her neighbours. We're a dull lot really. I looked round and couldn't think of a single interesting person to ask to meet her. I suppose Clare will be interesting when she comes. I wonder . . ."

"What about old Mrs. Ferring? She's interesting enough."

"I know, but she wouldn't come. She hardly ever goes out now, you know. And she wouldn't come just to meet anyone. Her visiting list is still very exclusive. We're on it *ex officio*. I don't think we'd pass muster otherwise."

"She's a marvel."

"I know. She's a museum piece. The last of her kind. Perfect to the last detail. . . . All the same, I'm sorry for those girls. Here's my first guest. Mrs. Helston, I think."

Lettice looked round the drawing-room with interest. It was a pleasant room, with three long windows reaching to within a few inches of the ground, curtains and chair-covers of flowered cretonne that was a little faded but fresh and cheerful. The furniture belonged to the least offensive period of the Victorian era, and the proportions of the room, spacious and high-ceilinged with delicately moulded cornice, robbed it of that air of clumsiness that small rooms impart to it. The well-polished surfaces shone like crystal, and books and sewing materials lay about on table and chair arm, showing that it was the living-room of the Vicarage. There was about it an atmosphere of unassuming serenity that reminded Lettice of its mistress. The leaping flames of the log fire in the wide old-fashioned grate deepened the bronze and ruby of the chrysanthemums that stood in a china bowl on the grand piano, and outlined the shadow of a tall jar of autumn leaves on the wall behind it. Lettice sat down in one of the deep cretonne-covered arm-chairs. Her head ached and she felt tired and dispirited. She had enjoyed settling into the little house and last night had had, for the first time since Harvey left her, a sense of peace and security. She would summon her resources to face the future. She would read ... take up her music again. ... There had stirred within her the beginnings of a new zest for life. And this morning it had all gone. She had dreamed of Harvey last night and had awakened to the old agony of longing and regret, the old soul-poisoning bitterness. She had given in to it without a struggle, almost welcoming it because of its familiarity. She knew it so well, had lived with it so long. It was easier to take refuge in self-pity than to fight against it. ...

Mrs. Skelton had begun her work in the cottage – still with the man's cap skewered into her hair and looking more than ever like a pantomime dame – and Harriet had gone back to London.

Lettice had found the brusque kindliness of Mrs. Skelton unexpectedly stimulating. She was a good worker, and there was little for Lettice to do after she had gone but get her own tea, which she found a novel and quite interesting occupation. She had put her name down at a Servants' Registry Office in Beverton, but so far had had only one applicant for the post of maid – a small child with adenoids and an extremely dirty face, thickly plastered with cosmetics, who announced with obvious pride that she suffered from "queer turns" and could do no rough work. It had not needed Mrs. Skelton in the background shaking her head and ramming the skewer home with unnecessary violence to persuade her to refuse the application. The applicant had lingered only to enlarge further upon her symptoms before taking a friendly farewell. When she had gone, Mrs. Skelton, who seemed to know intimately everyone within a radius of ten miles or so, gave Lettice a highly spiced account of the family's medical history. Guiltily, Lettice rather enjoyed the mixed cargo of local gossip that Mrs. Skelton carried with her. There was a rich humanity about the large grotesque figure that was irresistible. But this morning, sick in soul and body, she greeted her so coldly that Mrs. Skelton, who was quick enough to take a hint, had worked in silence, looking at her occasionally with an air of understanding that Lettice found slightly embarrassing.

She started as the door opened and her hostess entered.

"I'm sorry to have kept you waiting," said Mrs. Fanshaw. The cool keen gaze rested on her for a few moments in silence. "You don't look well. Are you all right?"

Lettice gave what was meant to be a casual little laugh, but that turned unexpectedly into a gasp. The tight band round her heart made her feel dizzy and breathless.

"Yes, I'm all right," she said. "I didn't sleep very well last night, that's all."

There was tenderness, amusement, and understanding in the faint smile.

"My dear, is he worth all this unhappiness?"

Somehow the question didn't seem an impertinence.

"No," said Lettice, "but that doesn't make it any easier."

Mrs. Fanshaw sat down by her.

"I suppose it doesn't. ... Well, how are you liking Pear Tree Cottage?"

"I like it," said Lettice. "I still haven't any idea why I came, but – I like it."

She looked at the piano, and Mrs. Fanshaw followed her gaze.

"Do you play?"

"A little."

"Do you play the organ?"

"I used to. We lived right in the country when I was a girl, and I used to play the organ in church. At Poleham in Essex. Do you know it? It seemed miles away from anywhere, though I suppose it wasn't."

Her thoughts went back to it with a sudden stab of homesickness. It had seemed so dull. Harvey had been the prince who broke into the mildewed castle and rescued the sleeping princess. Her father, she remembered, hadn't liked him, had even in his quiet courteous fashion tried to prevent his visits to the house. But Harvey had swept her off her feet. She would listen to no objections, no criticism of him. She had worshipped him – had continued to worship him in spite of everything. That, of course, had been her mistake. She had spent herself lavishly, keeping nothing back, and he had despised her for it. . . .

"Poleham . . ." Mrs. Fanshaw was saying reflectively.

"Yes. My father had no son and the estate's gone to a cousin, a Colonel Everett."

Her father had died the first year of her marriage. She had a sudden vivid picture of him – tall, thick-set, with bushy white eyebrows and moustache. She wished suddenly that she had been kinder. . . . She had always been impatient with him even as a child, irritated by his slowness of speech and action, his narrow horizon and interests. She had hardly thought of him once all these years. Harvey had, as it were, blocked her view, and, now that Harvey had gone, she saw him again quite clearly – stiff, inarticulate, unfailingly honest and kind, content to live the life of a country squire as his father had lived it before him, hating change of any sort. She'd neglected him unforgivably since her marriage. She'd been abroad with Harvey when he died. Again the bitterness of regret flooded her heart.

"I'm afraid you'll be on Mrs. Ferring's visiting list," began Mrs. Fanshaw, but Lettice turned on her with a vehemence that took them both by surprise.

"I don't want to be on anyone's visiting list. I came here because I wanted to get away from people. . . . Please may I go now? I didn't know that you were having other people. I know it's rude of me. You don't understand. I can't – meet people. I don't belong anywhere."

The shadowy smile did not fade from Mrs. Fanshaw's lips.

"Oh, but you do," she said. "My heart leapt for joy when I heard that you played the organ. Would you rather play at matins or evensong?"

"Neither," said Lettice, disconcerted and ashamed of her outburst. There was something hard and unsympathetic about the woman, after all, she decided resentfully.

"I've played the organ at matins and evensong every Sunday since I married Paul," said Mrs. Fanshaw. "And taken choir practice every Wednesday evening. It's a hand-bellows, and occasionally the boy who blows it lets the air out. There's nothing monotonous about our services. I remember, when one of Mrs. Skelton's boys was blowing, he used to go to sleep regularly during the sermon and someone always had to go in to wake him up before the last hymn could start. By the way, is Mrs. Skelton coming to you?"

"Yes," said Lettice a little sulkily. "She seems quite a good worker."

"She was a young mother when I first knew her," said Mrs. Fanshaw dreamily, "with eight or nine small children. Her husband was a farm labourer earning eighteen shillings a week, and I don't think she ever sat down from morning to night except for meals – if then. But she made life a sort of game for them all. There was often hardly enough food to go round, but she used to hide their platefuls in the most ridiculous places and make them hunt for them. She turned everything into a game. You could hear them laughing right across the green sometimes. They were a gang of young hooligans, of course. . . . I remember her once telling me that she bought a penny mask and put it on in bed to make her husband laugh when he came up. . . . He was killed by a threshing-machine at Crewe Farm about six years ago. She got no compensation because they made out it was his carelessness. I daresay it was, but he'd been up all night with a mare that was foaling. . . ."

Lettice was silent for a few moments, then said:

"I'm sorry I was so peevish. . . . Tell me about the other people who're coming."

"Mrs. Webb and Mrs. Turnberry. They're not at all formidable.

They each live alone with a son, but Mrs. Webb's is a model son and Mrs. Turnberry's isn't. It gives Mrs. Webb the advantage in conversation, but she's a little stupid and can't make the most of it, though she does her best. She has an uncomfortable suspicion that Mrs. Turnberry's laughing at her, and she generally is. . . . They've always disliked each other, but they've enjoyed their dislike so much that it's been as good as a friendship. You haven't any children, have you?"

"No," said Lettice.

She remembered suddenly that Olga had a child – a little girl called Susan. Olga had divorced her husband last year and been given the custody of the child, but she had always managed to dispose of her somehow, and hardly ever saw her. Lettice had met her once – a solemn dark-eyed child, not sad-looking but with that intense gravity that one often sees even in quite happy children.

Harvey would hate that, she thought with slightly malicious satisfaction. He had always disliked children and had made it quite clear from the beginning that his scheme of married life did not include them. Her lips curved into a bitter smile. It was amusing to think of Harvey saddled with Olga's child. . . .

"Mrs. Webb," announced the housemaid.

"Well, it wasn't so bad, was it?" said Mrs. Fanshaw. "They're dull, of course, but I generally find dull people more interesting than interesting ones, don't you? Most of the interesting people I've met have been unspeakably dull. . . . What did you think of them?"

Lettice's thoughts went back over the afternoon. Mrs. Webb, a plump little woman with smooth unlined skin and fair frizzy hair, slightly overdressed in beige georgette and pearls, conveying in voice and manner the elusive suggestion of the second-rate, had talked incessantly about her son, enlarging on his devotion to her and by implication on her own perfection as a mother. Mrs. Turnberry was dressed in a shabby navy-blue costume and not over-clean striped blouse. She had a swarthy gipsy face, bright brown eyes alive with humour, and she poked fun demurely but incessantly at Mrs. Webb, deflating her pretensions one by one as she tried to impress Lettice, and making sly little digs that were yet devoid of ill-humour. She ate a large tea with undisguised relish, while Mrs. Webb toyed delicately with a piece of bread and butter, little finger elegantly cocked.

"Well," Mrs. Webb had said at last, rising to her feet with a complacent smile, "I must be going now. I always like to be home before Colin gets back from work. Only once in all his life has Colin got back to an empty house without his old mummy to welcome him" ("Poor boy!" put in Mrs. Turnberry ambiguously), "and that was when I'd sprained my ankle in Beverton," went on Mrs. Webb, ignoring the interruption. "Such a state he was in! He didn't know what to do."

"I'm sure he didn't," Mrs. Turnberry had twinkled.

"I liked Mrs. Turnberry," said Lettice.

"Yes," agreed Mrs. Fanshaw. "She exists on an allowance made her by her elder son, who grudges every penny of it, and lives with her younger son, who drinks and – well, pilfers, let's say, and can't keep a job for a week, and yet she enjoys life; and Mrs. Webb, who has a devoted son and everything she wants and yet lives in a state of constant discontent, can't quite forgive her for it."

Lettice smiled suddenly.

"You do enjoy people, don't you?" she said.

"Yes, don't you?"

"I don't know. Harvey always stood in the way. He either liked them or disliked them. He was terribly rude to them when he disliked them. . . . He couldn't bear my not seeing things and people exactly as he saw them, so I got into the habit of seeing things through his eyes. . . . I suppose it was foolish of me."

"No," said Mrs. Fanshaw slowly. "I think it was wise of you."

Lettice turned her head away. The mention of Harvey had brought again that feeling of leaden constriction, that dull ache of despair.

"It wasn't," she said. "I've been a fool from the beginning. . . ." She rose. "I ought to go now. . . ."

"Not yet," said Mrs. Fanshaw. "Sit down and have another cigarette. . . . Tell me about Harvey. Tell me—"

There was a sudden gust of laughter in the hall, and two girls burst into the room. They wore schoolgirl coats of navy-blue, their cheeks were flushed with the cold air, their eyes bright with laughter. They stopped abruptly at sight of Lettice.

"This is Mrs. Helston," said Mrs. Fanshaw. "This is Thea and Lavinia Ferring. Now what do you two monkeys want?"

"We've heard from Sylvia," said the elder one breathlessly after greeting Lettice. "Gran said we could come and show you her letter."

"You've not come alone?" said Mrs. Fanshaw incredulously.

Their laughter rang out again – excited, slightly hysterical, suggesting release from some almost unbearable tension.

"Yes, we have," said the elder one. "Hannah was to have come with us, of course, but her rheumatism was so bad that even Gran daren't send her out. So she let us come alone. We begged her to. We said you ought to see her letter at once because you might not have heard and you might be worrying."

"We never thought she really would."

" 'You will go straight to the Vicarage and straight back,' " said the elder one, drawing herself up, tightening her lips, and speaking in precise clipped tones. " 'Do not stay there longer than half an hour. I shall expect you back not later than six o'clock. Come to me at once when you return.' "

They broke into fresh gusts of laughter.

"Gran's grim just now," said the younger. "We've not been allowed to speak at meals for two days. We got the giggles at lunch on Wednesday. Thea said—"

Again laughter seized them at the memory.

"You ridiculous children!" said Mrs. Fanshaw. "I don't know what Mrs. Helston will think of you. . . . Yes, I've had a letter from Sylvia, but I'd love to see yours."

The elder girl handed her a letter, and, perching each on an arm of her chair, they chattered like magpies as she read it.

"Isn't she lucky!"

"She's seen the desert."

"I never thought of Egypt as a real place till now. I just thought of it as something in the Bible – all plagues and flesh-pots and things."

"She's having marvellous food."

"And dancing every night."

"She's going up the Nile."

"I can't believe she won't see Moses in the bulrushes."

"Gosh! I wish I was with her."

"Lavinia," in the stilted precise tone, "I should be grateful if you would kindly refrain from using vulgar expressions."

Lettice watched the two girls as they sat there, chattering and laughing. The elder one was well-built and handsome, with regular features, fair hair, which she wore in a thick plait down her back, and level, laughing, rather reckless blue eyes. The younger was slight and graceful, with dark eyes, set wide apart beneath delicately marked brows, dark curly hair that fell onto her shoulders, and a wistful childish mouth. She turned suddenly and, meeting Lettice's eyes, smiled shyly.

"You've come to live at Pear Tree Cottages, haven't you?" she said. "Do you like it?"

"I think I'm going to like it very much," said Lettice.

"Ma Skelton told us about you," put in the elder. "We get all our local gossip from Ma Skelton. Gran says that a lady should never show interest in her neighbours' private affairs, but we've noticed that she's not above a gossip with Ma Skelton herself, if we're safely out of the way."

Mrs. Fanshaw folded up the letter and handed it to Thea.

"Thanks. . . . I love it." She smiled. "Especially the sting in the tail."

Thea opened the letter again and read aloud :

"P.S. – Please keep an eye on Mummy for me and don't let her go about looking too dreadful."

She examined her closely.

"You've got your brooch on crooked. . . . Your collar's not

straight ... Your cuffs aren't buttoned properly. ... Let's put her right, Lavvy."

They leaned over her laughing – pinning her brooch again, straightening her collar, buttoning up the long narrow cuffs.

"You little idiots!" she smiled. "I've buttoned every other. It's quite enough. Even Sylvia lets me off if I've done every other."

Suddenly Thea noticed the tea-table and sprang up.

"Oh, you've had a party! Can we finish the cakes? We're starving. There were only two tiny pieces of bread and butter each for tea. Who have you had?" She munched happily at a piece of iced cake. "Mrs. Helston, of course. Did you have Mrs. Morrice?"

"No, she couldn't come."

"I wish she'd been here. Ma Skelton says she's going to have the baby christened. We're *dying* to see it. We've never seen a baby christened. ... I like Mrs. Morrice. I wish we were allowed to know her. Gran doesn't like her trousers. She says they're indelicate. And she doesn't like her drinking at the 'Fox and Grapes.' But we shouldn't be allowed to know her, anyway, even if she didn't wear trousers or drink at the 'Fox and Grapes.' We're never allowed to know anyone interesting." She smiled at Lettice. "Shall we be allowed to know you? You look interesting, so I expect we shan't."

"Yes, I think you will," said Mrs. Fanshaw.

"Good! May we come to tea?"

"Of course," said Lettice.

"Thanks. We'd love to come. Not just for the sake of the meal, though I won't pretend that it doesn't count for a good deal. We'd better warn you that Hannah will bring us and fetch us back. It isn't that we're mentally defective or blind or lame or anything like that. It's Gran's idea of propriety." She looked at the table again. "Who were the other two?"

"Mrs. Webb and Mrs. Turnberry."

"Mrs. Webb!" They broke off into giggles again. "We ran into Colin Webb just now. We were running down the road. It was such fun to be out alone, and I said to Lavvy, 'I'll race you to the green,' and at the bend we ran into Colin Webb and nearly knocked him down."

44

"He was carrying some parcels."

"We knocked them right into the ditch."

"Thea was dreadful. She just stood there and roared with laughter at him."

"Lavvy helped him pick them up. He took off his hat and dropped that, too. He was all pink and flustered."

"Well, you were dreadful, Thea. You just stood and laughed at him. It was enough to make anyone flustered."

"One of the parcels was a box of chocolates. He was taking them home to mummy. He gets into a row if he doesn't take chocolates home to mummy. Ma Skelton says he can't call his soul his own."

"Thea, darling, that's quite enough of Mrs. Skelton's gossip," put in Mrs. Fanshaw.

"All right," said Thea, unabashed, "but don't judge us too harshly. Remember it's our sole contact with life. . . . Mrs. Turnberry wasn't wearing her amethyst necklace, was she?"

"No, I don't think so," said Mrs. Fanshaw. "Why?"

"Frank took it into Beverton last night and pawned it and came home drunk."

"Who ever told you that?"

"Ma Skelton," laughed Thea.

Mrs. Fanshaw took her by the shoulders and shook her.

"You little wretch!" She glanced at the clock. "You'll never be back by six."

A look of anxiety came into Lavinia's pale face. Now that the flush of excitement had faded from her cheeks, Lettice was struck by her pallor and air of delicacy.

"We'll run all the way."

"You won't be back by six even if you run all the way. It's six now. I don't suppose you came straight here, did you?"

"Well, no," admitted Thea with a grin. "We hadn't been out alone for years, and we had to do something to celebrate it. We went all round the green and peeped in at people's windows. We looked through the window of the 'Fox and Grapes.' Frank Turnberry was there just getting nicely tipsy. I wanted to go in and have a drink, but we hadn't any money, and, anyway, Lavvy wouldn't."

"I should think not!" said Mrs. Fanshaw. "And you'd better run off now, hadn't you? Will you get into trouble?"

"It'll probably be a case of going to bed early, but we'd rather do that than stay up. We can have fun upstairs, but sitting downstairs with Gran is like death."

Mrs. Fanshaw glanced at Lavinia.

"Would it help if I wrote a note to your grandmother to say that I kept you?"

Relief flashed into the small expressive face.

"Oh, thanks!"

Mrs. Fanshaw sat down at the bureau and began to write the note.

"It's Lavvy who's frightened of Gran," said Thea. "I'm not."

"I'm not really *frightened*," said Lavinia. "I admire her in a way. Whenever I read of people doing terribly brave things in history, I always think 'Gran would have done that.' If she'd been an early Christian, she'd have let them cut her up into little bits without making a sound. I'd have given in before they touched me. . . . I think if I hadn't to live with Gran I'd be almost fond of her."

Mrs. Fanshaw put the note into an envelope and addressed it.

"Here you are, and now off with you!"

"Don't forget to ask us to tea," said Thea to Lettice as they went out.

She heard their laughter as they ran down the drive.

Mrs. Fanshaw came back to the drawing-room, looking a little worried.

"Their father's dead," she said, "and their grandmother's brought them up. The mother's a Frenchwoman, who is only too glad to be relieved of the responsibility. . . . Mrs. Ferring's a charming old lady, but she hasn't moved with the times. She hasn't even tried to. . . . She brings up those girls exactly as she was brought up herself." She shrugged. "Oh, well, there's nothing we can do about it."

"The younger one's charming," said Lettice.

"Most people like Thea better," said Mrs. Fanshaw. "Lavvy's so shy as a rule, but she was a little over-excited today. ... Mrs. Ferring's sure to call on you, so do have the girls to tea. You've no idea what a thrill it would give them."

"Very well," said Lettice, a little ungraciously, shrinking, in the absorption of her self-pity, from even the shadow of responsibility. She rose. "And I really must go now."

Mrs. Fanshaw made no further demur.

"It's a terribly old-fashioned organ," she said as they went into the hall, "but it was a good one in its time, and it's quite easy to play."

Lettice turned to her.

"I'm sorry, but nothing on earth would induce me to play the organ. It's years since I touched it, anyway."

"All right," said Mrs. Fanshaw. "I won't worry you any more," and added, "just now."

When Lettice had gone, she went to her husband's study. He was sitting at his desk writing. He looked up with a smile as she entered.

"The party sounded almost rowdy," he said.

She looked down at him, frowning abstractedly.

"The Ferring girls came," she said. "I'm worried about them, Paul. Thea's nearly eighteen. How much longer does the old woman think she can treat them as if they were in the nursery? Well, children in the nursery are allowed far more liberty nowadays than she allows them. ... What's to happen to them? Won't you speak to her again?"

He considered.

"I got pretty badly snubbed the last time I tried," he said. "She told me, you remember, that naturally she would make arrangements for their being presented in due course. I suppose she has connections who might see to it."

"That doesn't really solve the problem, does it?" she persisted. "What's to happen after that? There's no money."

"I wonder if it's any good trying to get in touch with their mother," he suggested.

She shook her head.

"I don't think she can do anything. I'm not sure that she would if she could. . . ."

"She's very charming."

"Yes, that's the trouble. It's so much easier to be charming unattached. Two great girls in attendance would considerably detract from her charm. It isn't as if she had any money, either. . . . One feels that Thea can look after herself, but I'm worried about Lavvy. . . . They both took a great fancy to Mrs. Helston. I'll ask the old lady to call on her. She likes to call on all newcomers who are socially above reproach, and evidently Mrs. Helston quite safely belongs to the landed gentry – by birth, at any rate. . . . The more people those girls know, the better."

"You like Mrs. Helston?" he asked.

"Yes. . . . She's going to play the organ at matins, so that I can sit with the Sunday School."

He looked at her with a twinkle.

"Does she know she is?"

"Well, no," she admitted, "not yet."

Chapter Four

COLIN WEBB walked slowly across the green to Eastnor. He was thinking of Lavinia, seeing her again as she stood looking at him with that shy apologetic smile.

The apology was partly for their running into him and partly for her sister's mocking laughter. The laughter wasn't only youthful high spirits. There was in it, in a cruder form, something of her grandmother's arrogance – the arrogance that classed as "the village" everyone beneath her own social class. She could safely laugh at him, crediting him with no feelings to be hurt, no social position to be respected. Angry resentment flooded him afresh at the memory ... then the anger faded, and he remembered only Lavinia, with her wide grey eyes and wistful drooping mouth. What a child she had looked, so small and sweet and – "unprotected" was the word that occurred to him. And what a fool *he* must have looked – red and gaping, plunging about, picking up his parcels and dropping them again! He flushed hotly at the picture of himself that rose in his mind, contrasting it with another imaginary picture of a self-possessed young man, smiling easily, greeting them affably, joining in the laughter. Why could one never be the sort of person one wanted to be, he thought despairingly. At least he'd said "Thank you" when she handed him back the parcels she had picked up for him – or had he? The whole episode was a wild confusion of bewilderment and mortification in his mind.

"I'm so sorry," she had said in a breathless, rather frightened little voice as she handed them back. Her eyes had met his with compunction, with shy hesitating friendliness. Then her sister had dragged her off again on their madcap race across the green.

He had known them, of course, from a respectful distance ever since he had come to live at Steffan Green, had heard endless stories of the comfortless *ménage* up at the Castle – the place falling to pieces for lack of repairs, the two or three servants where at least a dozen were needed, the rigid unvarying routine imposed on the two girls by their grandmother. Oh yes, he thought, resentment invading him again as he remembered the older girl's mocking laughter, they might find the village an object of amusement, but he could assure them that the village found them the same. . . .

Almost against his will, his thoughts went to the old lady who, though she seldom now appeared in person, seemed still to dominate the village. Despite her terrific dignity, the diamond hardness of her would sometimes melt and reveal glimpses of a charm that made one credit the legendary stories of her youthful conquests. She was always very punctilious in her relations with the village, greeting the inhabitants with her aloof impersonal courtesy, asking after their families and concerns. Colin had thought her very kind to his mother and himself when they came to live at Steffan Green, but his mother had been resentful.

"Thinks of us as dirt beneath her feet," she grumbled. "We're nothing more or less than vermin to her. She couldn't call on me, could she? And she'd sooner be cut in little pieces than ever ask me up there."

"I thought she was very nice to you," ventured Colin.

"Oh yes, she was," said his mother, "just as she is to Mrs. Skelton. . . ."

Somehow, the thought of Mrs. Ferring had driven even the thought of Lavinia out of his mind. Odd to think of her living up there, old and poverty-stricken, in the house where she had queened it as a bride. Legends were still handed down in the village of the comings and goings of those days, the parties and dances and festivities – the road blocked with carriages, the old house ablaze with lights. . . . She now fulfilled her social duties to such of her neighbours as were on her visiting list by an occasional tea-party, for which, they said, one of the outdoor men put on the footman's uniform, and at which the provisions were painfully inadequate.

There was something lonely and isolated – never pathetic – about her. . . . Her two sons were dead. The girls' father had been killed in a railway accident soon after Lavinia's birth, and the other son – something of a ne'er-do-well, according to report – had gone out to Canada and died soon afterwards. Colin had seen their mother once or twice on her visits to the Castle – a Frenchwoman, tall and beautiful, with the Frenchwoman's traditional elegance. She lived in France, staying with her relations in turns, paying her way, people said, by her looks and charm, existing precariously. . . . She had always disliked England.

He shook the thought of the Ferring family impatiently out of his mind as he reached the gate of Eastnor. It was meeting the girls that had made him think of them. He wondered where they had been going. One didn't often see either of them in the village unless accompanied by Hannah, old Mrs. Ferring's maid.

A man was coming across the green from the direction of Beverton. He glanced at Colin with set unsmiling face, said "Good evening" shortly, and disappeared down Crewe Lane. Clifford Turnberry going to The Moorings. . . . He came over to see his mother on Wednesdays, and she took care to have Frank out of the way.

He put his key in the lock and entered the hall, glancing with almost unconscious anxiety at the clock. It was all right. He wasn't late. He always hurried from the bank to get back to her. . . . It he was later than the time she expected him, she would sulk most of the evening. If ever he deliberately spent an evening away from her, she would be coldly, icily angry for days. He suspected that the other clerks at the bank knew this and made fun of him behind his back – but he had inherited his father's love of peace, and few things in life seemed worth fighting for. Moreover, he honestly loved his mother and his home and, as a rule, preferred to spend his evenings there than anywhere else. All day he had been glad to think that she was going out to tea. Her occasional complaining "I've had such a long dull lonely day" always made him feel vaguely guilty.

"That you, dear?" she called.

He was relieved to hear that her voice sounded cheerful.

"Yes. . . ."

She came downstairs. She had taken off the beige georgette and put on a pale blue knitted jumper-suit that she had made herself and that was just a little too tight for her. She was round and plump and double-chinned, with rather shapeless ankles. She took a lot of pains over her appearance and always looked very neat and trim.

"Brought you some goodies," he said, taking the box of chocolates out of the paper bag and handing it to her.

He was a little ashamed of his habit of bringing home presents for her. She was always ingenuously pleased and gratified, but he was secretly aware (though he tried not to face the knowledge) that it was cowardice rather than affection that prompted the gifts.

Often, when he came home, he would find her in a state of brooding depression over some delinquency of the "woman" or some imagined slight of the neighbours, and the gift would restore her equanimity. Or, if he were a few minutes late, it would mitigate her annoyance.

"Oh, thanks, darling," she said. "How nice of you!"

He held the paper bag in his hand for a moment, seeing Lavinia's face as she picked it up from the ground and handed it back to him, then on a sudden impulse slipped it into his coat pocket. It seemed desecration somehow to throw it away as if it were just an ordinary piece of paper.

He followed her into the sitting-room, where a bright fire burnt on a clean hearth. She was "house proud," and the little house was always spotlessly clean. She was as fond of comfort, too, as a cat – liked deep chairs and warm fires, clean hearths, plentiful well-cooked food. She took a good deal of trouble to make his home pleasant and comfortable, and he recognised her unspoken contention that it was ungrateful of him not to spend all his leisure time in it.

She sat down on the settee by the side of the fire, opening the box of chocolates, and he stood on the hearthrug looking down at her. He was of slender build, with fair hair, a pale narrow face, and prominent cheek-bones over which the skin seemed to be tightly drawn. He looked over-serious for his youth and a little worn.

"Did you have a nice time at the Vicarage?" he said.

She selected a chocolate and put it into her mouth.

"Oh, I don't know," she said, munching it. "I can't stand that Mrs. Turnberry. Common, I call her. She was dressed like nothing on earth. You should have *seen* her blouse. Filthy. She looked as if she'd do with a good wash herself, too. She always does. And the way she ate!" She wrinkled up her snub nose in aloof disgust. "You'd have thought the woman was actually *hungry*."

He sat down and lit a cigarette.

"Was Mrs. Helston there?"

"Yes. Can't say I took to her much."

"I thought she looked rather nice," he said tentatively.

When new-comers came to the village he always hoped that his mother would make friends with them. It would relieve him of a part of his responsibility. He needn't think then of her waiting all day for him to come home in the evening. . . . But she seemed determined that this should not happen. There was something almost perverse in the way in which she immediately proclaimed disapprobation of every new acquaintance, as though a secret part of her were bent on blocking that particular means of escape to him. She had never, as far as he remembered, had any intimate women friends. Her attitude seemed to be that she had devoted herself entirely to her husband and now was devoting herself entirely to her son, and that nothing must free them from the guilt of her "loneliness" if they neglected their duty to her. He hardly remembered his father, but sometimes, when he brought home presents to assure him of a welcome or paid her insincere compliments to stem the flood of her complaining, he wondered rather ashamedly if his father's "devotion" – so often vaunted by her – had had its roots in the same feeling.

She selected another chocolate.

"I thought she was stuck-up. Gave herself airs. I've no use for that sort."

Her father had been a small draper in Beverton and the fact

invested her social consciousness with a certain aggressiveness. Generally speaking, she disliked her social inferiors just for being her social inferiors, and disliked her social superiors for "giving themselves airs."

"Perhaps she's shy," he suggested.

"Shy?" she said. "Oh no, she isn't shy. Just stuck-up. I believe she's quite friendly with those horrid fast Morrices. Birds of a feather, I suppose. Mrs. Skelton says she's divorced her husband. That probably means she's no better than she should be herself. I'm old-fashioned, I suppose, but I've no use for that sort of thing. I've got high standards. Your father never so much as looked at another woman."

Her eyes went complacently to the photograph of her husband that stood on the mantelpiece. He had been a large, gentle, uxorious man – a willing pupil to her training, believing that his every halfpenny, his every thought, his every minute, were less than her due. She considered her son's relation to her to be pretty much the same. As her son, he owed her all his money, care and time, and she took for granted that he should give them readily. Indeed, as her son, he owed them even more than her husband had done, because of the "sacrifices" that she considered she had made for him. She honestly looked on her expenditure of time and thought and money during his childhood as a debt that could only be repaid by a lifelong devotion. She had felt outraged when he had insisted on keeping his salary and paying a sum for housekeeping instead of giving her the whole sum and receiving pocket-money from her as his father's custom had been. For a week she had barely spoken to him, but when she saw he was determined she had surrendered. It was her only defeat, and she still had a sense of angry aggrievement when she thought of it.

"I asked Mrs. Turnberry how Frank was getting on," she said with a little malicious smile. "She changed the subject pretty quick. ... I told her about that necklace you got me for my birthday, too."

He said nothing. He knew that she was constantly boasting of his devotion. She told everyone how he got her a cup of tea in bed in the morning and put on her slippers for her in the evening. She often did it when he was present, causing him agonies of embarrassment. It was, of course, more her own merit than his that she was lauding. He had to steel himself to the secret amusement that he knew this caused their acquaintances.

"Well, I'll go and have a wash," he said, rising.

On his way upstairs his thoughts went back over the day – past the meeting with the Ferring girls, to the lunch hour, when he had met Greta Dorking in Beverton and she had cut him. All afternoon he hadn't been able to think of it without secret agitation. Now quite suddenly he could think of it calmly – think calmly, indeed, of the whole episode. It was as if the memory of his meeting with Lavinia stood by him, giving him new courage.

Greta Dorking was one of the assistants at the Beverton Free Library. She had got several books for him that he had wanted for his banking examination, and had generally tried to attend to his needs herself. One day, on an impulse, he had asked her to have lunch with him. She was pretty and high-spirited, with blue eyes, a pert *retroussé* nose, and a quick provocative impudence. He laughed more than he had done for years and began to feel – a strange thing for him – young and high-spirited himself. They met several times after that, and at last he found courage to ask his mother if he could bring her to tea one Saturday. It needed a good deal of courage, for he knew that she would consider it an insult to her. He kept telling himself that it was the most natural thing in the world for him to have a girl friend, and that she couldn't reasonably resent it, but he knew all the same that she would resent it. And she did. . . . She felt, in fact, almost as she would have felt towards her husband had he begun to show interest in another woman.

She became icily cold and distant in her manner to him, ignoring his presence, not speaking to him unless it were necessary. Greta came to tea, but even her vivacity could make little headway against the atmosphere. Colin's fighting spirit, however, had been aroused. He saw himself suddenly as that despicable subject of farce and caricature, the woman-ridden man. He determined to fight not only her domination of him but his secret fear of her. The battle was between the two of them. Greta didn't really come into it. He went to the pictures with her several times. His mother's icy silence continued, and her plump face took on a drawn pinched look. He knew that she was really suffering, and that her angry resentment would not let her sleep or eat. The state of things began to tell on him, too. He was kind-hearted, sensitive, and peace-loving. He could not endure the thought of giving her pain. He had always blindly accepted her estimate of the "sacrifices" his upbringing had entailed. He fought desperately against it, but he couldn't help feeling – as indeed she meant him to feel – ungrateful and unkind. The worst of it was that, once the novelty of the friendship had worn off, Greta began to bore him. The charm of her slang and cheap back-chat exhausted itself. She laughed too loudly and too frequently. The intimacies she attempted in the darkness of the picture-house embarrassed him. He went to dances with her once or twice, but his mother refused to go to bed till he returned, and the thought of her waiting up for him, a wan reproachful ghost, troubled him all evening. He began to make arrangements to meet Greta at times when he knew that his mother was going out herself and so would not know of it. Greta was quick-witted and saw how things were. She turned up her *retroussé* nose and her impudence became less provocative than sneering.

"Thursday? Oh yes, certainly. I suppose your mother's going out then, is she?"

"Saturday afternoon? Yes, I'll come. Sure your mother can spare you?"

There came the inevitable day when she said bluntly:

"No, thanks. I've had enough of it. I'm not so hard up for boys that I've got to take one out of its mummy's lap."

That was the end. He gave in finally and completely. His mother did not reproach him. She merely took him back in an atmosphere of loving forgiveness, putting herself out for his comfort and entertainment more than she had ever done before. He felt grateful and self-reproachful and, secretly, deeply humiliated by the whole episode. He decided to cut girls – and indeed friends altogether – out of his life. After all, he told himself, it was the least he could do. He owed everything to her. And what could he ask for beyond her kindness and companionship? She needed him, and, he told himself, he needed her. He had met Greta several times since the ending of their friendship, and she had always given him a distant nod of recognition, raising the *retroussé* nose in disdain. Once he heard her say "Mother's pet" to her companion as they passed him.

Today was the first time she had cut him. And today, oddly enough, was the first time he could look back on the episode without a feeling of sharp humiliation. It seemed to belong to a part of his life that was over and done with. It was strange, the feeling he had of starting a new life today. He didn't examine or analyse it. He only knew that he looked forward with an excitement he had never known before, but he didn't know what he was looking forward to. . . . There was nothing, after all, to look forward to but days and weeks and months of work at the bank in the day-time and his mother's companionship in the evening. . . . He washed his hands in the bathroom, then went to his bedroom.

His desk stood between the windows, and on it were the text-books and note-books he was using for his banking examinations. He brushed his hair at the mirror, then sat down at his desk and took up *Practice and Law of Banking*, opening it at the place where the marker was. He sat there, his eyes fixed unseeingly on the page, surrendering himself to this new secret sense of delight, this heady feeling of anticipation. . . .

When he returned to the sitting-room, his mother still sat by the fire, nibbling chocolates. Though middle-aged, she looked, soft and sweet and kittenish in the firelight. She smiled at him as he entered, and a sudden warm rush of affection for her flooded his heart. He remembered how, when he was a little boy, she used to make up stories for him about the adventures of an imaginary trio of friends – a mouse, a rabbit, and a pig.

"It's Saturday tomorrow, isn't it?" she said. "Shall I meet you in Beverton for lunch and we can go to the pictures in the afternoon?"

"I'd thought of going for a walk," he said. "I want to stretch my legs."

"All right," she said. "We'll go for a walk instead."
He hesitated for just a second, then said:
"Good! That'll be fine!"

Chapter Five

MRS. TURNBERRY crossed the green on her way home from the Vicarage tea-party. She had enjoyed her tea. With Frank, of course, you couldn't have things dainty, and it was nice to have things dainty once in a while. Mrs. Webb had amused her, too, cracking up Colin's devotion when everyone knew that the poor lad hadn't any choice. He'd got to be devoted or go through the hoop. . . . One couldn't dislike the boy, but he was a spiritless sort of creature. Her Frank wasn't anything to boast about, she knew, but she'd rather have him than Colin Webb any day. It had been as good as a play to see Mrs. Webb, all dolled up in her pearls and beige georgette, cocking her little finger as she drank her tea and talking in her put-on voice. She had enjoyed the entertainment without the faintest tinge of malice or bitterness. She had been amused, too, by Mrs. Helston, and here there was the faintest tinge of bitterness. Looking like death (and a pretty little thing really, too), just because her husband had gone off with another woman. My goodness, thought Mrs. Turnberry, I wish that was all I'd had to put up with. I'd think myself a lucky woman, all right. The late Mr. Turnberry had been consistently unfaithful throughout his married life, and, though she had suffered a good deal in the early years, she had finally become so accustomed to this state of things that she would have felt embarrassed and disconcerted had he returned to his allegiance. Men, said Mrs. Turnberry to herself . . . and let her thoughts run over the whole gamut of bitterness, tolerance, amusement, contempt, reluctant admiration. They get away with it every time. . . . Oh well, I suppose we couldn't do without them. . . .

She would have liked to drop in on Crewe Cottages, but there wasn't time. It was the evening Clifford came to see her, and Frank might be at home. She didn't like leaving Frank alone in the house. You never knew what he'd take. There wasn't much of value left, but he'd take anything to pawn for a drink. Once last summer he'd picked every flower in the garden, tied them into bunches, and stood in the market-place in Beverton selling them at sixpence each. She'd never seen Clifford as angry as he was when he heard of that – Clifford, a respectable Beverton solicitor. He'd come over to Steffan Green, his face grey with fury, and said that if ever she let such a thing happen again he'd stop her allowance. That had amused her. ... "Let it happen again." As if she or anyone else could prevent its happening! She was glad she'd found out about the amethyst brooch in time. She'd been down to Beverton this morning to get it out of pawn. ... It had taken most of her house-keeping money, but she didn't want to leave it till next week. Sometimes Clifford made her show him all her jewellery – such as it was – to make sure that Frank hadn't taken any of it. She slackened her pace as she passed the last of Crewe Cottages, where Mrs. Barton lived with her six children, the eldest only nine years old. The temptation to go in was very strong, but she resisted it. She'd have liked to call at Mrs. Skelton's, too, and find out when that novelist woman was expected and what wages Ivy was going to get. ... But she must get home quickly, so as to be ready for Clifford. ...

Mrs. Turnberry loved popping into the cottages and was always welcomed by their inhabitants. Her known poverty, the straits she was put to in order to keep her home together, the public scandal of her younger son, seemed somehow to bridge the social gap that would otherwise have divided her from them, and they accepted her as one of themselves. She was almost as shameless a gossip as Mrs. Skelton herself. She would sit in the little cottages, talking, listening, laughing (for life had not yet succeeded in damping her good spirits), hearing all about them and their neighbours. They sent for her when they were sick and applied to her when they were in need. There was nothing of the ministering angel about her – she teased them and joked with them and her jokes were often extremely ribald – but she never failed them. They knew that she had no money herself, but she went round and got it for them from other people, begging for them where she had never begged for herself, however desperate. ... She collected the money for Mrs. Barton's baby clothes. She collected subscriptions every week for extra milk for little Lily Peters, who was tubercular. At need she would even beard old Mrs. Ferring at the Castle and force her to open her reluctant purse-strings. And she did it all because she enjoyed doing it, because she took a deep rich interest in humanity. Despite her own experience, she gloried in marriage and childbirth, rallying courting couples in a way that used to shock her elder son inexpressibly.

A fat little Barton child came toddling down to the gate and stood grinning at her through the bars. She smiled back at him – a large smile that showed her gaping yellow teeth (Clifford had given her money once for a false set, but somehow or other the money had found its way to Frank) – and, taking a small rosy apple from her basket, handed it to him. In the autumn she generally carried a supply of apples from the tree at the bottom of her garden to give to the village children. When she could afford it, she carried sweets for them, too. She loved children, and perhaps the happiest time in her life had been when Clifford and Frank were children. They had been fond of each other in those days. Frank was the younger and had always looked up to and admired Clifford. Even now, despite all that happened, he was fond of Clifford, and ingenuously proud of his success. ... She had reached the gate of The Moorings, and stood there for a moment breathing in the crisp acrid smell of autumn. She enjoyed these days of late October – the faint tang of frost in the air, the morning mists, the mingled smell of garden fires and dead leaves, the flaming loveliness of the woods that surrounded the little village on all sides. In the gardens, ladders stood high against the apple trees, and the last chrysanthemums flaunted themselves bravely in the dying borders. A man was coming down the road from the direction of the woods, a pile of firing under his arm, dragging behind him a branch that had been blown down in last night's gale. Some children passed with baskets of blackberries. A small boy stopped to show her the "conkers" he had gathered.

"Fine!" she said. "My word, aren't you lucky!"

As she turned from the gate, Frank came round the side of the house, carrying a spade and beaming a welcome. He was big and clumsy and powerfully built, with a long face and heavy features, generally more or less dirty. For special occasions, his mother would clean him up as though he were a little boy, washing his face and ears and neck and brushing his hair, though she scarcely reached his shoulder.

"Hello, Mother," he said affectionately.

The odd part of the whole thing was that he really was fond of her. His affection didn't prevent his stealing from her and lying to her, but, for all that, it was real enough. When she was ill, he would look after her as tenderly as a woman, putting eau-de-Cologne on her head, shaking her pillows, bringing up her meals on a tray covered by the best tray-cloth. He would often work with her in the house, scrubbing, scouring, cooking. She would tease him and he would bellow with laughter, and the two of them would be as happy together as if he were a little boy again and she a young mother. Then the craving for drink would come on him. . . . She always knew the signs. He would become silent, a far-away look would replace the ingenuous smile on his large good-natured face, and it would be a battle of wits between the two of them – he trying to get money, she trying to circumvent him. Even when he was drunk, he was never unkind to her – or to anyone. He merely became stupid and fuddled and more bewildered than ever, accepting her reproaches without resentment, promising to amend.

"Been digging the potato patch," he said, still smiling at her, waiting for her commendation.

He enjoyed working in house and garden because it was something within his powers. He didn't have to puzzle his brains over it. He wasn't continually making mistakes or being badgered by other people.

"Good boy!" she said. "Have you had your tea?"

"I waited," he said. "I wanted to have it with you."

"But I've been out to tea."

"I thought you might want some more."

She smiled at him.

"I never say 'no' to a cup of tea," she said, "but we'll have to be quick. Clifford's coming, you know."

They went round to the back door and into the stone-flagged kitchen where they had all their meals. She watched him as he stood scraping his boots on the scraper. He looked disgracefully shabby – his suit shapeless, frayed at the cuffs and trouser-ends. It wasn't any use trying to make him look decent. She'd bought him a new overcoat at the beginning of the winter with money saved from Clifford's allowance, and he had pawned it the next day. She took it out of pawn and he pawned it again two days later. Now he went about in a torn and greasy raincoat.

"I put the kettle on all ready," he said. "You sit down, Mother, and I'll make it."

He had set the kitchen table for two, with loaf of bread, jar of jam, and a milk bottle.

"I expect you're tired," he said, taking an earthenware teapot and putting tea into it. "I'll soon have it ready. . . . I'll turn over the rest of the vegetable ground tomorrow. We ought to have some frost soon."

She remembered suddenly that he had been alone in the house before she came.

"You've not taken anything, have you, Frank?" she said.

"No, Mother," he said.

He didn't seem annoyed or surprised.

He made the tea and poured her out a cup.

"What time did you get back?" she said, watching him narrowly.

She had found him a job loading delivery vans at Bruce's, the big grocers at Beverton, and she got up at five every morning to see him off – cooking his breakfast, preparing his lunch and tea for him to take with him, giving him money for the journey and a packet of cigarettes. Though he still went off at the same time every morning and came home about the same time in the evening, she'd had a suspicion for some days that he'd lost the job. Yesterday was the day he should have brought her his pay, but he'd told her a long involved story about leaving it for a moment in his raincoat pocket on the bonnet of one of the vans and finding it gone when he came back. He had said that he had dug the potato patch this afternoon. . . . That meant that, knowing she was out to tea, he hadn't waited till his usual hour for coming back.

"Have you lost your job, Frank?" she said.

"No, Mother. Why?" he asked in a tone of innocent surprise.

She said nothing.

She knew that he'd lost it. He couldn't hide anything from her. She'd go round and see Mr. Bruce tomorrow and find out what had happened. Perhaps it was just that he was too clumsy and stupid. He might quite easily have tired of the job and stopped going of his own accord. If only it weren't that he'd – taken things. . . .

"It's colder, isn't it?" he said, changing the subject. "I think it's going to freeze." He heaped sugar into his tea, stirred it up, took a great gulp, and went on, "Old Wilton brought round that mare he's worrying about. You can see her ribs standing out. I told him it was teeth trouble. I've told him so before. She's not digesting her food. And he shouldn't feed her on wheat chaff. Straw's no good to a horse. It's different with cattle. . . ."

Despite his large clumsy hands, he had a wonderful touch with animals. He could handle a broken leg as skilfully as any vet, and all the farmers around consulted him about their animals' ailments. She had tried to have him trained as a vet once, but a curious lack of coordination of his faculties had made him fail at that, as at everything else. He couldn't memorise anything or pass the simplest exam. His gift was instinctive. The rules and science of it bewildered him. He couldn't concentrate so far as to take in even a paragraph of print. And he couldn't stay away from home. He ran away from school to come home. He ran away from the veterinary college and came home. They sent him as a pupil to a farmer in Surrey and he ran away from there and came home. In the end her husband had given up all hope of settling him in life and solved the problem

64

by ignoring his existence. He lived at home, working in the garden and helping his mother in the house, careful to keep out of his father's way. Those had been quite happy years for both mother and son. He was company for her. They got on well and had endless little jokes together. He drank occasionally as a solace, but had not yet turned to it to keep his sense of inadequacy permanently at bay. . . . Then her husband had died, his affairs in wild confusion, and Clifford had taken charge. He said that he would allow her two pounds a week and that Frank must get a job and pay her a pound a week towards housekeeping. They both stood in awe of Clifford – Clifford, in a good position, with a smart wife and comfortable house in Beverton. But the smart wife and comfortable house took a good deal of money, and Clifford, naturally perhaps, resented the two pounds a week, and couldn't endure the suspicion that any of it went to keep his ne'er-do-well brother in idleness.

Frank was taking enormous bites out of a thick slice of bread and jam with obvious relish. There were traces of the jam all round his mouth.

"Jam on his fingers and jam on his nose," she said, quoting a parody of a nursery rhyme that she had made up for them when they were children.

They began to laugh together childishly, irrepressibly, laughing finally at nothing, enjoying the laughter for its own sake. They had always been able to do that. . . . Suddenly she heard the click of the garden gate and put out a hand to stop him.

"Hush!" she said. "What's that?"

"The post," he suggested.

Anxiety descended on her spirit. She dreaded the post. Only last week she had received a bill from a Beverton poulterer for two ducks, and, when she called to say she had never had them, he told her that Frank had bought them and asked for them to be put down to her. Frank had denied it, of course, but she had had to pay. Things like that were always happening. . . .

There came four sharp knocks at the door.

"It's Clifford!" she said, rising hastily. "Don't let him see you. Go out at the back and wait till he's gone."

"All right." He took his old raincoat from behind the kitchen door, then turned to her. "Give me sixpence, Mother," he pleaded. "I haven't got any money."

She took up her shabby black bag, the leather worn grey, the clasp broken, and, burrowing into it, brought out four coppers.

"It's all I've got," she whispered urgently. "Now go. . . . Quickly!"

He slipped out of the back door into the dark.

She opened the front door and gave a well-simulated start of surprise.

"Why, it's Clifford!" she said brightly.

He wore a neat, well-tailored navy-blue overcoat and a bowler hat. His bowler hat always faintly amused her. It seemed to express his personality as no other headgear could have done.

He came into the hall, took off his hat, and, bending down, kissed the air in the region of her cheek.

"You were expecting me, weren't you?" he said, discounting her pretence of surprise.

"Well, yes, I suppose I was, but I thought you might be later. Come into the drawing-room, dear."

She took him into the tiny drawing-room, and put a light to the gas-fire. The room had a stuffy unlived-in atmosphere. She and Frank always sat in the kitchen, and she never entertained nowadays.

He sat down wearily and uncomfortably on a low plush-covered chair.

"How's Marcia?" she said.

"Quite well, thanks."

"And you?"

"Yes, thanks."

"I've just been to tea to the Vicarage," she went on chattily. "Mrs. Webb and me and Mrs. Helston. She's taken one of Pear Tree Cottages, you know. . . ."

He nodded absently, and she prattled on about local affairs, telling him that a novelist had taken Honeysuckle Cottage and that Mrs. Skelton's Ivy was going there as maid. He watched her, frowning. He knew that bright artless manner of hers. It meant that she had something to hide.

"I'm sorry, Mother," he said, cutting her short, "I can't stay long. ... May I see your accounts?"

"Yes, of course, dear," she said, getting up and going to the little bureau.

He took the paper she gave him and studied it, his frown deepening. It accounted for last week's two pounds religiously. If only he could be sure that none of it had gone on that wastrel Frank! Tooth-brush ... soap flakes ... lard ... shoe blacking – small sums that he couldn't check (she'd learnt to avoid things that he could demand to see), but he was pretty sure that they all represented doles to Frank. She cooked her accounts shamelessly, he knew, and she was as slippery as an eel. There was no getting upsides with her. He felt tired and baffled.

"Have you got receipts for all these things?" he said.

"Well, dear," she said, "not the little things. ... One couldn't. ..."

He examined the list again. She sat watching him. Isolated irrelevant memories of his childhood flashed into her mind. She remembered how once he had crawled along the bed of the muddy ditch that ran under the entrance to the front gate in a new white sailor suit. She'd been so annoyed that she'd smacked him. The memory made the sight of him, sitting there pompously in judgment on her, so funny that she couldn't help smiling.

"Has Frank given you his pound this week?" he said, looking up sharply.

There was sudden tension in the air. They were coming to the crux of the matter.

"Why, yes, Clifford," she said innocently, "of course," then wished she hadn't added the "of course." It seemed just to overdo it.

He fixed his eyes on her intently, but long practice had taught her to meet his gaze without flinching.

"Has he still got his job?"

"Oh yes," she assured him.

"It's nice for Marcia and me," he went on with sudden bitterness, "to think that my brother's loading vans at Bruce's."

"Well, Clifford," she said, "it's a job, and it's the only one he could get."

"I know." He looked at her again. "You're *sure* he gave you his pound?"

"Of course."

"And you don't owe any bills?"

"No, none."

He took out his pocket-book and handed her two pounds.

"Not a penny of that is to be spent on Frank, mind," he sad sternly. "He buys his own clothes, of course?"

"Of course," she said, and added as she put the notes into her pocket, "Thank you, Clifford."

He looked at her again, wondering how much she owed, certain that Frank had never bought himself an article of clothing in his life. Her eyes slid from his at last as she said conversationally:

"It's gone colder, hasn't it? But then it's been such a mild autumn till now. Haven't the trees been lovely?"

She made as if to get up, thinking the visit at an end, but he still sat there, gazing at her sombrely.

"Look here, Mother," he said at last, "Marcia and I have been talking things over. We can't go on like this."

Her heart began to beat unevenly, but her expression of innocent surprise did not alter.

"Like what, dear?"

"You know," he said shortly. "It's not too easy for me to spare this two pounds a week and it's not very pleasant to know that a good proportion is spent on that" – a look of savage dislike came into his face – "good-for-nothing lout. We've got more bedrooms than we need at Brookfield, and it would be cheaper and more comfortable for you to come and live with us."

She had gone white and was trembling a little. Brookfield – that smart, shining, newly-built house just outside Beverton, with its modern furnishings, its up-to-date labour-saving devices, its comfortless comfort. She visited it as seldom as she could and always said to Frank on her return, "Well, I shouldn't like to live there, that's all." And Marcia – hard and smart and bright, like the house, with her social pretensions, her thinly veiled contempt of her mother-in-law, her open resentment of the fact that her husband had to give her money that might have been spent on his wife. Living on sufferance with Marcia in that grand cheerless house. . . .

"I couldn't leave Frank, Clifford," she said, clutching at the nearest excuse.

"Of course you could," he said impatiently. "It'll do that wastrel good to have to stand on his own feet. It's just what he needs. . . . He'll get on all right."

"He won't, Clifford. . . ."

Without her, she knew, Frank would sink to – she couldn't bear to think what he'd sink to. And he wasn't a wastrel. Clifford didn't understand. It wasn't his fault that he was like that. . . .

"I couldn't leave this house, Clifford," she said breathlessly. "I've lived here ever since I married your father. It's everything to me. The garden—"

A faintly indulgent smile came into his face.

"Of course you can leave it, Mother," he said. "It may be a bit of a wrench at first, but you'll soon get used to it. I've given a good deal of thought to the subject and I'm quite sure it's the best for us all. In any case, you're getting old and you need someone to look after you. You might be taken ill at any time. Marcia will be like a daughter. . . ."

Mrs. Turnberry smiled wryly. However ill she was, she'd rather have Frank's loving unskilled care than Marcia's cold efficiency.

"I'm sorry, Clifford," she said. "It's kind of you and Marcia, but – I'm not coming."

He rose.

"There's no hurry," he said. "Of course you need time to get used to the idea. When you've thought it over I'm sure you'll see it's for the best. . . . Well—"

She followed him into the hall, where he put on his overcoat, kissed the air near her cheek again, put on his hat, said, "Goodbye, I'll be round again next Wednesday," and vanished into the darkness.

She went back to the kitchen and began to clear away the tea things and wash them up. She was still trembling. "They can't make me go," she said aloud as she put the saucers on the drying-board. "They can't make me. . . ." Frank would be nothing but a tramp if she left him. Well, she'd rather be a tramp herself than live in that house with Marcia. She saw herself and Frank tramping along the high roads with their belongings in an old pram. She was frightened and unhappy, but at the picture her irrepressible spirits welled up in a sudden gust of laughter. What a sight we'd look, but I shouldn't mind. I'd like Marcia to see us, though. I'd like to see her face. . . .

The back door opened suddenly, and Frank came in. He looked a little fuddled. Probably they'd all been treating him at the "Fox and Grapes."

"Clifford's gone," she said.

"I know. . . . I met him in the lane."

"Did he see you?"

"Yes. I said, 'Hello, Cliff,' and he took no notice."

She wiped her hands on the roller towel behind the scullery door and followed him into the kitchen.

"Perhaps he didn't see you."

"Yes, he did. It was just under the lamp. I said, 'Hello, Cliff,' and he just looked at me as if – as if – and walked on without speaking to me." He sat down at the table and looked up at her unhappily. "He hates me, Mother."

"Nonsense!"

"He does. . . ." He put his head on his arms on the table and began to cry. "Cliff . . ." he said brokenly. "Old Cliff . . ."

She laughed at him.

"You great silly!" she said. She stood by him and, drawing his head onto her breast, kissed his rough untidy hair. "There . . . you great silly!"

Chapter Six

OLD Hannah's footsteps re-echoed through the big empty hall as she hobbled across it, carrying a candle in one hand and shading the flame with the other. She wore a black dress and plain white apron and had thrown a short black woollen shawl over her shoulders. The candle threw gigantic shadows onto high walls of mildewed stone, where pieces of ragged tapestry bellied in the draught from the open fireplace.

When she reached the front door – scarred and blackened and almost as old as the house itself – she paused for a moment as if to gather her strength before dragging back the heavy iron bolt.

The two girls entered with a gust of cold air. Their run from the village had brought colour into their cheeks and brightened their eyes. They were laughing breathlessly as they entered. The old woman closed the door and shot home the bolt, then turned and peered at them, drawing the shawl closer over her shoulders. Her wrinkled skin was covered with brown "liver spots," and her pursed mouth worked in a curious circular movement as she stood looking at them.

Something of their exuberance faded. Lavinia shivered as if the chill of the old house had already struck through her spirit. Thea still laughed, but there was an edge of defiance in her laughter.

"Well, Hannah," she mocked, "have you missed us?"

"You're late," said the old woman dourly. "She'll have a word to say to you."

"No, she won't," said Thea. "Mrs. Fanshaw's written a note."

The old woman shrugged.

"She's in the drawing-room. You're to go to her there."

She hobbled back across the stone-flagged hall. Thea followed her, hobbling in mimicry, laughing over her shoulder at Lavinia. Lavinia smiled, but her heart was beating rapidly. She had never been able to conquer her fear of her grandmother's displeasure, never learnt to make a joke of it, as Thea did.

The old lady was seated at a small rose-wood desk in the drawing-room, writing a letter. The rigidly upright pose gave the slim slight figure a delusive appearance of height. The face, deeply lined, was hardly less white than the elaborately dressed hair. The dark, almost black, eyes were keen and searching, the lips sunken and compressed. She wore a black silk dress with a collar of old Mechlin lace.

She looked at them for a moment without speaking, then:

"You're late," she said.

"I know," said Thea, unabashed. "Mrs. Fanshaw sent you a note."

She handed her grandmother the envelope, throwing a quick conspiratorial wink at Lavinia as she did so.

The large bare room, unheated, stone-walled beneath rotting silk hangings, was ice-cold. The fire here was seldom lighted, as they usually sat in the library. But even in the library the fire was never large enough to warm the room. So long was it since the old house had been adequately warmed that its damp and musty atmosphere struck with the sharpness of a sword thrust. There was even a faint suggestion of corruption in it, as if the slow death of stone and woodwork were taking actual physical form. The old lady seemed impervious to the cold, and even Thea was little affected by it, but Lavinia found it almost unbearable. Though she had come in warm and glowing from her run, already the chill seemed to have invaded her very bones. A spasm of shivering shook her, and her teeth chattered audibly.

Mrs. Ferring glanced up from the note she was reading.

"Kindly control yourself, Lavinia," she said, "and hold yourself properly."

Obediently Lavinia straightened her drooping spine.

The old lady put the letter aside, silently accepting the excuse it contained.

"Well, my dears, sit down and tell me about it," she said. "You went straight there and back, of course."

"Of course," said Thea, faintly daring mockery in her eyes.

"Had Mrs. Fanshaw heard from Sylvia?"

"Yes. . . . She told her all about the Pyramids. She's going to Luxor. . . . Oh, wouldn't it be lovely to go to places like that! Everything here's so horribly ordinary."

The rather grim expression of Mrs. Ferring's face relaxed, and something that was almost a twinkle came into the black eyes.

"Les esprits médiocres," she quoted, "condamnent d'ordinaire tout ce qui passe leur portée."

Thea shrugged and looked rather sulky. She loved making fun of people, but she didn't like being made fun of herself.

Mrs. Ferring turned to Lavinia.

"Was Mrs. Fanshaw alone?"

"Yes," said Lavinia, trying hard to stop her teeth chattering, "but she'd had Mrs. Webb and Mrs. Turnberry and Mrs. Helston to tea."

"Mrs. Helston?"

"She's come to Pear Tree Cottages next door to Mrs. Morrice," explained Thea, who generally recovered her good humour as quickly as she lost it. "Her husband's left her for another, and she's divorced him."

The old lady tapped her fingers sharply on her desk.

"I will not permit gossip, my child." She glanced at the old-fashioned gold watch and chain that lay by her on the desk. "It's time you went up to the schoolroom. You have your work to do for tomorrow."

The two girls rose with alacrity and went from the room, running across the hall and up the wide curving staircase.

" 'I will not permit gossip, my child,' " said Thea in excellent imitation of the old lady's thin precise voice. "But she adores it really. She took care to let me finish before she chipped in. She always does."

The schoolroom was a small room on the second floor. The traditional family schoolroom, tucked away on the top floor so as to leave the rest of the house clear for the gay social life that had once filled it, now let in the rain so badly that it had to be abandoned, but the heavy oak bookcase and the scarred, scored table, at which innumerable little Ferrings had learnt their alphabet and done their sums, the ramshackle basket arm-chair and ancient toneless piano, had been brought down and put into the same places they had occupied in the original schoolroom. A small cheerless fire smouldered in the grate. Lavinia went to it and knelt down, holding out her hands.

"I think I shall die of cold one of these days," she said through chattering teeth.

Thea sat on the table, swinging her legs and watching her.

"You'll only make your chilblains worse, doing that," she said. She jumped down. "Shall I take your hat to the bedroom?"

"Oh, thanks," said Lavinia, looking up at her gratefully. "I know it'll be there again if I go."

Thea laughed.

"You are a little coward," she said. "I don't mind them a bit."

"I know I am," said Lavinia humbly. "I just can't help it."

"I'll ask Hannah to put the trap there tonight."

"No, don't," shuddered Lavinia. "That's worse. I'd rather hear them running about than in the trap."

"Well, it's not much use, anyway. It never catches any."

"I'd almost got used to them on the ground – well, no, I hadn't really—" said Lavinia, "but it was seeing one on the dressing-table. . . . I just daren't go into the room again."

"You'll have to," laughed Thea, "unless you want to sleep in here and they're just as bad in here at night."

The old house was overrun by rats, and they were becoming more and more daring. Old Mrs. Ferring majestically ignored them, Thea noticed them only to throw at them whatever was to hand when they appeared, but Lavinia had a sick horror of them. They invaded her dreams, brown, loathsome, creeping. . . . This morning she had found one on the dressing-table in their bedroom and had not dared to go to the room since.

Thea opened the door. Old Hannah was passing along the corridor outside.

"Hannah," she said imperiously, "the fire's almost out. It's as cold as Christmas. Can't we have some more coal?"

The old woman stopped her slow painful progress and looked at Thea from under her brows.

"No, you can't, Miss Thea," she said shortly, "and you know well enough you can't. You've had your scuttle today."

"Scuttle!" said Thea contemptuously. "It wasn't more than a shovelful. We've got to be here till dinner and the fire'll be out in five minutes."

"I can't help that," said the old woman with a shrug. You've had your scuttle for today, and you're having no more."

"Look at Lavvy. She's frozen."

Lavinia, still crouching by the dying fire, turned her wan face to them.

"Get up from there, Miss Lavinia," said the old woman.

She spoke from habit, not expecting to be obeyed. She had ruled them sternly enough as children, but now they ignored her. She had no affection for them. She had no affection for anyone in the world except her mistress. She had gone to her as personal maid for her first London season sixty years ago and had followed her devotedly through the triumphs of her youth, the turmoils of her maturity, to her straitened old age. Once she had held her place as lady's-maid in the complicated hierarchy of a large staff. Now she kept the old house going as best she could, hobbling painfully about from morning to night, scrubbing, scouring, cooking, with the help of Mrs. Skelton and a young girl from the next village, lying awake each night puzzling out ways and means, wondering whether she would be able to get through the next day.

"All right, you old skinflint, if you won't, you won't, I suppose."

The old woman went on her way as if she had not heard.

Thea pulled a face and muttered, "Mean old bitch," under her breath.

Lavinia giggled.

"*Thea!* She'll hear you and tell Gran."

"No, she won't. She's as deaf as a post, and she *is* a mean old bitch." Her eyes danced suddenly. "Serve them right if we hacked up the furniture for firewood. I will, one of these days. . . ."

Lavinia looked round the room.

"I don't suppose you *could* hack it up," she said. "It's as hard as iron – all of it."

"All right. Throw me your hat. You'll keep your coat on, won't you?"

When she came back Lavinia was sitting where she had left her, her head resting on her hands.

"Starting one of your headaches?" she said.

Lavinia looked up and smiled reassuringly.

"No – not a real one. It's just the cold that makes it ache a bit."

"Well, don't start a cold in your head, that's all. Gran can just put up with your headaches, but she can't stand your colds. There's something essentially vulgar, in Gran's eyes, about a cold in the head, you know."

Mrs. Ferring had never been ill herself and had little patience with illness in other people. Thea had inherited her iron constitution, but Lavinia was delicate, continually catching cold, and subject to devastating sick headaches. The sick headaches were not so bad from the old lady's point of view, as Lavinia stayed in bed, tended erratically by Thea and Hannah, but it irritated her to see the child going about red-eyed, snuffling, constantly blowing her nose.

"A little self-control, my dear," she would say, "is all that is needed."

"It really is going out," said Lavinia, watching the dying embers. She leant forward and blew them into a faint glow. "That's the last of it."

Thea went across to the bookcase, and, taking her wooden pencil-box from the top shelf, emptied its contents onto the table. Then she knelt down, her thick fair plait hanging over her shoulder, and placed the lid on the red ash.

"I'll put the bottom part on when that's caught," she said.

"Thea!" gasped Lavinia. "She'll find out and be furious."

Thea sat back on her haunches laughing triumphantly, her eyes fixed on the tiny flames that lapped the edge of the wooden lid.

"I don't care," she said. "I'll tell her why I did it. . . . I'd like to burn everything in the house."

She got up and carefully laid the box on the top of the lid.

"You're crazy," said Lavinia, torn between delight at Thea's daring and apprehension of its results.

"I know I am. I think it must be going out alone. It's gone to my head."

The flames caught box and lid and blazed up, throwing out a fitful warmth. The girls held out their hands to it. . . .

"What ought we to be doing?" said Lavinia dreamily. "I've forgotten."

"French exercise," said Thea. "We needn't start yet."

The ruling passion of old Mrs. Ferring's life had been pride of race (she had, in fact, married a cousin, not because she loved him, but because she could not endure the thought of leaving her family for any other), and in the wrack of the family fortunes – for her husband had tried to increase his dwindling income by speculating wildly – she considered that the sole duty she could still perform to it was to bring up her two granddaughters as she had been brought up. The expense of school or a governess was out of the question, so she taught them herself. She was an intelligent, cultured, well-read woman, and she taught them excellently. If the curriculum was a little old-fashioned, it was none the worse for that. Despite themselves, the girls generally enjoyed their lessons. Lavinia was the more intelligent of the two, but she was nervous and seldom did herself justice. Thea, though more stupid, was her grandmother's favourite. In her the old lady recognised something of the independence and fearlessness of her own character. Lavinia she secretly despised for her timidity and delicacy. Their lives were organised on a rigid and comfortless routine, but the old lady took her full share in it, getting up each morning at six-thirty to supervise their practising, having all her meals with them, shirking none of the governess' duties, except the walk in the afternoon, which they took with Hannah, while the old lady attended to her correspondence and to the business of her housekeeping and now sadly diminished estate.

"Isn't it lovely!" said Lavinia, kneeling forward to the blaze. "It seems to go right through you. . . . I'm almost warm now, aren't you? . . . Let's look at the album again."

"All right," said Thea.

She went to the bookshelf and took down a large old-fashioned family photograph album, bound in worn leather. They had found it when they were rummaging in the attics and were never tired of poring over it. There were photographs of Mrs. Ferring as a beautiful young woman on horseback . . . in presentation dress . . . sitting in a dog-cart holding the reins with a groom behind and another at the horse's head . . . in every conceivable costume and on every conceivable occasion – house parties, shooting parties, picnics, skating parties. The photographs had a sort of fearful fascination for the sisters, to which they surrendered half reluctantly. They resented the domination that the old woman's personality exercised over them, but they couldn't resist it. Over and over again they would recount to each other the stories they had heard of her from various sources – stories of her arrogance and recklessness and charm. She had ridden her horse up the staircase of her London house and driven tandem down Piccadilly. . . . A royal personage had been passionately in love with her and had treasured a glove of hers till he died. . . . Thea tried to break the spell by mockery. She would dress up in the faded old-fashioned dresses kept in a trunk in the attic and act imaginary scenes with the royal personage, hiding her face coyly behind her fan, saying in a high-pitched affected accent: "Oh, lor, your royal highness! No, really, I couldn't. . . . I protest I couldn't . . ." while Lavinia laughed in shocked delight.

But the spell was too strong to be broken and they always lingered over the photographs.

"Which was the ambassador who was in love with her?"

"The Austrian."

"I'd love to have been there when she drove a bath-chair with a donkey through the Park for a wager."

"Wouldn't she be wild if she knew we knew about that?"

"And the time she hit that man across the face with her riding whip."

"I love to think of her doing that. He was thrashing his dog, wasn't he?"

"Doesn't she look a sight in the one with the bustle!" said Thea, trying again to defy the spell, and added almost against her will, "She had lovely hair. . . ."

They turned over another page.

"I love this one of the chalet, don't you?"

They looked at a faded old-fashioned photograph of a shooting party – bewhiskered, gaitered, violently tweeded – posed outside a gay little wooden chalet on the side of the lake in the park.

"The chalet must have looked jolly when it was new," said Lavinia.

"It's quite jolly now," said Thea, "if only Gran would let us go into it."

"Grandfather brought it from Switzerland, didn't he?"

"No, you idiot. He'd spent his honeymoon in Switzerland and had the chalet made here when he got home for picnics and things. People used it quite a lot before Gran took a dislike to it. I wish I knew where she kept the key."

"You wouldn't dare," said Lavinia.

"Perhaps I shouldn't," admitted Thea with a grin, and added, "I bet she doesn't know that this photograph's here. She'd have taken it out and torn it up if she did. Do you remember how she tore up that other one you showed her?"

Lavinia turned another page.

"Here's Uncle Simon. . . . He looks nice. I wish he hadn't gone to Canada."

"He'd probably have died here just the same if he hadn't, you little silly, and we shouldn't have known him even then."

Thea glanced at the old wooden table, where, among scratchings and scorings and ink-stains, the name Simon showed deeply incised.

"I bet he got into a row for doing that," she said as she turned back to the album.

"Here's Father. . . ."

They looked at the pale characterless face with slight embarrassment. Though they did not remember him, they had a vague idea that they ought to feel emotion of some sort at sight of his photograph and they couldn't. They felt no curiosity about him, no interest in him. No one had been able to tell them anything to arouse either. Gerald Ferring had been as pale and characterless as his face. They looked at the photograph in silence, and Thea paid it the tribute of refraining with some difficulty from exercising her wit on it. The long moustache, wavy hair, and large vapid eyes were tempting.

"Perhaps if we'd known him . . ." said Lavinia uneasily and did not finish the sentence.

They turned over the page with a sigh of relief.

"Mother . . ." they said, and gazed in silent admiration at the beautiful face.

"It's nearly a year since she was here last," said Lavinia wistfully.

"She said she'd come again soon," said Thea.

Mrs. Gerald Ferring led a busy life and seldom found time to visit the daughters of whose charge her mother-in-law had so conveniently relieved her. When she did come she got on excellently with the old lady. She belonged to that school of French aristocracy that teaches almost exaggerated deference to the head of the family. Moreover, she was convent-bred, and the austere routine of the old house differed little from that in which she had been brought up. She was as much at home in it as she was in the world of fashion and luxury. Her family was almost as impoverished and quite as old as the English one into which she had married, but it had its wealthy members, who were willing to give her hospitality and protection in return for the cachet that her looks and charm lent to their establishments. She gambled discreetly and was a good bridge player. Discreetly she advertised her dressmaker, who, in return, never sent in a bill. It was a precarious life, but fortunately a slightly haggard air enhanced rather than detracted from her beauty. Lavinia's dark eyes dwelt on the photograph adoringly.

"She doesn't look as serious as that really," she said.

"No, but I've seen her look just like that. Then she smiles – quite suddenly."

"Oh, wouldn't it be lovely if the door opened and she came in now? I dreamed of her the other night, and when I woke up I could almost smell that lovely smell she has."

"Yes, I know. Mrs. Helston smelt nice, too. I liked her, didn't you?"

"Yes. She was like Mother, but not so beautiful. She reminded me of her. And didn't she look *rich*! I'm sure that dress she had on must have cost pounds and *pounds*."

"Wouldn't it be marvellous to be rich, Lavvy? If you had lots and lots of money what would you buy with it?"

Lavinia dug her elbows into her sides and seemed to snuggle into herself with a little shiver.

"Coal," she said. "I'd have fires and fires and fires everywhere. In every room. I'd be *warm*. When I think of rich people I always think of them being warm."

Thea laughed.

"You little pig!"

"I know," said Lavinia with a smile, "but I do. And food. Lovely food. Not the awful stuff that Hannah cooks that makes you feel you'd rather starve."

" 'Kindly eat up what is on your plate, Lavinia,' " said Thea in her grandmother's voice.

Lavinia laughed.

"What would you do if you were rich, Thea?" she said.

Thea threw out her arms in a vague all-embracing gesture.

"I'd go out into the world. I'd meet people. Lots of people. I'd have adventures. I'd be a fêted woman. I'd have lovers. . . ."

"*Thea!*" said Lavinia in shocked amusement.

The laughter faded from Thea's face, leaving it hard and sullen.

"And I will soon," she said, "whether I've got money or not. I'm nineteen next month, and I'm not going to stay here and be bullied by two old women much longer. . . . I'd marry anyone just to get away. I'd even marry" – her laughter bubbled out – "Colin Webb."

Lavinia felt a sudden rush of anger that took her by surprise. She saw him again standing there, holding out his hand for the parcel she had picked up. There had been something so – kind about his thin plain face. People laughed at him for his devotion to his mother, but that only showed how little they understood. It must be lovely to have someone to take care of one. That must be the nicest part of being married, having someone to take care of one. He'd looked kind and humble and – yes, he'd looked as if he liked her.

"Or Frank Turnberry," went on Thea. "He'd be no trouble at all because he'd be at the 'Fox and Grapes' all day."

She put on an expression of vacant good humour and raised an imaginary glass with the gesture they had seen him making in the "Fox and Grapes" that afternoon.

Lavinia stood up and went to the old fly-blown mirror that hung between the windows.

"What are you looking at?" said Thea.

"I'm wondering if I'm pretty," said Lavinia.

Thea came and stood by her.

"Yes, you're pretty," she said and added complacently, "I'm more handsome than pretty. Gran was handsome. She was big, too, like me. Isn't it funny how people get smaller as they grow old? . . . Oh, why do we always come back to Gran?"

Suddenly they heard the sound of the old lady's voice on the stairs, and, hastily seizing some books from the bookshelf, sat down at the table, as if intent on study. Mrs. Ferring opened the door and stood in the doorway. Her keen eyes flashed round the room, missing nothing.

"Pick up that book, Theodora," she said, pointing to a book that they had dropped in their hasty onslaught on the bookcase.

Then she glanced round the room again and went out.

As the door closed on her Lavinia looked at the fireplace, where the pencil-box was now an undistinguishable mass of grey ashes.

"Good thing she didn't come in earlier!" she said.

Thea, who had picked up the book, threw it down angrily onto the floor again.

"Mr. Fanshaw told Gran she'd no right to keep us boxed up here like a couple of children."

"How do you know?" said Lavinia.

"Sylvia told me. She heard her father and mother talking about it. Gran said she'd have us presented in due course. Can't you *see* it? She'd expect us to wear our old nun's veiling dresses and *walk* to London. . . . Oh, it's not so bad for you!"

"Why isn't it?" challenged Lavinia.

"You like this sort of thing." Her arm swept out vaguely in the direction of the bookshelves. "It bores me stiff. You don't really mind lessons and you like reading. You even like the awful stuff she reads aloud to us after dinner."

"Well," admitted Lavinia apologetically, "I do like it sometimes. I like it when it's Shakespeare. The words are so lovely. . . ."

Thea pulled a face.

"It makes me want to be sick . . . but it's better than when she holds forth about the family. I *loathe* the family. All that bunk about being here before the Normans came. As if it mattered to anyone on earth."

The door opened and old Hannah stood in the doorway.

"Time you young ladies went to dress for dinner," she said sourly. "I've put out your things," and withdrew, giving the door a little bang as if to preclude any argument.

Lavinia looked guiltily at the books in front of them.

"We've done nothing," she said.

"Oh, we'll do it tonight in the bedroom," said Thea easily. "It never takes you long and you can help me with mine." She was silent for some time, then said suddenly, "I know what I'm going to do. I've made up my mind."

"What?"

"I'm going to write to Mother and say that if she doesn't *do* something about me soon, I'm going to run away. And I will run away, too. . . ."

Dinner was served in the library, for the large dining-room with the twenty-foot mahogany table was never used nowadays. The girls wore badly-fitting dresses of white nun's veiling, made for them by the sewing woman who came in occasionally from Beverton. They had grown considerably since they were made, and Thea's wrists protruded several inches below the cuffs. Old Albert, the odd-job man, who had been with the family ever since the girls remembered, and had always seemed as old as he was now, put on his shapeless suit of Ferring livery every evening and waited at dinner, shuffling noisily about, too short-sighted to see what was wanted and too deaf to hear what was said to him. The dinner was elaborately served on the family plate, but it consisted of an inadequate supply of mince, with grey and watery boiled potatoes, followed by a blancmange. Lavinia's hands were so numb with cold that she could hardly hold her knife and fork. Sometimes the old lady would be a cheerful and entertaining companion, but tonight she seemed tired and out of humour.

"These potatoes are disgusting," said Thea sulkily.

Mrs. Ferring raised her eyes from her plate.

"There is no need to make comments on your food, Theodora," she said. "If you do not like anything you may leave it."

"I don't like any of it," said Thea, "but I can't starve."

"Kindly remain in silence for the rest of the meal," said Mrs. Ferring.

"Well, there's not much inducement to talk, is there?" said Thea impudently.

The black eyes snapped in sudden anger.

"Leave the room," said Mrs. Ferring shortly.

"With pleasure," said Thea.

Her sulkiness departed and her eyes danced in childish daring as she flung the final impertinence before making a somewhat hasty retreat.

Mrs. Ferring and Lavinia continued the meal in silence. Old Albert hovered about them, removing their plates with unsteady bungling fingers, dropping a knife and fork, knocking over a glass, setting down the silver dish containing the blancmange so clumsily that the loose white mass split and fell apart.

Heavy depression descended on Lavinia. While Thea was there, her high spirits made everything, even discomfort, seem a joke. Now that she wasn't there, to wink across the table, to throw sudden laughing glances, everything seemed terrifying somehow. I'm a coward, she thought. ... I'm always afraid without Thea. She looked at her grandmother, sitting at the head of the table lost in her thoughts. She was so old, so far away ... she seemed to belong to another world. ... Her depression deepened to a panic of loneliness, and it was all she could do not to get up from the table and run after Thea. ... Suddenly there flashed into her mind the memory of Colin Webb as he had stood in the road by the green looking at her, young, kind, shyly admiring. ... It was like a warm ray of comfort shining into the coldness of her heart. The panic feeling of loneliness left her, and a new confidence filled her spirit. The old lady seemed to rouse herself with an effort.

"Have you finished *Lorna Doone*, Lavinia?" she said.

Lavinia straightened herself as she answered:

"Nearly. I'm in the last chapter."

"Do you like it?"

"Yes ... but I'm reading *Silas Marner*, too, and I think I like that best."

"Better," corrected Mrs. Ferring and added, "We will read a little more of *Hakluyt's Voyages* after dinner."

Chapter Seven

THE snow, which had been falling all night, had stopped now. It lay over the garden like a soft white cloud that had drifted down from the sky, outlining the bare branches of the trees with delicate tracery of silver threads. At the bottom of the garden a bush of jasmine was coming into flower, and the starlike golden blossoms peeped like sleepy children from the blanket of snow. On the stone terrace in front of the vicarage a small space had been cleared, and crumbs scattered round a saucer of water. Across the white surface of the snow, tiny criss-cross marks radiated to this spot. A company of sparrows, robins, and tits were busily at work.

Mrs. Fanshaw watched them for a few moments from the study window, then turned back to the room, where her husband stood on the hearthrug, his back to the fire, his coffee cup in his hand.

"I think winter's the best time to be in the country," she said. "The summer's nice in the town, but the winter's such a mess. At least we get our winters clean. Just think of this" – she waved her hand towards the snow-covered garden – "in a London street." She sat down on the settee and took her coffee cup from a small table beside it. "Have I done all the things Sylvia told me to? I've fed her birds, I've taken cuttings of her pet chrysanthemums, I've bought some malt extract for Johnny Barton, and I've oiled her bicycle. What else did she tell me to do?"

He looked down at her.

"She told you to be specially nice to me so that I shouldn't miss her."

She smiled.

"Well, I'm doing my best, aren't I? Do you miss her?"

"Of course. Don't you?"

"Yes. I'd hate not to. Everything seems to be waiting for her to come back. It's terrifying to realise how much one's life is bound up with the people one loves. I feel now that I haven't any individuality at all apart from you and Sylvia. How I'd have despised myself in the old days!" She stirred her coffee thoughtfully. "Which is the real person, I wonder – the one I am now or the one I was then? I meant to be absolutely free all my life, and I went and delivered myself bound hand and foot to you."

"I suppose that it's one of the mistakes of youth to think that freedom exists," he said reflectively. "Actually there's no such thing. I believe that the only really free man in the world is a lunatic. The older one grows the more one realises that perfect freedom, if it existed, would lie a horrible thing." He was silent for a moment, then went on, "It's a man's ties – his loyalties, his responsibilities, his affections – that give him any reality he has."

She sighed.

"Yes ... but it seemed a lovely idea then – so inspiring and exciting. Perhaps it was a kind of slavery in itself. Slavery to freedom. What nonsense it sounds! Oh, she told me to ask the Ferring girls to tea. I'll ask them next week."

"What about Mrs. Helston?" he said with a faint twinkle. "Have you broken the news to her that she's to play the organ at matins?"

"Well, not yet," she admitted. "I'm still at work on the foundations. I want them to be well and truly laid. Yesterday she came to blow while I practised, and then I got her to play and I blew. She quite enjoyed it. We're going to do it again next week. It's a kind of chloroform, and she'll wake up from it quite suddenly to find herself playing at matins."

He looked down at her with his quizzical smile.

"I believe it," he said. "I don't think I've ever known you fail."

"Oh, I'm quite good with people," she admitted modestly. "It's things that bore me – figures and accounts and household mending. Sylvia beats me hollow at things. It's good for one to feel humble before one's child."

He put his coffee cup on the mantelpiece and came to sit by her on the settee.

"Old Rollings called to see me this morning."

"I know."

She made it a rule never to question him about his parishioners' visits, however curious she might feel.

"I suppose you guessed what he wanted?"

"Money?" she hazarded with a faint sigh.

He nodded.

"He was in debt again. He said they were going to 'County Court' him. I lent him five pounds."

" 'Gave,' you mean."

"Well, 'gave,' then."

"Oh, Paul! He's shiftless and extravagant. . . . You gave him five in the spring."

"Yes . . . that was for a new harrow. His old one was literally in pieces and unmendable."

"Moralists all warn us against promiscuous charity."

"I don't call it promiscuous charity, and I've not much opinion of moralists."

"What about that young man who came to you for the train fare to his dying mother in the summer? You found that he was a fraud after you'd given him – two pounds ten, wasn't it?"

"I'd always rather risk helping someone who doesn't need it than not helping someone who needs it," he said. "I read a book lately in which one of the characters said that you must pay rent for your faith in human nature. He said that the confidence trick was the work of man but the want of confidence trick was the work of the devil."

She put her hand over his.

"You're incorrigible," she said.

"I daresay I am," he admitted.

She rose, laying her hand on his shoulder in a fugitive caress.

"I ought to go over and see Clare," she said. "She was moving in today."

"And I ought to go over to Baglett End," he said, "to see old

Mrs. Bertram and talk about the New Jerusalem. She believes so utterly and literally in streets of gold and harps and white robes that I've never liked to throw any doubts on it. I think she sees it as a rather tawdry transformation scene out of a second-rate pantomime. But the prospect of it is ample compensation for what she's suffering now, and I suppose that's all that matters."

"It's about four miles, isn't it? I wish you had a car."

"I don't want a car. There's something in walking that gets one in tune with elemental things. We ought to keep contact with the earth. It's not just a question of exercise. It's something much deeper than that."

"You'll be dead tired."

"I enjoy being dead tired. People miss a lot who don't get dead tired."

She laughed – her rare laugh, soft and musical.

"Well . . . I'll go and see Clare," she said.

Clare Lennare – a thick-set, middle-aged woman, with strong features and a luxuriant crop of short white hair, beautifully waved and taken straight back from her brows, opened the door. She wore a dark coat and skirt and was smoking a cigarette in a long ivory holder.

"Hello, Helen," she said. "Good to see you. Come in. It sounds a miracle, but we're absolutely straight. Ivy's been a little brick."

Mrs. Fanshaw stepped into the small low-ceilinged parlour and looked round approvingly.

"Um. You've made it look nice," she said. "Very nice. . . . You're as horribly capable as ever, I see."

"And you're the same untidy old maypole as ever," said Clare affectionately. "Come and look over it and then have tea with me. Ivy's just making it."

In the little box-like room next the parlour that was to be Clare's study, a pile of new books stood on the knee-hole desk by the window. Clare waved her cigarette at them carelessly.

"Gardening . . . birds . . . nature," she said. "I know nothing whatever about them at present, but I'm going to study them. I've always meant to do the country, but I never seem to have had time till this year. I've done Egypt and India, most of the Continent and the Arctic region, but never till now the English countryside. I always thought that it could wait for my old age, and, as I see my old age looming in the distance, I'm now embarking on it. I'm joining all the bird and gardening and nature societies I can find, and I've ordered every periodical on the subjects that's printed."

"You always were devastatingly thorough," said Mrs. Fanshaw.

"Yes, and you were always dreamy and unpractical, and yet," enviously, "somehow you got away with it. You could do what you liked with people. I used to be jealous of you. I often think of those days. Do you?"

"Sometimes," said Mrs. Fanshaw dreamily. "It was a glorious mixture of idealism and sex repression and exhibitionism, wasn't it? Half of us were honest-to-God St. Georges out to slay dragons, and the other half——"

"Honest-to-God dragons out to slay anyone they could lay hold on," ended Clare. "Anyway, they were great days. I loved them. I've never got such a kick out of anything since."

"I rather hate to think of them," admitted Mrs. Fanshaw, "though I suppose I'd do exactly the same if I had my life to live over again. . . . Sometimes even now I dream that I'm being pushed about by policemen. I wake up dripping with sweat."

"I always knew you were a coward at heart," said Clare with satisfaction. "The knowledge consoled me for what I used to think of as your undue influence over people."

"You're one of the few of us who've done something after it."

"Yes," admitted Clare judicially, "but I'm still doubtful as to whether it was worth doing. So are my publishers in their less optimistic moments."

In the little parlour Ivy was setting down teapot and hot-water jug on the low tea-table by the fire. She wore her red knitted dress and a string of pearl beads.

"Good afternoon, Ivy," said Mrs. Fanshaw.

"Good afternoon, Mrs. Fanshaw," said Ivy, smiling at her shyly.

Mrs. Fanshaw glanced at the red knitted dress.

"Didn't your mother get your uniforms finished in time?" she asked.

Ivy blushed.

"Oh yes, Mrs. Fanshaw, but, please, Mrs. Fanshaw——"

"I told her not to wear them," put in Clare. "They were dreadful things, weren't they, Ivy? Navy-blue drill and several times too large. I like her best in her red dress, don't you?"

Ivy withdrew, smiling in shy delight.

"Isn't she a pet!" said Clare as the door closed on her. "She's one of the prettiest things I've ever seen in my life."

Mrs. Fanshaw looked at her with a slight lifting of the eyebrows.

"You mustn't spoil her," she said. "Class distinctions are rather rigidly observed in the country."

Clare shrugged impatiently.

"I've no use for that kind of thing," she said. "I like to treat people as human beings and I like them to treat me as a human being. . . . Have one of those scones. Mrs. Skelton sent them in by Ivy. They're delicious."

"I know. She's a marvellous cook, but she prefers charring."

"I'm quite a good cook myself," said Clare modestly. "I did housewifery one winter and quite enjoyed it. I did it in order to give my domestic stories a convincing background."

"I'm afraid I'm not much use at cooking, but as Paul never knows what he's eating it doesn't matter."

"I can't imagine you a parson's wife, Helen."

"Why not?"

"There was never much of the meek saint about you."

"Why should there be? You know, the old artists who painted those pictures of a sad, meek, effeminate Jesus had got it all wrong. Remember that He was the man who drove the money-changers out of the Temple and overthrew their tables. What sort of a physique does that suggest? And can't you see the twinkle in His eyes when He said, 'Neither tell I you by what authority I do these things'? Have you ever read 'The Ballad of the Goodly Fere'?"

"I don't think so."

"I don't remember it all now, but I used to know it by heart. It's supposed to be said by Simon Zelotes.

"When they came wi' a host to take Our Man,
His smile was good to see,
'First let these go!' quo' our Goodly Fere,
'Or I'll see ye damned,' says he.

Aye, he sent us out through the crossed high spears
And the scorn of his laugh rang free.
'Why took ye not me when I walked about
Alone in the town?' says he."

"How odd!" said Clare. "Go on. Do you know any more?"
"A little:

"Oh, we drank his 'Hale' in the good red wine
When we last made company,
No capon priest was the Goodly Fere
But a man o' men was he.

I ha' seen him drive a hundred men
Wi' a bundle o' cords swung free,
That they took the high and holy house
For their pawn and treasury.

I'm afraid that's all I can remember."

Clare considered.

"No, I don't like it," she said at last. "I prefer 'Gentle Jesus, meek and mild.' "

"Oh, well," smiled Mrs. Fanshaw, "I expect we each see Him as we want to see Him and it's all true. . . . You're going to write here, aren't you?"

"Y-yes," said Clare, "but I haven't got a plot yet. I'm waiting for inspiration. The background, of course, is quite simple. It's to be a novel of the countryside. That's why I've come here. By the way, are there any real characters in the place?"

"I'm afraid not," said Mrs. Fanshaw. "Characters went out with the carriage and pair, you know."

"Well, tell me about the people who do live here, anyway."

"I'm afraid there's nobody interesting. Across the green at Pear Tree Cottages there are the Morrices with one child, and a Mrs. Helston who's just come to live here. She's divorced her husband."

Clare considered this, then shook her head.

"I'm tired of that plot," she said. "The heroines of my last three books have divorced their husbands. Who else?"

"Next to them lives Mrs. Webb with one devoted son."

Clare considered this.

"N-no," she said at last. "That's too old-fashioned."

"Down Crewe Lane at The Moorings there lives Mrs. Turnberry, also with one son – quite devoted but a little unsteady."

Clare considered this, too, with pursed lips, and shook her head.

"N-no, it's been done too often. Who else?"

"There's old Mrs. Ferring who lives up at the Castle with her two granddaughters."

"Is she a member of the aristocracy?"

"Yes."

"I'm no good at the aristocracy. I've often tried." She passed a cigarette to her guest and fitted one into her long holder. "I make the butler do the things that the footman ought to do and get the titles wrong. You've no idea till you've tried how full of pitfalls titles are." Her short rather stubby fingers struck a match and held the light to Mrs. Fanshaw's cigarette, then to her own. "My grandfather was a blacksmith and what's bred in the bone will come out in the pen. . . . What about you and Paul?"

Mrs. Fanshaw looked with amused interest at the earnest heavy-featured face, the firm prominent nose, fine grey eyes and big humourless mouth. If she had been a little taller and thinner, Clare would have been a strikingly handsome woman.

"I'm afraid not," she said. "There aren't even the glimmerings of a plot about Paul and me."

"Besides," said Clare meditatively, "I've done you, haven't I? In *Amazons*."

Her visitor shuddered.

"You have indeed," she said. "I still go hot and cold all over when I think of that book."

"I idealised you, I admit," said Clare. "I certainly idealised you."

"Libelled's a better word," said Mrs. Fanshaw.

Clare had got up suddenly from her seat and was standing at the window.

"Quick, Helen!" she said excitedly. "Tell me who that is."

Mrs. Fanshaw joined her. Miss Pendleton was walking across the green. The tattered black cape covered her thin stooping shoulders, and the ancient black bonnet was perched askew on her wispy grey hair. Her wrinkled, clay-coloured face was twisted into a malevolent grimace, and she muttered to herself as she walked.

"She's wonderful," said Clare with a gasp of ecstasy. "She's a character. She's got atmosphere. She's got everything I want. She's just what I'm looking for. Who is she? Where does she live?"

Mrs. Fanshaw watched the bedraggled figure with an anxious frown.

"She's a Miss Pendleton," she said. "She lives with a cousin just outside the village. She used to live in one of Pear Tree Cottages. . . . I'm afraid she's on her way there now. . . . Do you mind if I go, Clare? She'll be worrying Mrs. Morrice, and she's got one baby and another on the way."

"I'll come, too."

"No, don't. . . ."

"My dear, I must. She's the central character of my book. I must start studying her at once. There's not a moment to be wasted." She slipped a note-book into the pocket of her coat. "I'm ready. . . ."

"I'd rather you didn't come. You might upset her."

"Of course I won't upset her."

Mrs. Fanshaw shrugged.

"Oh, well. . . ."

They went out onto the green. The bent, emaciated figure stood a moment in front of Pear Tree Cottages, staring fixedly in at the window, then disappeared down the path that ran by the side of the house to join the lane behind.

Mrs. Fanshaw knocked at the front door. She felt rather annoyed with Clare for insisting on accompanying her. Clare, however, was already following the old woman down the path.

Lydia opened the door. A cigarette drooped as usual from lips carefully coloured to match the red jumper. She pushed a strand of dark hair back from her forehead.

"Hello," she said. "I was just going to have a drink. Come and join me."

Mrs. Fanshaw entered the hall.

"I saw Miss Pendleton coming along," she said. "I only wanted to make quite sure that she wasn't bothering you."

"Damn the woman!" said Lydia angrily. "If she starts again I'll have her locked up."

"P'raps she's just come to have a look. . . ."

"I'll send her away, then. I won't have it. She ought to be in an institution."

They went through the house to the back garden.

"There the old devil is," said Lydia, throwing her cigarette onto the ground. Miss Pendleton was standing at the gate, holding the top of it with both hands, her head craned forward on her long scraggy neck. As soon as she saw Lydia coming down the garden, she raised herself and began to speak in the thin cackling voice that somehow had the effect of a scream.

"Not good enough for you, is it? Altering everything about, are you? Where's my arbour? That's what I want to know. What've you done with it? You've got no right. . . . Who are you and where've you come from? I know the likes of you! Coming into decent folks' houses and changing their things about. Whose place is it by rights? Not yours, you painted hussy, you! I'll pay you out. I'll——"

Mrs. Fanshaw went up to her.

"Now, Miss Pendleton," she said briskly, "you can't talk like that. You'll be getting yourself into trouble. It's all nonsense, too, and you know quite well it is. This used to be your house, but you live with your cousin now. Mrs. Morrice has bought it and it belongs to her. You must never come here and annoy her again."

At Mrs. Fanshaw's voice something of the old creature's rage seemed to desert her.

"She's no right to touch my things," she whined. "You're a good lady, Mrs. Fanshaw. You've always been kind to me. You did ought to stop her moving my things. My father made that arbour with his own hands." She peered around with bleared short-sighted eyes. "Where's my pussies' graves? If she's dared to lay hands on my pussies' graves. . . ."

"Your pussies' graves are still there," said Mrs. fanshaw. "I'm sure Mrs. Morrice will let you come in and see for yourself, won't you, Mrs. Morrice?"

"No, I won't," said Lydia angrily. "I won't have her inside the place."

"Well, you can see quite well from here," said Mrs. Fanshaw. "Just move a little to one side. There! You can see them, can't you? Under the pear tree. You can count them. There they are – all ten of them."

"If she touches them," muttered the old hag, "if she dares touch them. . . . What call had she to go and lay hands on my arbour? The slut she is – the painted bitch——"

"Now, listen to me, Miss Pendleton," said Mrs. Fanshaw firmly, but the old woman broke in again.

"To see her there, in the place where I was born, dressed up like a man, the shameless thing! They used to flog women like her in the old days. They——"

Clare stepped forward suddenly.

"Come with me, my dear," she said. "Come and rest in my cottage. You're tired. I'll give you a cup of tea."

The old woman turned small malignant eyes slowly upon her.

"Who are you?" she said.

"Just a friend," said Clare. "Come . . ."

She put her hand on the rusty black shoulder, and the old woman allowed herself to be led away, still muttering. Lydia had turned white with anger.

"How *dare* she come here!" she said in a low furious voice. She gave a little breathless laugh. "I'm sorry. I don't know why it gets me on the raw like this. . . . I suppose it's Jemima." She looked towards the gate. "Who was that other woman?"

"Clare Lennare. That novelist friend I told you about. I haven't seen her for over twenty years, but we used to burn churches together. Didn't you like her?"

"No, I didn't. . . ."

Chapter Eight

THE sun had come out for the first time that day, showing up the rich tints of the fourteenth-century window that was the chief treasure of the little church. The Flamboyant style had lingered in this part of England long alter it had been replaced by the Perpendicular in other parts, and the graceful flowing lines of the tracery looked exquisitely beautiful in the pale spring sunshine.

Bowls of snowdrops and crocuses from the vicarage garden stood at the foot of the font. Mrs. Fanshaw and Lydia had arranged them together that morning. For one excuse or another, Lydia had put off the christening from November, when she had first suggested it, to January, but now she was throwing herself heart and soul into the preparations and had spent all yesterday afternoon ironing a shawl of old Chinese embroidery that had belonged to her grandmother, and in which Matilda was to make her appearance.

"Play something *cheerful*!" she had admonished Lettice, when she heard that Mrs. Fanshaw had asked her to play a voluntary before the service. "I suppose you couldn't play some nursery rhymes? Matilda loves 'Pussy's in the Well.' "

Lettice sat at the organ, looking around her with idle interest. It was years since she had been in an empty church. The church itself was rather dark, but the sunlight that filtered through the windows played upon marble monuments of dead and gone Ferrings, and turned the mellow stone of the Norman pillars to gold. In the silence and emptiness was something oddly consoling – perhaps because the silence spoke so clearly, and the emptiness was so full. Here countless generations had brought their troubles and disappointments and received comfort. How trivial and petty one's own troubles seemed in face of it all! But one couldn't hold that point of view for more than a few moments. One's troubles soon began once more to dwarf everything else – even Eternity. ...

On a small table by the west door was a small pile of booklets that Mr. Fanshaw had had printed at his own expense. One of them gave the history of St. Elphege, to whom the church was dedicated, and the other the history of the church. Mr. Fanshaw loved his church with a mixture of mystical devotion and pride. It was he who had discovered the tempera painting of the Virgin beneath the plaster on the south wall and the old glazed red-and-buff tiles beneath the floor of the porch. Thanks to its poverty, the place had escaped the terrors of a Victorian "restoration" and still had its (none too comfortable) pews of blackened oak and its fifteenth-century timber roof. In the porch hung the old fire-hook once used for pulling down burning houses. Its lych-gate led into a cobbled courtyard, surrounded by cottages, hidden from the road by trees and a high bank. Passers-by were often mystified by the square Norman tower appearing as it seemed from nowhere above the trees.

She looked round the church again. Strange how deep a peace seemed to brood over it. The peace of God which passeth all understanding. ... She remembered how as a child she used to hail the words with relief because they meant the end of the service, then one day the beauty of them had struck her suddenly, bringing tears to her eyes. Her father always sat in the second pew from the front. It upset him terribly if any stranger, unfamiliar with the customs of the place, took his seat. He liked to do the same thing at the same time in the same way day after day. It used to irritate her almost beyond endurance, but now at the memory her heart ached with tenderness and remorse. It was as if some hard core of bitterness that had been in her spirit were slowly melting. But even so – she daren't let herself think of Harvey. Her new-found peace was too precarious for that. Consciously and with an effort she kept the thought of him at bay. There were moments, of course, when she couldn't keep it at bay any longer. She fought those off as long as she could, filling her mind with the little trivial interests of the country, which were yet so oddly consoling. She had begun a piece of tapestry work, remembering how, in Balzac's *Lys dans la Vallée*, Madame de Mortsauf had found solace for her grief in needlework. "L'action de lever le bras en temps égaux berçait ma pensée et communiquait à mon âme, où grondait l'orage, la paix du du flux et du reflux, en réglant ainsi mes émotions."

She glanced at the piece of music before her – a Bach fugue, infinitely satisfying in its union of emotion and balanced formulae. ... She hadn't meant to play the organ for this christening of Matilda's. She didn't exactly know how she'd let herself in for it. Mrs. Fanshaw had asked her so casually (saying that she herself was to be godmother and so couldn't play the organ, too) and taken her acceptance so for granted that before she realised it she found everything settled, and it would have seemed childish and churlish to try to back out. It didn't occur to her till afterwards that there was no reason at all why Mrs. Fanshaw should not have played the organ before the service and taken her part as godmother as well. ... She had felt horribly nervous when first she sat down at the organ – so nervous that her hands had trembled uncontrollably – but these few minutes alone in the empty church had taken away her nervousness. Imperceptibly the peace of the place had stolen upon her spirit. ...

With an important clatter of heavily-nailed shoes the small red-haired boy who was to "blow" for her (by name Noah Popplecorn, but generally known as Sandy) came up the aisle, said "Good afternoon, mum, they're just comin'," and dived into the small cupboard-like aperture where he carried on his – often unnecessarily noisy – activities. He started up the bellows with terrific energy. She waited a few moments, then put her hands onto the keys. ...

Philip and Lydia came in first, Lydia carrying Matilda. She looked smart and unlike herself in a navy-blue two-piece suit and a small blue hat with wings that looked as if it had just alighted on her head. Philip wore a morning coat and striped trousers. Matilda slept peacefully, resplendent in the embroidered Chinese shawl.

"If I'm having it at all," Lydia had said, "—and I *am* having it – it's got to be the real thing."

She had gone up to London to buy her new two-piece and hat, and had insisted on Philip's digging out the morning suit that he had not worn since their marriage. She had been furious because Maurice and Pepita – two members of the old Chelsea set, whom she had asked to be godfather and godmother – had wanted to get out of their town clothes and don shorts and trousers as soon as they arrived.

"But – *gosh*!" Maurice had said, "it's the *country*, isn't it? And it's only a *christening*. . . ."

Lydia had for a moment been too angry to speak, and when she did speak she spoke to some purpose. They still looked sulky as they followed her into church.

"Living in the country always makes people queer," Maurice had whispered to Pepita as they entered the porch.

He was a plump highly-coloured young man who specialised in the history of the marionette, and Pepita was a cadaverous Rossetti type, who dyed her lovely auburn hair a distressing blonde and contributed cookery recipes (culled from standard cookery books) to the cheaper women's weeklies. She considered that her own inability even to boil an egg added piquancy to the situation.

"Queer?" said Pepita viciously. "It's turning Lydia *crackers*."

Mrs. Fanshaw followed them, sending a reassuring smile to Lettice as she entered the church. She wore brown shoes and a brown hat with a navy-blue costume, and Lettice had a suspicion that the hat was back to front. She was conscious of a sudden pang of sympathy with the absent Sylvia. Lavinia Ferring came in behind her. Lettice wondered why Thea had not accompanied her. One seldom saw either of the Ferring girls alone. The school-girl felt hat threw a shadow over the pale oval face framed by the soft dark curls. Lettice thought that she looked paler even than usual. . . . Mrs. Turnberry was there, in an old raincoat, standing by Lydia, beaming down on Matilda, her yellow teeth showing, her gipsy face alight with tenderness.

Clare Lennare entered somewhat noisily, her short figure seeming more thick-set and ungraceful than usual in a new suit of heavy check tweed. With her, rather surprisingly, was Ivy Skelton, looking pretty and defiantly self-conscious in a dark well-tailored coat and skirt with a white shirt-blouse and a halo hat, perched at a smart angle on her golden curls.

Lettice remembered that on the day she went to London last week Clare and Ivy had been on the platform – Ivy dressed in the new costume and hat. She had supposed that one of Clare's friends had given her the outfit. It could not have been a cast-off of Clare's, and she could not possibly have bought it out of her wages.

Lettice had gone up to London on one of those sudden impulses which hold the unhappy and insecure at their mercy. She was "letting herself go," she had decided. She hadn't had her hair set or permed for months. She hadn't bought a new hat for months. She hadn't taken any pains at all with her appearance. Now that she lived in the same village as Mrs. Fanshaw and Mrs. Turnberry it hadn't somehow seemed to matter. . . . But, glancing at herself in the mirror on the landing as she went downstairs one morning, she almost heard the gloating comments of her friends, "Poor old Lettice! She's gone all to pieces," and imagined Harvey's triumphant amusement when he heard it, for Harvey, in his conquering-male fashion, had always taken for granted that her every effort at self-embellishment was made in order to attach him to her more securely. The part of her that was not enslaved to him had often been irritated by his unspoken assumption that the aim of every woman's life was to attract or secure some man's attention. The slight element of truth in the assumption made it all the more irritating.

So she had gone up to London and spent an exhausting day – having a hair perm, a facial, and buying a new hat, dress, and coat. She had lain back on the soft couch in the beauty parlour covered with a rose-pink blanket, while soft grease-covered fingers leapt about her face like the scampering of a tiny animal, and had thought suddenly how pathetic was woman's perpetual struggle to attain beauty. It was one of the pivots on which civilisation turned. Every magazine one took up was full of it. Advertisements of it covered the hoardings and filled the papers. Every shop window one passed bore witness to it in lavish display. Hundreds and thousands of men spent their lives in unending toil of hand and brain in order that a plain woman might appear pretty and a pretty woman beautiful. If every woman decided to be as God made her, the economic structure of the world would surely collapse. . . .

As she was going out of her cubicle she met another woman coming out of the next one. She had a smooth mask-like expressionless face – without a single line or wrinkle, but without the informing glow of youth. There was something horrible about it. . . . Lettice's mind turned with relief to the memory of Mrs. Turnberry's brown wrinkled skin, the deep lines carved across Mrs. Fanshaw's forehead and from the ends of her narrow humorous mouth.

A feeling of loneliness swept over her as she went out into the street. She felt like a ghost, with no place of her own. She didn't belong either to the old town life or to the new country one. She bought a hat she didn't like because the assistant told her that everyone was wearing that shape this season, and a dress that didn't suit her because the assistant told her that it was the "new colour."

Her depression increased each moment. . . . She took a taxi to her club for lunch, then, at the door, remembered that a friend of Olga's was a member, too, and was seized by terror lest she should find Olga and Harvey lunching there. She paid the man and walked away quickly to the Bond Street Stewart's, lunching in the shop on coffee and sandwiches. "Nannie" served her – the pleasant good-looking middle-aged woman in the old-fashioned uniform who presided over it so beneficently, making each of her customers, as it seemed, her special care, remembering their preferences, indulging their foibles. She had always reminded Lettice of a kindly devoted nurse presiding over a roomful of children. She and Harvey often used to go there for morning coffee. They had nicknamed her "Nannie," and all her friends had adopted the name. Watching her now as she moved about, "settling" her charges, answering their questions in that soothing reassuring voice that seemed to keep at bay a whole world of imaginary terrors, Lettice wondered despairingly how she had attained that serenity. Had she won to it through suffering and turmoil or did some people possess a secret amulet against life's unkindness?

"Lovely to get the spring again, isn't it?" said the woman, smiling at her as she took her money.

The smile heartened her, and she set her shoulders with new courage as she went out of the door that the commissionaire opened for her. Outside, she bought a bunch of violets from a man with one leg and pinned them into the collar of her short fur coat, then walked on vaguely down Piccadilly. The lunch-hour crowds on the pavement thronged about her, and her courage faded, giving place to a feeling of physical oppression that was almost panic. She had forgotten the surging crowds of the London streets and that sense of unprotectedness that had been one of the minor horrors of Harvey's desertion of her. Unreliable though he had been in so many ways, his manner had always held a suggestion of old-fashioned chivalry that she had loved. He was skilful in steering her through crowds so that no one jostled her, in piloting her across streets as though the traffic must wait her pleasure.

She got onto a 'bus and, mounting the steps, sat on the top watching the crowd below with a new detachment, as if seeing them for the first time. They were like a swarm of ants. . . . It was a strange and somehow surprising thought that each had been the object of pride and care on someone's part, had been painstakingly taught to walk, speak, blow his nose, observe the ordinary decencies of a civilised community. . . .

She got down at the end of Piccadilly and went to a News Theatre. The cartoon was depressingly grotesque, and a lengthy account of the life-story of a banana failed to interest her. The news was uninspiring, and the commentator's schoolboy facetiousness jarred on her so much that she got up in the middle and went out. She wandered idly down Regent Street for a few minutes, looking at the shop windows. She had meant to go back to Beverton by the last train, but she didn't know what to do with herself. The shop windows that used to be so full of interest in the old days seemed dull and monotonous. She wondered if the explanation were that their appeal had been chiefly to her vanity – she used to see herself wearing the clothes, the hats, the jewelry, moving among the elegant furniture – and her vanity had not yet recovered from the devastating blow of Harvey's desertion. She wished now that she had asked one of her old friends to meet her, and yet she felt terrified of running into one of them by accident. . . . If she met Harvey and Olga, of course, she would hurry past, pretending not to see them. But suppose he stopped and spoke to her. It was just the sort of thing he would do. Her heart began to beat violently at the thought, and her knees felt suddenly unsteady. Her pride forced her to walk almost to the end of Regent Street, but gave out abruptly when she reached Liberty's, and she took a taxi to Liverpool Street, where she had to wait three-quarters of an hour for the next train.

On her return, the little cottage had seemed home to her for the first time, and she had been glad to take refuge in its peace and serenity. Almost as soon as she got back Mrs. Fanshaw arrived with a bunch of Christmas roses from the vicarage garden.

"I didn't know you'd be home so soon," she said. "I meant to have them in your room waiting for you."

She glanced at Lettice's white weary face and went on to tell her how Freddie Barton had fallen into the midden at Crewe Farm and emerged coated with manure from head to foot, and how old Amos Hall, who would be ninety next month, had walked six miles to Pulleston Fair and brought home a coconut.

When she had gone Lettice wondered how it was that she never asked her about her troubles or offered sympathy and yet somehow left the impression that she had done both.

After tea she went for a walk through the woods. They were as still and quiet as if they had been laid under some enchantment, but she no longer felt that panic of loneliness that she had felt in London. Perhaps it was only among people that one could feel really lonely. . . .

Her unseen "blower" had evidently let his attention wander and allowed the small dangling weight to stray above the chalked danger line, for a loud discordant groan told her that the supply of air had abruptly ceased. Mrs. Fanshaw threw her a little grimace of sympathy, but at that moment Mr. Fanshaw came out of the vestry in cassock and surplice, and at the same moment Mrs. Webb entered by the west door dressed in her gala attire – fur coat, beige georgette dress, and feathered hat. She smiled self-consciously and complacently around her, as she joined the group at the font.

Lettice dropped her hands from the keys. Sandy opened his cupboard door, pushed out a red perspiring face, and began what was evidently an explanation of his lapse in dumb show. Lettice reassured him with a smile.

"Suffer the little children to come unto me, and forbid them not: for of such is the kingdom of heaven." Maurice fidgeted uneasily with his feet and flushed sulkily when Mrs. Fanshaw nudged him to remind him of the bowls of snowdrops at the foot of the font. "And He took them in His arms, put His hands on them, and blessed them."

Pepita's voice rose high and rather shrill in the responses, drowning Mrs. Fanshaw's soft voice and Maurice's mumble. She had inexhaustible powers of self-dramatisation and saw herself as the central figure of a deeply moving ceremony. Matilda opened wide blue eyes as the water was poured gently on her brow, uttered a faint whimper of protest, then lay there gazing serenely about her.

"We receive this child into the Congregation of Christ's flock, and do sign her with the sign of the Cross, in token that hereafter she shall not be ashamed to confess the faith of Christ crucified, and manfully to fight under His banner against sin, the world, and the devil, and to continue Christ's faithful soldier and servant unto her life's end. Amen."

Lavinia was watching with breathless interest, her small face earnest and intent. (I didn't know how beautiful it was. I suppose Thea and I had it done when we were babies. I suppose everyone's had it done. I wish one could remember it. It ought to make one try so hard to be good. . . . I must try not to be so discontented and not to mind about the rats. . . .)

Mrs. Turnberry's eyes never left Matilda. Her brown wrinkled face was fixed in an unconscious smile of tender delight. (Isn't she lovely! Frank had blue eyes, too. Clifford's were brown. That was the happiest time of my life – when they were babies. Clifford means well. He's quite fond of me in his own way. It's just that he doesn't – understand.)

Clare Lennare watched with an abstracted frown. (No, I don't think I could possibly bring it in. The only child in the book's illegitimate, and I don't think that they have christenings. They may have, of course. I must find out. I'll make a few notes when I get back, anyway. It may come in useful. . . .)

Ivy's small pointed face still wore its faintly defiant expression. (Got a sauce, he has, carrying on like what he did last night. I never said I'd marry him this year. I'm not sure I'm going to marry him at all. He's only a common labourer. . . . I had a fine time in London with *her* last week going to the pictures and all. She didn't tell me how much she paid for the coat and skirt. She laughed when I asked if it was more than a pound. She thinks a lot of me, she does. It's fun being with her and her helping me with the housework and teaching me typing. What call has George to get mad at it? If he loved me he'd like me to have a good time. Selfish. That's what he is. Same as all men. She said so. She said all men are selfish, and she ought to know. Got a bit of sense, she has. Companion-secretary, that's what she wants me to be. Goin' to pay me well, too, an' take me about with her. Says she'll probably take me abroad next year. I'd be a proper mug to go marryin' George Harker when I got the chance of that.)

"Ye are to take care that this child be brought to the Bishop to be confirmed by him as soon as she can say the Creed, the Lord's Prayer and the Ten Commandments in the vulgar tongue and be further instructed in the Church Catechism set forth for that purpose."

They were all going out of church now.

"Was it necessary to bring Ivy?" said Mrs. Fanshaw to Clare as they went beneath the lych-gate.

"Not necessary perhaps," admitted Clare calmly, "but you know I'm a communist, don't you? I've no use for social distinctions.

And she's such a pretty intelligent little thing. It's almost incredible that that dreadful old woman should have produced her. It's like——"

"Don't say a lily on a dung heap," put in Mrs. Fanshaw. "I couldn't endure it."

"N-no," agreed Clare regretfully. "The expression had occurred to me and I think it very apt, but I agree that it's a cliché."

"Seriously, Clare, do you think you're doing the child any good by all this?"

"All what? By helping her to rise above the deplorable conditions in which she happens to have been born? Certainly I do."

Mrs. Fanshaw shrugged.

"I suppose it's no good warning you, but you're making trouble for her and yourself. Her mother came to see me last night. She's worried. . . ."

"Really," said Clare with pity in her voice, "it's tragic, when one remembers what you once were, Helen, to see you engulfed like this in prejudice and convention."

"Well, never mind that," smiled Mrs. Fanshaw. "How's the novel going? Got a plot yet?"

Clare's heavy face lit up.

"A marvellous one. It's a secret, of course. I never betray my inspiration by talking about my plots. I got it from Miss Pendleton."

"Miss Pendleton?"

"Yes. It's wonderful. Stark. Goes most beautifully with all the background I've been collecting."

Clare had by this time made herself an object of amused interest in the neighbourhood. She would sit on a stile or sometimes on top of a gate and take lengthy notes of the landscape in a large note-book balanced on her knees. She was proud of what she called her technique.

"I'm an artist in words," she would say. "I make pictures in words as painters make pictures in paint. And, like a painter, I study every detail of the scene I'm painting. It takes me as long to find the right word as it takes a painter to find the right tint. And, without the actual scene I'm describing in front of me, I should lose the inspiration."

By the village in general Clare was considered more than a little mad, and George was not the only one who had been hurt and offended by the airs that Ivy put on as her protégée. Mrs. Fanshaw was secretly worried by the situation. She knew what a conflagration a small spark can cause in a narrow community. . . .

Lettice was standing just outside the lych-gate talking to Lavinia, who was explaining in her soft shy voice why she was without Thea and the ubiquitous Hannah.

"Thea had toothache all last night, so Gran said she must go into Beverton and have it seen to, and, of course, Hannah had to go with her, and at first Gran said I mustn't come alone but I *begged* her to let me because I couldn't have *borne* not to come, and in the end she let me. She said that, as I was coming to tea with you, I'd be all right, and perhaps you'd send me home with someone. That's *silly*. I can go home by myself perfectly well. . . . But she sent you a note about it, and I'll get into trouble if I don't give it you, I suppose."

"Of course, I'll see you back," smiled Lettice. "I'll go with you myself. I'd like the walk."

Lavinia's face lit up.

"Oh, that'll be lovely!" she said.

Mrs. Ferring had called on Lettice the week before, and had kept her enthralled by the stories she told her of the old days, when, it turned out, she had known Lettice's grandmother. Witty, cultured, entertaining . . . there was yet something terrifying about the stiff, small, rigidly upright, shabbily dressed figure, with the piercing black eyes and the silver hair dressed in the fashion of the last generation. While enjoying the visit, Lettice found herself nervously anxious not to offend the old lady, vaguely fearful of a displeasure of which the smiling face and pointed pleasant speech gave no sign. She understood for the first time why the two girls submitted so docilely to their grandmother's tyranny.

It was partly because old Mrs. Ferring accepted Lettice socially that Mrs. Fanshaw had suggested having tea at her house after the christening. It was convenient for Matilda, and the Ferring girls would be allowed to go there. (Old Mrs. Ferring did not recognise the Morrices' existence.) Lydia, for her part, was only too glad to be relieved of the burden of entertaining a party that would probably overlap with Matilda's bedtime, a ceremony that, despite all her protestation to the contrary, was the culminating peak of the day's activities.

"You're coming to tea, aren't you?" said Lettice as Clare joined them.

Ivy was tripping mincingly back to Honeysuckle Cottage. She was going to practise typing till Clare came home. She enjoyed sitting at the typewriter in the little parlour and pretending that she was a famous novelist like Miss Lennare. . . . She tossed her golden head as she opened the cottage door. Well, after all, people who could type didn't marry common labourers like George Harker. Only ladies typed. Everyone knew that. . . .

"Thanks," said Clare absently.

She was still wondering if she couldn't drag a christening into her novel by hook or by crook.

She walked across the green towards Pear Tree Cottages with Lettice. Lavinia dropped behind with Mrs. Fanshaw. The rest of the party had already gone on.

"I've got a message for you from Thea," said Lavinia in a low voice. "She said I was to be sure to give it you. She was simply *sick* that she couldn't come and ask you herself."

"What is it?" smiled Mrs. Fanshaw.

"It's a secret," said Lavinia. "I've got to make you promise not to tell anyone before I tell you."

"I'm not sure that I ought to promise that," said Mrs. Fanshaw.

"*Do* promise," pleaded Lavinia earnestly. "I've promised not to tell you unless you promise not to tell."

"It seems a perfect tangle of promises."

"It's nothing you need mind promising. It's nothing *wrong*. . . ."

"All right," said Mrs. Fanshaw. "I promise."

"Well," Lavinia lowered her voice still more and glanced round in a conspiratorial fashion, "she's written to Mother and told her that, if she doesn't take her away from Gran, she's going to run away, and she told Mother to send the answer to you because Gran opens all our letters at home, and so the answer's coming to you, but you're not to tell a soul about it or show it to anyone. Just ask us to tea when it comes and tell us. . . ."

Mrs. Fanshaw's rare laugh rang out.

"What *ridiculous* children you are!" she said, but she took Lavinia's hand in hers with an affectionate pressure, realising how serious and dramatic the situation was to her. Then suddenly she grew grave. "I promise on one condition – that Thea doesn't run away without telling me first."

"But you'd stop her."

"I'd try. . . ."

"She *can't* go on. . . . She says so. It's worse for her than me."

"Why?"

"She's older, and – she's got more spirit."

"I should have thought that made it worse for you. But never mind. Tell Thea that, of course, I won't say anything to her grandmother, but she mustn't do anything so silly as running away. She'd only make herself and everyone else very unhappy."

"I think she'd enjoy even that," said Lavinia slowly. "She says she's so sick of nothing happening, and that as long as *something* happens she doesn't much care what it is."

The others were waiting for them at the gate of Pear Tree Cottage. Matilda lay in Lydia's arms, gazing around with limpid blue eyes and blowing bubbles with her saliva.

"She has the most *disgusting* instincts . . ." said Lydia, wiping the soft rosy mouth with a clean handkerchief.

Philip was pretending to be interested in Maurice's latest theory of the origin of the marionette, but his answers were distrait and his eyes were fixed proudly on Matilda, who calmly continued to blow more bubbles as fast as Lydia wiped them away.

"Do come in," said Lettice, arriving breathlessly. "I'm so sorry I wasn't here. . . ."

They went into her little sitting-room, where tea was laid and a large christening cake stood in the centre of the table.

Mrs. Skelton had herself found a maid for Lettice – the daughter of a local farmer, a plump, good-natured girl of about twenty, called Bella, almost embarrassingly eager to "suit" and a good worker, if a little heavy-handed with the crockery.

"Let Matilda cut the cake," pleaded Lavinia.

"That cretin?" said Lydia. "She'd *dribble* over it."

But Philip held the small hand gently under his and cut large untidy wedges of the crumbling sugar-coated mass.

"Where's Mrs. Turnberry?" said Lydia, looking round.

"She said she couldn't be here for tea," said Lettice. "Her elder son was coming to see her."

"Clifford?" said Lydia with a grimace. "Poor old soul!"

She put Matilda down on the settee, where she lay, still blowing bubbles and playing with her dimpled hands. Lavinia knelt by her, worshipping, putting a finger into the tiny hand and feeling a thrill of delight as the fingers closed round it tightly.

"Won't you have some tea, Lavinia?" said Lettice.

"Oh, not yet," said Lavinia softly. "She's so lovely. . . ."

"You're looking much better than you did when first you came, Mrs. Helston," said Mrs. Webb in her making-polite-conversation voice. She had thrown her fur coat open and sat preening herself and fingering her pearls.

Lettice glanced at her reflection in the mirror on the wall.

"Am I . . .?" she said vaguely.

Yes, she was looking her best today. In the old days she would have been glad, because Harvey would have been proud of her. She had looked terrible, she knew, those last few weeks when she had been fighting that desperate losing battle to win him back from Olga. Sleepless nights and days of sick suspense had drained her beauty, leaving her haggard and heavy-eyed. In her despair, she had even tried to use that as a spur to his dying love, appealing mutely to his pity, though she knew in her heart that pity can kill love. Well, that was all over. . . . There was no one left in the whole world to care what she looked like, to cherish her beauty, to feel pride in it. At that thought the expected wave of un-happiness engulfed her spirit, but beneath it stirred a tiny unexpected feeling of relief. No longer need she strain every nerve to keep herself, as it were, in top gear, no longer need she view with apprehension every sign of approaching middle-age. The woman Harvey loved could never rest on her laurels. She must continue unremittingly to be the most attractive woman he knew. For the first time she thought of Olga without bitterness, – even with a faint pity.

"I suppose the country suits me," she said.

"You've not been here long, of course," said Mrs. Webb. "Personally I find that one's powers *rust* in the country." She spoke in a tragic voice and smiled a bright, brave, mirthless smile. "I'd always rather have lived in the town, but I've had to sacrifice myself, first to my husband and now to my son."

Clare had gone over to the window and stood there looking out. There were drifts of snowdrops under the trees. The sky was a clear pale rain-washed blue. . . . She took her spectacles from her pocket and put them on.

"Is that a starling or a blackbird on the lawn?" she said rather petulantly.

"A starling," said Mrs. Fanshaw, glancing out of the window.

Clare took out a note-book and made a few notes.

"I find birds more difficult to learn than I thought I should," she said.

Clare was systematically and with the help of her text-books studying birds and gardening. She found the birds particularly difficult. Even with her spectacles she was rather short-sighted, and their refusal to allow her to approach near enough to compare them with their descriptions in the text-books exasperated her. Gardening was simpler. One just followed the gardener about with one's book and told him what he ought to be doing. The first gardener she employed had given notice at the end of a week and the second had given notice yesterday.

"So stupid," she complained to Mrs. Fanshaw. "I mean, what's the good of my buying all those books if they won't do anything they say?"

"Gardeners have their own ways of doing things," said Mrs. Fanshaw.

"But there must be a right and a wrong way," persisted Clare, "and one may be sure that these people who've written books have got up the subject thoroughly."

"It's inevitable, I suppose," said Mrs. Fanshaw with a sigh, "that you should have an exaggerated opinion of the importance of the printed word."

Maurice and Pepita had taken their leave and set off to catch their train.

"All this," said Maurice, on the way to the station, with a gesture that included the whole countryside, "is picturesque enough, but it's slowly *ruining* Philip and Lydia. I don't think that anyone I've told that new theory of mine to has shown less interest of it. Before he went in for – all this," repeating the gesture, "he'd have been nothing short of *excited* over it. After all, it's epoch-making in its way."

"I quite agree," said Pepita. "I love the country myself – in its right place – but they're letting it kill their sense of proportion. Why on earth she objected to my wearing my new Daks – After all, what's the sense of coming into the country if you can't do it properly?"

"The child was rather sweet," said Maurice.

"But, my *dear*!" protested Pepita. "Think of the *expense* and how it *ties* one and how it's *ruined* those two."

"Of course, of course," he agreed hastily. "I wasn't suggesting . . ."

Lydia and Philip had taken Matilda home, and Mrs. Webb was the next to go.

"I'd like to," she said in answer to Lettice's not very sincere invitation to stay a little longer, "but I can't do as I like. A mother never can. . . . I must be back in time to welcome Colin home from work. I've always done that, however inconvenient it's been, and I always will."

The little mouth was set tightly in the flabby rounded cheeks, and suddenly Lettice realised that this plump, over-dressed little woman wasn't quite as negligible as she seemed. I shouldn't like to annoy her, she thought, and, I'm sorry for her son.

"Now, Lavinia, have some tea," said Lettice, when she came back from seeing off Mrs. Webb. "You've had nothing at all."

"It was all so terribly exciting," sighed Lavinia.

"Well, don't let it take away your appetite," said Mrs. Fanshaw. "Look at all these lovely cakes. . . . I'm sure Mrs. Helston will let you start now and wire in."

"Do," said Lettice. She touched the bell. "Let's have some fresh tea made and all start again."

Lavinia threw her a grateful look. It made her feel one of the grown-ups – not a child going on eating after everyone else had stopped.

She settled down happily on the hearthrug at Lettice's feet.

"Do you mind me sitting here? Gran won't let us sit on the floor at home."

Lettice laid her hand on the dark curls in a passing caress and moved the cake stand nearer.

"Now eat away . . ." she smiled.

Lavinia munched away contentedly, throwing occasional glances of admiration at Lettice as she did so. She had admired Lettice ever since she first saw her. Her beauty and elegance had invested her with something of the glamour that had always invested her mother in her eyes. The faint perfume that hung about her, too, reminded Lavinia of her mother. Wouldn't it be lovely to be like that, she thought, but I never could be. I'm not pretty enough and I'm too shy, and even if I had scent it would just smell like scent, not seem part of me as theirs does. As she ate she was trying to store up in her memory every detail of the afternoon to tell to Thea afterwards.

"Thea will be furious that she missed it," she said.

"We must send her some cake," said Lettice. "Some of each sort. . . ."

"Oh, thank you," said Lavinia eagerly. "She'll be terribly pleased. We only get bread and jam at home." She flushed hotly and bit her lip as if conscious of disloyalty. "That's not Gran's fault, of course. It's because we haven't much money. The only time Thea and I really enjoy tea," she went on quickly as if to correct the slip, "is when we can take it down to the chalet, and of course we can't do that in winter."

"Where's the chalet?" said Lettice, handing her the cake stand. "Have one of those little meringues."

Lavinia selected one rather diffidently.

"I'm afraid I'm being *terribly* greedy. . . . You see—" she stopped and went on lamely, "I wasn't very hungry at lunch."

Lettice looked at the pale transparent cheeks and the hollow blue-veined temples in the shadow of the dark curls. The child's half starved, she thought compassionately.

"Tell me about the chalet," she said.

"Oh . . . it's by the lake," said Lavinia. "Gran hates it. I don't know why. She'll never go near it. It's a lovely little place. It's got an upstairs and a downstairs and furniture, but it's locked and Gran won't give us the key. We have tea just outside it by the lake and pretend we live in it. Grandfather built it for fun when he came back from his honeymoon in Switzerland. . . . Sylvia comes and has tea with us there sometimes. . . . Will you come the first fine day . . . and you?" she turned to Mrs. Fanshaw. She was flushed and bright-eyed with excitement, her usual shyness forgotten.

"We'll both come," said Mrs. Fanshaw, "and we'll bring the tea."

"Oh, how lovely!" said Lavinia, her slender body tense with eagerness.

Mrs. Fanshaw noticed for the first time that Clare had turned from the window and was listening with rather a curious smile.

"Once Thea and I found a photograph of Uncle Simon standing by the chalet," went on Lavinia. "We showed it Gran, and she just tore it up without saying anything. I can't think why she hates it so. Hannah says it's because grandfather got pneumonia from sleeping there and died in a few days. Thea makes up ridiculous stories about it. She says that Gran's murdered someone and buried their body under the chalet. It's a darling little place. We could have such fun there, if only Gran would let us have the key."

"It has fir-cones carved over the doorway, hasn't it?" put in Clare.

Mrs. Fanshaw looked at her in surprise.

"Have you seen it?" she said.

Clare laughed. She had a harsh, unpleasant laugh.

"Oh no, I've never seen it."

"How do you know, then?" said Lavinia wonderingly.

"A little bird told me," teased Clare.

Lavinia flushed. She hated being treated as a little girl. She hated this large stupid woman in check tweeds. Everything was suddenly spoilt. She looked at the clock and rose from the hearthrug.

"I ought to go," she said. Shyness had enveloped her again. She felt ill-at-ease and half afraid, she didn't know why. "Gran said I mustn't be late. . . ."

Mrs. Fanshaw threw a reproachful glance at Clare, but Clare had turned again to the window with such a sharp exclamation that Mrs. Fanshaw rose and joined her. The witch-like figure of Miss Pendleton stood at the Morrices' gate, fumbling at the latch with hands encased in shreds of black cotton gloves, from which the end of each finger showed white.

"That woman *again*!" groaned Mrs. Fanshaw. "I won't have Lydia worried by her today."

She was starting towards the door, but Clare laid her hand on her arm.

"She was coming to see me," she said, "and, I suppose, found I'd not come back and couldn't resist coming on to the Morrices. She'll be all right with me. I can manage her. . . ."

They watched her go down to the wispy inhuman creature, who was crouching over the gate, craning her neck to see into the nursery, where Lydia was putting Matilda to bed. Lettice opened the window wider, and the thin shrill voice floated into the room like a wraith of evil.

"You and your dirty brat! Got a ring. . . . Oh yes. . . . Any dirty slut can get a ring. Where's your lines? That's what I'd like to know. And your fancy man! Don't come down to you often, nowadays, does he? Carryin' on in my father's house! He'd have had the likes of you whipped till your Simon wouldn't know you. . . . Spewing your dirty bastards where my mother said her prayers! Simon! I'll Simon ye. . . ."

Philip Morrice was going down to the gate, his face white with anger, but Clare reached it first. The old woman straightened herself, and, as she did so, a gust of wind blew back the rusty draperies, showing a body so thin and unsubstantial as hardly to suggest a human body at all. As Clare spoke to her, the toothless gums parted in an ingratiating smile, and the two of them went off together down the lane.

Mrs. Fanshaw turned from the window, a look of anxiety and apprehension on her face. Not the least unpleasant part of the whole unpleasant incident had been Clare's evident influence over the woman. She thought of that toothless ingratiating smile with a shudder. . . .

Lavinia's eyes were dark with horror. Lettice had drawn her away from the window, but the shrill voice had been penetrating, despite its ghost-like thinness.

"She said, 'Simon,' " said Lavinia slowly. "What did she mean?"

Mrs. Fanshaw shrugged her shoulders.

"I don't know," she said shortly. "She's been drinking. . . . I'll go to see her cousin again tonight."

Lettice was smiling reassuringly at Lavinia.

"Don't look so upset, darling," she said. "Drunk people are horrible. The old creature didn't know what she was saying. Forget all about it. . . . Don't let it spoil your day."

Lavinia looked at her and smiled tremulously.

"No, I won't," she said. "It's been so lovely. . . ."

"And now we'll walk back to the Castle together. Run up and get your things on. They're in my bedroom."

Lavinia ran upstairs, a happy child again.

"You've cut me out with Lavinia," said Mrs. Fanshaw when the door had closed on her. "I'm so glad you have. I'd like dozens of people to cut me out. The child's starved for love."

"And for food, I should say," said Lettice dryly.

"Yes, but that doesn't matter quite so much. It's love that's so important to a child. Hannah dislikes her. Her grandmother would do her duty by her whatever it cost, but hasn't a spark of real affection for her or for anyone else. Her son, Simon, is the only person in the world she ever loved."

"That old woman mentioned Simon."

Mrs. Fanshaw shrugged.

"I don't know where she manages to get drink from. Not from her cousin. ... And she's no money. She'll have to be put in an institution."

Philip Morrice entered unceremoniously. He had changed into city clothes. His absurdly boyish face looked set and stern.

"I'm sorry to barge in like this," he said, "but that old devil——"

"I know," said Mrs. Fanshaw. "We heard. Has it upset Lydia?"

"It did a little. She's all right now, but with Jemima coming it makes me feel a bit anxious."

"Of course."

"I'm going to the police in the morning."

"It won't do any good," said Mrs. Fanshaw. "Miss Pendleton's known the police since they were babies. I don't think they could do anything."

"We'll see about that," he said grimly. "But what I really came about – I've got to go up to town, and I don't like leaving her in case the old fiend comes back." He looked at Lettice. "You'll be in all evening – won't you? – just in case—"

Lettice hesitated.

"I'd promised to see Lavinia home, but I'll come straight back."

"I'll stay till she comes back," said Mrs. Fanshaw. "I'll sleep with Lydia if you like. ..."

"That's awfully decent of you, but – I just want to be sure that there's someone within call. She doesn't know I've come." He was silent for a moment, and his fair face flushed in sudden anger. "When I think of the things the old bitch said to her——"

"Don't think of them," said Mrs. Fanshaw. "She'd been drinking."

"That's no excuse."

"I know."

Lavinia entered, wearing her hat and coat.

"I'm ready – Oh, it's Mr. Morrice."

"Call me Philip," smiled the young man.

As the father of Matilda and the future father of Jemima, he felt pleasantly paternal towards her. It would be nice when Matilda was about seventeen – shy and sweet, with that untouched look about her, though he had a shrewd idea that Matilda wouldn't be this type at all. She'd be athletic and downright and domineering. Perhaps Jemima would be this type. . . . He'd like one of them to be.

"Philip . . ." said Lavinia, and her solemn face broke into its slow sweet smile.

"Come along, child," said Lettice. "My coat's in the hall, and I won't put on a hat."

They walked down to the gate with Philip.

"Goodbye," he said. "I'm getting the 'bus into Beverton." He looked anxiously at Lettice. "You'll keep a look-out?"

"Of course," she assured him.

They watched him walk away and stop at the corner of the green to speak to a man who had just got off the Beverton 'bus.

Lavinia heaved a deep sigh.

"I don't want to go home," she said. "It's been such a wonderful day. . . . I shall be telling Thea about it for weeks, and even then I shall never make her understand how wonderful it's been."

"Some people would have found it dull," smiled Lettice.

"Dull!" echoed Lavinia.

"Mrs. Helston—"

Lettice stopped. Mrs. Turnberry was crossing the green. She was breathless, and her face looked pale in the dim light.

"May I speak to you?"

"Of course. . . ."

"No, I mean – I'm sorry, but it's terribly important. It'll take some time to explain."

"I was just going to see Lavinia home," said Lettice.

"Oh, it doesn't matter about me," protested Lavinia. "Really I can go alone."

The man Philip had been speaking to was coming towards them. It was Colin Webb. He raised his hat and blushed as his eyes fell on Lavinia.

"Oh, Mr. Webb," said Lettice. His presence seemed providential. He stopped. His heart was beating violently. He tried to think of something to say but could only stand staring at her. "Would you see Lavinia back to the Castle for me? I was going with her, but Mrs. Turnberry wants to speak to me and—"

Colin felt that it was all happening in a dream. He found his voice with an effort.

"With pleasure," he said, then cursed himself for the banality of the phrase. He changed it to, "Of course, I'd be delighted," then thought despairingly that that was even worse.

But Lavinia was smiling at him in shy friendliness.

"Why should you bother?" she said. "I can easily go alone."

There was no coquetry – only a child's reluctance to give trouble.

"Indeed you can't," put in Lettice. "Your grandmother would never forgive me."

"Well, I daresay I'd get into an awful row," admitted Lavinia.

"I – I'd love to," stammered Colin, wishing that he were carrying off the situation better. He wanted to seem the sort of person who would protect and cherish her – die for her, if needs be – and he seemed just a stupid schoolboy. "With pleasure" . . . "I'd be delighted" . . . "I'd love to," he mimicked himself savagely. How sweet she looked! He thought of Greta Dorking. It seemed incredible that they should inhabit the same world.

"Well, run off now, both of you," said Lettice.

They set off down the road, walking slowly, not speaking. . . .

Mrs. Turnberry watched them, and her brown face relaxed into a large beneficent smile, then clouded over again.

"I'm sorry to upset everyone's arrangements like this," she said. "It's Clifford. . . ."

They turned towards the gate of Pear Tree Cottage.

"Mrs. Fanshaw's there," said Lettice.

"That's all right," said Mrs. Turnberry. "I want to speak to her, too."

They went into the drawing-room. Mrs. Fanshaw turned from the window.

"What have you done with Lavinia?"

"Colin Webb's seeing her home."

Mrs. Fanshaw raised her eyebrows.

"I wonder what her grandmother will have to say to that."

"Oh . . ." said Lettice, taken aback. "Oughtn't I to have let him? But surely——"

"Mrs. Ferring doesn't 'know' the Webbs," said Mrs. Fanshaw with her faint smile, "and in any case she wouldn't have allowed Lavinia to go out with even the most socially unimpeachable young man without a chaperon."

"Oh, dear, how dreadful!" said Lettice.

"No, interesting," said Mrs. Fanshaw. "Quite interesting. And quite safe. Colin's too thoroughly mother-trained to make anything of the situation. Well, now you're here, I'll run over to Clare's. I'm worried about Miss Pendleton. You've got Mrs. Turnberry to keep you company."

"I'd like to speak to you, too, Mrs. Fanshaw," said Mrs. Turnberry. "It's Clifford. . . ."

"Sit down," said Lettice.

They sat down and Lettice looked from one to the other.

"It's Clifford," said Mrs. Turnberry again.

Her loose ungainly figure was slumped forward in her chair. Her hands, clasped loosely on her lap, were dirt-ingrained and work-roughened.

She smells, thought Lettice suddenly. I suppose there isn't a bathroom in that old cottage, and she just doesn't bother. But somehow it smells clean dirt, like the earth. She *is* rather like the earth. How silly that sounds!

"Yes?" Mrs. Fanshaw was saying gently. "What about Clifford?"

Mrs. Turnberry turned her eyes to Mrs. Fanshaw. They were without their usual twinkle, but they were not angry or bitter. She looks like an animal that's being ill-treated and doesn't know why, thought Lettice.

"He's just been to see me," said Mrs. Turnberry. "He's found out that Frank's lost his job with Bruce's, and he says I've got to go and live with him and Marcia. He says he won't do anything more for Frank. I—" she twisted her roughened fingers together in her lap. "Frank's all I've got. Clifford doesn't understand. It isn't Frank's fault that——"

"I'll talk to Clifford," said Mrs. Fanshaw.

"No, it's all right," said Mrs. Turnberry. "I mean – I begged him to let Frank try again. Clifford's a good boy, but he – doesn't understand. . . . He's proud, and he thinks Frank disgraces him. He's ashamed of us both. . . . He said that, if Frank can get another job before next week, he'll give him another chance, so——"

"Can he?" said Mrs. Fanshaw wonderingly. "Would Brace's give him a reference?"

Mrs. Turnberry shook her head.

"No. You see, he – took things when he was there. Clifford's only just found that out. That's what made him so angry. I don't think he means to be hard. Men *are* hard. I suppose they can't help it. . . ."

A mist seemed to close over Lettice, shutting out the pleasant little room and its occupants. Men are hard. . . . She saw again the faint complacent smile that had touched Harvey's lips when first he saw her blinded with weeping because of his rejection of her. Her distress had been food and drink to his vanity. She tasted again in memory the bitterness of that moment, and suddenly the old longing for Harvey – his easy charm, his gay tenderness – swept over her. She felt abased and humiliated by it. Would she never recover from her sickness? If he came to her now would she take him back, knowing him as she did? She daren't face the question, daren't even try to answer it. A feeling of dull despair assailed her. What was there to live for? What did other women live for ?. . .

Gradually the mist cleared, and again she saw the two women – Mrs. Fanshaw, her keen compassionate gaze fixed on Mrs. Turnberry; Mrs. Turnberry, her listlessness gone, speaking eagerly, pleadingly.

"Clifford won't like it, of course, but it'll be work. He said if he got work before the end of the week we could stay on. . . . I know you've got Thornham, but couldn't you just give Frank a day? He's always been good at gardening. And there wouldn't be the same – temptations. I suppose Clifford would say it was a disgrace to have a brother a jobbing gardener, but it wouldn't be the same as if he was in Beverton, where Clifford lives. That was what annoyed Clifford about his working at Bruce's. And I'd be able to keep an eye on him. I've always thought he'd do well as a gardener. . . ."

"I'll give him two days a week," said Mrs. Fanshaw in her crisp rather curt voice. She turned to Lettice. "How often does your man come?"

"Two days a week," said Lettice.

"Could you give Frank a day?" She went to the window. "He could dig up that waste bit and you could give him jobs in the house, couldn't you?"

"He's good in the house," put in Mrs. Turnberry eagerly and added, "Clifford wouldn't be so hard by himself. It's Marcia egging him on. She's never liked Frank, and, of course, she grudges us the money."

"I'll ask Miss Lennare," said Mrs. Fanshaw.

"And I'll ask Mrs. Webb," said Mrs. Turnberry, setting her lips determinedly.

"That's right," said Mrs. Fanshaw approvingly. "And you can tell Clifford tonight that he's got a job. We'll all arrange to pay his wages to you."

"Thank you," said Mrs. Turnberry. She looked into the distance and gave a little shrug of her shoulders, as if what she saw there made her heart fail. "Oh, well, it'll be all right for a bit, anyway. Clifford can't go back on his word. He said a job. He didn't say what sort. . . . I'd better go now. Thank you so much. I'm so grateful to you." As she rose her grim face suddenly lightened, and the old twinkle returned to her creased brown eyes. "Children are funny, aren't they?"

"I'll go and ask Clare now," said Mrs. Fanshaw, when the visitor had gone. "I wanted to see her in any case. I've got to have it out with her about Ivy, and find what she's playing at with old Miss Pendleton."

"You take everyone's worries on your shoulders," said Lettice.

"I'm only upholding tradition," said Mrs. Fanshaw. "A country parson's wife is supposed to be a busybody. I like to conform to type when possible."

Terror descended on Lettice. She was to be left alone again with those memories of Harvey that lurked in the shadows like hidden assassins waiting till she was unprotected. . . . The sanity and courage of her visitor seemed to keep them at bay.

"I wish I weren't such a fool," she said.

"We're all fools," said Mrs. Fanshaw. "Life would be very dull if we weren't. . . . Mrs. Skelton told me last night that Ivy was a fool and Clare was a fool and George was a fool and inferred that I was one, too."

"Ivy . . ." said Lettice, searching for something, anything, to say that would keep her visitor with her. "I don't suppose there's any harm in it."

"Oh, harm!" shrugged her visitor, rising and drawing on her gloves. "Not in the way you mean. Ivy's mother probably doesn't even know of the existence of that particular sort of harm. Her complaint is that Clare's spoiling her. Making a lady of her. She said most emphatically that she doesn't want her Ivy made a lady of. No, I think it's just an Emma and Harriet Smith affair, except that Clare lacks the saving graces of Emma, and Ivy the saving graces of Harriet Smith. Clare's stupid, and it's the stupid people who do the most harm in the world. By the way, when Frank Turnberry comes, don't have anything lying about that he could steal. Keep the windows closed at the bottom when he's working in the garden. I'm taking rather a responsibility in asking people to give him work, but I'm fond of his mother, and I've always disliked that vulgar little snob Clifford married. . . . Goodbye, my dear." At the gate she turned. "You played beautifully. You won't find matins any more difficult," and set off briskly across the green without waiting for Lettice's indignant protest.

The door of Honeysuckle Cottage was ajar. She pushed it open and went into the sitting-room. Clare was not there. Ivy, wearing her red woollen dress, her fair hair massed in curls round her small face, sat at a table in front of a typewriter, smoking a cigarette with exaggerated elegance. Seeing Mrs. Fanshaw, she lolled back in her chair defiantly, holding out the cigarette (Clare had told her she might smoke, but so far she was not enjoying the process) at an ostentatious angle. Mrs. Fanshaw stood looking at her in silence, and the years rolled back till Ivy was again a member of Mrs. Fanshaw's Infants' Sunday School Class, with the prospect of receiving a coloured Scripture card if she was good or of standing in the corner by Mrs. Fanshaw's chair if she was naughty. She rose to her feet and held the cigarette behind her.

"Good afternoon, Mrs. Fanshaw," she said in her little girl voice.

"Good afternoon, Ivy," said Mrs. Fanshaw, a faint flicker of amusement in the narrowed blue eyes. "Is Miss Lennare in?"

"Yes, Mrs. Fanshaw."

"Will you please tell her I want to speak to her ... and you needn't come back."

"No, Mrs. Fanshaw," said Ivy meekly.

Chapter Nine

A FLASH of blue and red crossed the path between the overhanging trees. "Twi – twi – twi."

Lavinia stopped abruptly and laid her hand on Colin's arm.

"A stone-chat," she whispered. "It's long past its bedtime. We must have disturbed it, and – Oh, look!"

With a rustle of undergrowth, a young rabbit appeared, stared at them unconcernedly, then lolloped along the path in front of them.

"Isn't he lovely! He's not a bit afraid of us."

Colin looked at the creature without seeing it. He was conscious only of Lavinia, her lips parted eagerly, her eyes fixed on the rabbit as it disappeared again into the undergrowth. She had the loveliest lips he'd ever seen. When they weren't smiling they drooped wistfully at the corners. When she smiled, the short upper lip lifted exquisitely, but always there was that suggestion of wistfulness. . . . She turned suddenly and met his eyes . . . then quickly looked away. They began to walk on.

"When Thea and I were little we used to pretend that we were princesses and that the birds were our pages," she said. "The thrushes and blackbirds were hers, and the robins and chaffinches were mine. We quarrelled about the skylarks, because we both wanted them. When they flew up into the air we used to pretend that they were going on messages for us. . . . We used to pretend that we understood what they said." She spoke quickly, nervously, as if she were afraid – not of him, but of what she had seen in his eyes in that brief instant when they met hers. "I love birds, but I wish that the people who call themselves bird lovers weren't always so dreadful ... like Miss Lennare. ..."

Her mind went back over the day. It had been perfect except for that one episode. She shrank from the memory of that witch-like figure leaning over the gate of Pear Tree Cottages, mouthing obscenities. Colin was looking at her again. The dim light emphasised her air of fragility. He noticed that her coat was shabby and that she had outgrown it. It was stretched tightly across her chest and frayed at the cuffs. His heart yearned over her with an unbearable tenderness.

"Look at the moon," she said. "Can't you see the man in it plainly tonight? Used you to talk to him when you were a little boy?"

"No," said Colin.

"I thought everyone did," she said. "He always seemed to come and comfort me the nights Gran had been cross with me. ... What were you like when you were a little boy?"

"I don't know. ..."

"I used to see you in church with everyone else every Sunday, and then, the night that Thea and I ran into you, you suddenly seemed to turn into a real person. You must have thought us dreadfully rude."

"No, I didn't."

"When you were a little boy, I suppose you used to come into these woods. Perhaps I've seen you here."

"We lived in Beverton then," he said. "I sometimes used to picnic here on Saturday afternoons."

"With other little boys?"

"No, with my mother."

The moon was rising higher and flooding the wood with silver light.

"It seems to put everything under a sort of spell, doesn't it?" she said dreamily. "I'm hardly ever out after dark. It's – exciting."

She wasn't afraid of him any longer. A strange new happiness that she had never known before upheld her. She surrendered to it gratefully, unquestioningly, as though she were holding out starved hands to a fire.

"Let's go slowly," she said. "It's so lovely being here. . . . I shall probably get into an awful row anyway, so a few more minutes won't matter."

She was surprised that she could think of her grandmother's anger without fear. It was as if the happiness that lit her heart like a flame had burnt up everything else. The path moved into the blackest of the shadows, and instinctively she drew nearer to him as if for protection. He could feel her arm against his through her thin coat.

"Moonlight's – frightening in a way, isn't it?" she said. "The shadows are so black that they seem to be moving."

When they came out into the moonlight again she saw that he was trembling.

"You're cold," she said.

Their eyes met again, and suddenly – it seemed to her with no movement from either – she was in his arms, his lips pressed down on hers. She put her arms round him and strained herself to him, her happiness like a sharp sword in her body. He released her with a quick jerky movement, as if he were being pulled away from her against his will. His face looked white in the moonlight.

"I'm sorry . . ." he said.

"Why are you sorry?" she said. "Let's sit down."

They sat on a fallen log that lay by the side of the path. Her hat had come off, and the dark curls were tumbled about her face. She pushed them back with a quick movement.

"I oughtn't to have done that," he said hoarsely, "but I love you so terribly. . . ."

"I love you, too," she said. "I've loved you ever since that night when Thea and I ran into you, but I didn't really know till just now. . . ." She fixed her clear childish gaze on him. "I suppose we can't get married for ages."

He thought of her grandmother, his mother, his position at the bank, and hopelessness swept over him.

"How old are you?" he said.

"Nearly eighteen. . . . We can wait, can't we?"

"I'd wait for you for ever and ever," he said, "but——"

"But what?" she persisted.

"I don't know. . . . They'll never let you marry me."

"They can't stop me," she said. "If we wait . . . if we love each other. . . ."

He looked at the small pale face in the frame of tumbled hair. He longed to rescue her from unhappiness, to protect and cherish her, to shower gifts upon her, and all he could do was – to wait.

"I wish I were someone different."

"I don't want you different . . ." he said. "You're so sweet and lovely."

He put his arm round her, and suddenly she crumpled up against his shoulder, her frail form shaken by sobs.

"Darling," he cried, "what's the matter? What is it ? . . . Tell me. . . ."

"Nothing," she said between her sobs. "Only I'm so terribly happy."

Mrs. Webb was enjoying the interview. She felt that she was getting her own back. . . . Shabby, poor, with a scoundrel of a son, the woman had dared to make fun of her all these years. It was only right that she should be here at last, humbly mendicant (surely that wasn't the old gleam of mockery in the brown eyes?), realising the difference between them. . . .

"I'm very sorry for you, Mrs. Turnberry," she said, tightening the tiny mouth in the flabby pink cheeks. "Very sorry indeed. Colin's never given me a moment's anxiety in his life, so that I really hardly understand what it must be to have a son like Frank. Of course, I brought Colin up carefully. There's a saying that your children are what you make them. Never a moment's anxiety he's caused me since he was a baby."

"I'm sure he hasn't," said Mrs. Turnberry meekly. "He's not the sort of boy to cause anyone anxiety. . . ."

Mrs. Webb glanced at her suspiciously. Yes, there *was* a flicker of the old mockery, just for a second. The small blue eyes hardened.

"Well, I'm very sorry I can't help you," she said, speaking with a kind of affronted graciousness.

Her eyes wandered to the gate. She couldn't think why Colin was so late. He was generally home long before this. She hoped that nothing had happened to him. If nothing had happened to him, she'd make him understand very plainly indeed that she wouldn't put up with this kind of thing. He must have left the bank at five. It was now nearly half-past six. If she let it go this time it would happen again. . . . She rehearsed the scene to herself ("I've been so anxious about you, Colin. I couldn't think what had happened. I've got a terrible headache with worrying. . . . You know that it always upsets me not to know where you are. It was most inconsiderate of you . . .").

The gleam of mockery had faded from Mrs. Turnberry's eyes. She hoped that Mrs. Webb hadn't noticed it. She knew she couldn't afford to make fun of people now.

"Half a day would help," she pleaded. "And he'd work hard. He's a good gardener."

Mrs. Webb shook her head.

"I'm very sorry," she said, "but, as I said, one has a duty to oneself. The things one's heard of Frank—"

The door opened and Colin came in. Mrs. Webb turned a reproachful gaze on him and offered him her cheek. He bent and kissed it absently. She noticed with rising indignation that he had brought no present for her. Her husband had established the tradition that the least the man of the household could do, when he came home late, was to arrive armed with a present (it did not avert punishment but it mitigated it), and she had taken care that the tradition was handed on to his Son. She would have liked Mrs. Turnberry to see him presenting her with a large box of chocolates and kissing her affectionately, and he hadn't done either. She glanced meaningly at the clock, but he didn't seem to notice. Generally when he came home late he was nervously apologetic and anxious to atone. Now he hardly seemed to realise that she was there. He was standing staring in front of him, frowning. . . . He looked different, somehow. She felt suddenly afraid. . . . A tremor – small, almost imperceptible – had shaken the foundations of her world. Her little mouth tightened till the lips hardly showed. If it was that Dorking girl again ... she'd soon put a stop to it. She'd have it out with him tonight. She'd cry. ... She could summon tears at will – large fat tears that welled up into her blue eyes and rolled down her soft little cheeks. ... He could never hold out against her tears. His father hadn't been able to, either. He'd be on his knees by her, comforting her, promising anything. ... She was astute enough not to use the weapon too often, but tonight, she assured herself, was an occasion for it. She'd never seen him look like this before.

"I came about Frank," Mrs. Turnberry was saying.

She had no hope that Colin would ever question any decision of his mother's, but she wanted, rather maliciously, to make him feel uncomfortable.

"Clifford's going to sell The Moorings and take me to live with him and Marcia if Frank doesn't get some work, so I'm trying to get him work as a jobbing gardener – a day here and there to make up the week – but your mother says she can't give him any."

Colin turned to his mother.

"I thought you said that you'd asked old Hoole to give you a second day and he couldn't."

She stared at him in amazement. The timid diffident boy had gone, leaving this unsmiling man in his place.

"Yes, but——" she stammered.

"Of course, we can give him a day." He turned to Mrs. Turnberry. "Tell him he can have a day's work here. Hoole's day is Tuesday, isn't it?" he said to his mother.

She didn't answer. A dark unbecoming flush had suffused her neck and was creeping in patches up her cheeks. That was always the first sign of anger in her. ... Colin didn't even appear to see it.

"Any day but Tuesday," he went on to Mrs. Turnberry.

"Thanks so much, Colin," she said gratefully.

She was watching him curiously. He'd grown up since last she'd seen him. And that was only an hour or so ago, when he'd set off to see Lavinia Ferring home. . . . Her eyes narrowed shrewdly. Ah . . . perhaps that was it. Do the boy good. Done him good already. What a royal rage the old lady up at the Castle would be in if she knew ! . . . Perhaps she did know by now. . . . And this little pussy-cat of a Mrs. Webb. She'd bite and scratch. She was ready to bite and scratch already, though she knew nothing of it yet. Life was suddenly full of interest again for Mrs. Turnberry, in spite of Clifford.

When she had gone Mrs. Webb turned a flushed face to her son.

"Colin, how *could* you?" she said in quivering reproach.

He was just going out of the door and swung round impatiently.

"How could I what?" he said shortly.

He was looking at her with that odd abstracted gaze as if he didn't see her. The solid ground seemed to shift beneath her feet. She began the process of "working herself up."

"First of all you come home nearly an hour late. I was literally *ill* with anxiety, thinking something had happened to you." Tears welled into her eyes. "And then you——"

He interrupted her.

"Don't be ridiculous, Mother. If anything had happened to me you'd have heard of it at once. And if I hadn't been coming home to dinner, I'd have let you know."

He'd gone out before she could recover breath to reply. She sat there staring in angry amazement at the closed door, the tears still coursing down her cheeks.

Chapter Ten

FEBRUARY had opened with snow and sleet and was ending in warm sunny days that lulled one into the delusion that winter was over. Catkins swung in the hedges among the "bread and cheese "of the hawthorn, and in the gardens the almond trees showed tight pink buds. . . . Coltsfoot bloomed in the meadows and the air was sweet with the courting songs of the birds. Every post brought seed catalogues, and everywhere the empty vegetable patches stood, freshly turned over, waiting for the next month's sowing.

Frank Turnberry plodded about his day's work from garden to garden of Steffan Green. He was happier than he ever remembered being. He loved gardening. . . . He could work at his own rhythm with no one to nag or badger him. Life in the open air suited him, too, and, though the end of the day's work generally found him making his way across the green to the "Fox and Grapes," he seldom got more than comfortably fuddled.

Clifford had been furious at what he called his mother's "trick," but he kept his word and continued to pay the two pounds a week to her. It was, he told her sternly, the greatest disgrace she had yet inflicted on him, and, though for the present he would make no practical objection, at Frank's first lapse he would fulfil his threat of turning him out and taking her to live with him in Beverton. She had never seen him so angry and so much in earnest, and for the first time in her life she was afraid of him. She was determined that Frank should keep this job. Several times a day she would make excuses to pass the garden where he worked to make sure that he was there, and she would turn out his pockets each night to make sure that he had "taken" "nothing. . . . Sometimes Clifford, paying her his weekly visit on Wednesday evening, would pass Frank working late at one of his "jobs" in the village and would avert his eyes as he passed, his face white with anger and humiliation. If Frank saw him he would never fail to smile a beaming welcome over the hedge and to be hurt afresh on every occasion by Clifford's ignoring him.

Thea and Lavinia had taken advantage of the unusual spell of warm weather to have the long-arranged picnic at the chalet by the lake. Mrs. Ferring had given her permission, together with strict orders that the girls were to be back in the house by six o'clock, and had written punctiliously to Lettice and Mrs. Fanshaw, asking them to excuse her presence, as meals in the open brought on her rheumatism.

"Rheumatism!" laughed Thea. "She'd rather die than come near the place. That's the reason why we like it. . . ."

The picnic was in the nature of a celebration, for Thea was going to a finishing school on the outskirts of Paris the following week. Her mother had left her letter unanswered for so long that she had been on the point of fulfilling her threat of running away, when at last the answer arrived. She wrote to say that she had persuaded Madame Bertier, the head mistress of the finishing school she herself had attended, to take Thea as a pupil without fee, in return for her recommendation.

There was no question of her taking Lavinia, too, but Lavinia was as glad of Thea's deliverance as if it had been her own. Indeed, she no longer wished to be delivered herself. She felt that without those stolen meetings with Colin she wouldn't have been able to live. Even Thea knew nothing about that. She would not have betrayed them but she would have laughed at them. To Lavinia this new – and first – love was more vital, more precious, than life itself. Thea's ridicule, though kindly meant, would have somehow besmirched it. The Sunday after he had seen her home through the woods, she had sat in the Castle pew next her grandmother, her gaze fixed on her prayer-book, her heart beating wildly, aware in every nerve of Colin next his mother, his face pale, his eyes seeking hers across the aisle. .... And the next evening she had looked out of the schoolroom window and seen him standing at the edge of the woodland that adjoined the neglected park. Somehow or other she had managed to get out to him without anyone's seeing her. And after that she had met him regularly. They had been short uneasy meetings, full of wild happiness and wilder fears.

"Don't be so frightened, sweetheart."

"I can't help it. I think Gran would kill me if she knew."

"We shall just have to wait."

It always came round to that. .... "We shall just have to wait."

Sometimes it was she who consoled him. "It will soon pass. .... I shall be twenty-one and you'll be earning enough money, and we shall be terribly happy."

"I can't believe it," he would say. "It's crazy of me to think of it. .... You're so lovely ... and so far above me. Everyone who sees you will fall in love with you."

"I shall never love anyone but you. Never, never, never."

Between disjointed protestations of love they would make attempts to solve the practical side of the problem, going helplessly round and round the same circle.

"I daren't tell Gran. She'd never let me marry you."

"I'm not supposed to marry till I'm earning four pounds a week. That won't be for years."

"If only we could run away together. .... Colin, would your mother help me if she knew?"

"No," he admitted reluctantly.

Somehow, after that one flare-up of defiance in the matter of Frank Turnberry, he had slipped back into the old relations with her. Frank still worked in the garden (she dare not risk defeat by trying issues with him again on that particular question), but Colin had become again propitiatory in his manner to her, anxious to please, terrified of her discovering his friendship with Lavinia.

"I wish there was someone in the whole world who could understand and help," she cried. "Gran's mother married before she was seventeen, and I *feel* terribly old."

Always the dark cloud of fear surrounded them. She would go

back from their meetings sick with terror lest her grandmother should have discovered her absence. Once, when her grandmother gave her a sudden keen glance after one of them, her knees trembled so violently that she could not stand and sank down on the nearest chair. She would hear of happy engagements and think, "Oh, it isn't fair. Why can't ours be like that?"

Among the discomforts and hardships of her daily life at the Castle, her thoughts would fly to him a hundred times a day for comfort and protection. The memory of his face – honest, loving, anxious – would somehow fill her with soaring rapture, sometimes plunge her into an anguish of despair. She lived in a state of acute nervous tension, excited and depressed in turns. If Thea had not been so taken up by her own affairs she would have noticed that new high-pitched tremulous quality in her sister. She was easily moved to tears or laughter and both were very near each other. She looked paler, thinner. She was more absent-minded than ever and constantly in trouble with her grandmother. . . .

But Thea was too full of her own concerns to be conscious of anything else.

"I can hardly believe it," she said excitedly. "This time next month I shall be there. It's wonderful waking in the morning and remembering it. . . . I don't see why I shouldn't have gone straight away, but, of course, I had to have what Gran calls an 'escort.' Can you imagine anything more stuffy and old-fashioned than an 'escort'!"

"As your escort to London," smiled Mrs. Fanshaw, "I thank you."

It had been arranged that Mrs. Fanshaw should take her to London and that there she should be met by a friend of the head mistress, who was also going over to Paris, and should spend a few days with her mother in Paris, buying the necessary clothes before joining the school.

"I'm sorry to miss Sylvia," she said. "I just had to write and tell somebody, so I wrote pages and pages to her last night. . . . I'm not jealous of her any longer. I wish she were here today, though. It's the first picnic we've had without her."

"I wish she were, too," said Mrs. Fanshaw. "I'm afraid she'll find me past hope when she does come back. I've forgotten what she told me to wear with what. I'm sure I'm wearing all the wrong things together."

"Yes, you are," said Thea. "Even I can see that."

"Don't tell her," pleaded Mrs. Fanshaw.

It had struck Lettice how friendless the girls must be that their only guests at the picnic should be herself and Mrs. Fanshaw. Mrs. Fanshaw had brought the tea, and the girls had carried down rugs and deck-chairs from the house. There was an almost midsummer warmth in the February sunshine, though the chill of evening warned one that winter was not yet over.

"Spring at last," said the optimists, and "We shall pay for it," the pessimists replied.

The lake lay calm and peaceful, the trees at the edge sharply reflected in the clear blue depth. From it the untidy neglected park stretched up to the belt of trees that in summer-time completely hid the castle. Now it could be seen through the leafless branches – grey, fortress-like, derelict-looking, the paint peeling off the woodwork, the windows of some of the rooms broken, one tower in ruins. It made the gay little wooden building beside which the girls had camped seem ludicrously incongruous. Lettice had not seen it before and was examining it with interest. It was an attractive miniature chalet, of the usual two and a half storeys, built of small pine logs, with a shingled roof and carved rafters. A carved balcony enclosed the second storey, and the roof projected as far as the balcony, completely hiding the upper windows.

"It's charming," she said.

"It's a copy of one that grandfather fell in love with in Switzerland," said Thea. "He had it copied, regardless. It's frightfully well built."

"It's furnished ..." said Lettice, looking in through the tiny windows at the chairs and tables that were stained with damp and covered with dust.

"He had most of the furniture sent from Switzerland," said Thea. "Oh, it's *maddening* that Gran won't let us use it. She goes all grim if we even mention it. There's the sweetest little bedroom upstairs, too. We've climbed up to look through the windows." Thea stood at the door and turned the door handle impatiently. "She's got a key somewhere. I wish I knew where it was."

"I love the little fir-cones carved round the door," said Lettice. . . . She frowned abstractedly. "Who told me that there were fir-cones carved there?"

"Miss Lennare," said Lavinia, shrinking away from the memory. "How did she know?"

"I've no idea," said Mrs. Fanshaw shortly. "She's an idiotic woman. She loves mystery for its own sake."

She thought with irritation of the interview she had had with Clare, when she remonstrated about Miss Pendleton and Ivy.

"My dear Helen," Clare had said, "Miss Pendleton's a friend of mine, and I'm getting a perfect plot from her, so please don't interfere."

She had been disarmingly meek about Ivy, promising to observe the social conventions in their relations, but the very next morning she had taken Ivy up to London again, dressed in the new coat and skirt. . . . Mrs. Fanshaw had washed her hands of her after that.

"A stupid woman," she repeated, and added, "And now let's have some tea. It'll get cold as soon as the sun goes in." She glanced at Lavinia. "Lavvy looks cold already."

"Lavvy's always cold," said Thea carelessly. "She's got a fresh crop of chilblains this week. It makes Gran furious. She thinks that if she'd use a little self-control, she wouldn't have chilblains or colds or coughs or anything. Oh, how lovely!" she went on as Mrs. Fanshaw unpacked the tea basket. "Food's one of the things I'm looking forward to most at Madame Bertier's."

Mrs. Fanshaw glanced at the handsome classical-featured young face and wondered if her position at Madame Bertier's would cause her any humiliation. She decided that it wouldn't. Thea was a kind-hearted girl, but already you could see her grandmother in her – dominating, insensitive, even a little ruthless. No one could doubt her affection for Lavinia, but she had no thought to spare for her in the excitement of her own good fortune, no compunction at leaving her to face the dreary routine alone. She had the selfishness that so often forms part of a strong character.

"You'll be lonely, won't you, Lavinia?" Lettice was saying gently.

"Yes . . ." said Lavinia.

She thought of the long days without Thea's high spirits to lighten them, without Thea's laughter to take the nightmare quality from life in the grim old house. . . . Colin seemed suddenly as far away as if he were part of a dream. She felt cold and helpless and despairing.

"You must come and see me often," said Lettice.

"Oh, thank you," said Lavinia gratefully.

She had suggested to Colin that they tell Lettice of their "engagement" (she tried hard to think of it as an engagement), but Colin had been insistent that they shouldn't.

"Colin, she's so sweet. She'd – understand. She'd help."

"She wouldn't," Colin had said. "I know she's kind and perhaps she'd understand, but she'd think it her duty to tell your grandmother. They all hang together."

Lavinia had sighed and agreed. They were children alone and unprotected in a hostile world of grown-ups.

"None of them would understand," he had said. "They've – forgotten, I suppose."

"Oh, Lavvy will be all right," Thea was saying easily. "She likes reading and she's good at lessons and goes crazy over sunsets and trees and things. Lavvy will be all right."

It was convenient for her to believe that Lavvy would be all right – so, easily and light-heartedly, she believed it.

"Mother's meeting me in Paris to buy clothes," she went on. "Won't it be marvellous to buy *clothes*! And with Mother. . . ."

Lavinia's thoughts went to the exquisite elusive creature they called Mother, idealised by time and distance. On Mrs. Gerald Ferring's rare visits to the Castle, Lavinia, though wildly happy, was shy and constrained, overwhelmed by the suggestion of an unknown world of elegance and fashion that the visitor always carried with her. But, when she was not there, Lavinia always seemed to draw nearer to her in spirit, to pour out confidences, to receive understanding and sympathy. And her thoughts had been turning more and more to her mother as the solution of her problems. She would understand about Colin, even though no one else in the whole world understood. She would help her, as she had helped Thea. . . . She imagined her – radiant, loving, without that something of weariness and aloofness that hung about her when they actually met. Once or twice Lavinia had thought of writing to her as Thea had done, had even written several confused accounts of the situation on pages torn out of an exercise book, but had been prevented by some almost subconscious sense of reality from sending them. It was so difficult to express things properly in writing. . . . Suppose Mother didn't understand and just sent back her letter to Gran. . . . Lavinia's whole body burnt with mingled humiliation and terror at the thought. For a long time she had hoped that her mother would decide to come to England herself to fetch Thea, but that hope had now faded. Still – she was bound to come over sooner or later. It was nearly a year since she'd been, and she had never let so long a time elapse between her visits before. She would be coming soon, and then – everything would be all right. She didn't consider the details of how everything would be all right. It would just be all right. . . . She clung to this hope – delusive though some secret part of her knew it to be – as an amulet against the fear and unhappiness that assailed her. Mother would come home and everything would be all right. . . .

"Wake up, Lavinia!" said Mrs. Fanshaw.

The little spirit kettle had boiled, and she was pouring the water into the teapot. Thea had spread the picnic table-cloth and was arranging the food on plates, with cries of delight.

"Sausage rolls! How lovely! Peaches! Ooo! And what a dream of a cake. Where *did* it come from!"

"I had it sent from a place in London," said Lettice. "It's called a Lady Baltimore cake."

"It looks too wonderful to eat."

They set to work happily, and soon Lavinia forgot her anxiety. . . . The warm spring sunshine seemed to creep into her bones, the tea was a delicious blend that a cousin of Mrs. Fanshaw's had sent from China, the pastry of the sausage rolls was the flaky crumbly sort she loved. Everything was going to be all right. . . .

"I meant to make some queen cakes for it last night," said Mrs. Fanshaw, "but Miss Maple called and stayed for hours and I hadn't time when she'd gone. Perhaps it's as well," she added with a sigh. "Sylvia says I can't make cakes. She makes them beautifully, of course. And her pastry's almost as good as my mother's used to be. I suppose pastry skips a generation, like drunkenness."

"Do tell us about Miss Maple," said Thea, selecting another sausage roll. "She's not coming back to St. Elphege's, is she?"

"I'm afraid she is," said Mrs. Fanshaw.

"Never mind," said Lavinia with her gentle smile. "It's never for long."

"Mr. Fanshaw will step out of the pulpit with the wrong foot or something," added Thea. "Then she'll go somewhere else."

"Yes, but not before she's made our lives a misery," said Mrs. Fanshaw ruefully.

"Who is she?" asked Lettice.

"Oh, don't you know about Miss Maple?" laughed Thea. "One forgets you're a new-comer. You fit in so well."

"Have a Devonshire cookie, Lavinia," said Mrs. Fanshaw. "You always used to choose them for your birthday tea at the vicarage when you were a little girl, do you remember?" She turned to Lettice. "Miss Maple is the thorn in our flesh. Her uncle used to be Vicar of St. Elphege's before we came here, and she lives in Beverton. She used to come to St. Elphege's regularly just in order to see that Paul did everything exactly as it had been done in her uncle's time. If he didn't she walked out of church and then came round to the vicarage and made a scene. We used to dread the sight of her. Then, to our relief, she shook the dust of us off her feet and began going to All Saints in Beverton."

"And made *his* life a misery," put in Thea.

"Exactly. I think that his final offence was to have a server at Holy Communion. She went on somewhere else and the same thing happened everywhere. She's gone the round of all the churches within reach of Beverton several times over. The first thing they ask at the ruridecanal meeting is 'who's "got" Miss Maple now?', and whoever has is commiserated by everyone. I gathered from her that she has exhausted the circle once more and is starting on us again."

"Did she say so?" asked Lettice with interest.

"Oh no, she never says so. She just pays you an ordinary social call and as she goes says pleasantly, 'Well, see you on Sunday.' It's a sort of challenge. It means that if you've made any innovations in the service you must quickly unmake them or take the consequences."

"I shall look forward to seeing her," said Lettice.

"She's worth seeing," laughed Thea.

"She always wears rush hats trimmed with raffia," put in Lavinia, "and she always has a raffia handbag."

"And she wears holland dresses that she makes herself," said Thea, "and she covers them with embroidery all over and they don't fit anywhere."

"And she's very well off and very mean," added Lavinia.

Mrs. Fanshaw smiled.

"Actually," she said, "she's exactly like the stage caricature of a rural spinster, overacted by an amateur. But," she grew serious, "she was rather interesting yesterday. She was talking about the old days here."

"Anything interesting about us?" said Thea, munching a piece of Lady Baltimore cake.

"Or Gran?" said Lavinia.

"Not much one didn't know. . . . She was a little girl when your grandmother came here. No one for miles around talked of anything but your grandmother and her doings. Later she was sometimes asked up to the Castle to have tea with the two little boys."

"Father and Uncle Simon?" said Thea.

"Yes. . . . She said that as Simon grew older all the girls in the village were in love with him. He was so attractive and good-looking. They were even jealous of Miss Pendleton's sister because she was sewing-maid at the Castle."

"Miss Pendleton's sister?" said Thea. "I didn't know she had one."

"I remember vaguely hearing that she had," said Mrs. Fanshaw. "A half-sister young enough to be her daughter. According to Miss Maple, Miss Pendleton brought her up very strictly. She was a very prim and proper Miss Pendleton in those days. Quite different from the one you know. The sister died while they were away on a holiday. Miss Maple said she was pretty and very superior, and such a clever dressmaker that your grandmother used to let her make her dresses. She was quite a pet of your grandmother's, she said."

"A pet of Gran's!" groaned Thea. "Can you imagine Gran having a pet of any sort – much less a pet dressmaker."

"It's funny she never told us," said Lavinia.

"Why should she?" said Thea.

"Well, we've often mentioned Miss Pendleton. You'd have thought she'd have told us about her sister. And Hannah . . . Hannah's told us about all the other people in the village who used to work here – she was proud of there being so many servants here in the old days – but she never mentioned Miss Pendleton's sister."

"Well, it's time we packed up," said Mrs. Fanshaw firmly, "unless we're all to get into trouble. . . ."

Chapter Eleven

LETTICE crossed the green to Pear Tree Cottages. After the picnic they had all walked together to the edge of the wood, then Lettice had turned back towards the village and Mrs. Fanshaw had accompanied the two girls across the park to the Castle.

As she lifted the latch of the small green gate, Lettice glanced up at the next door window. Odd to think of Miss Pendleton living there with the pretty half-sister. Impossible to imagine a "prim and proper" Miss Pendleton. For a moment she seemed to see a pale wistful face looking out between the muslin curtains, then it turned into Lydia Morrice's bright vivacious face, the inevitable cigarette between the reddened lips. She held Matilda on the crook of her arm. When she saw Lettice, she came from the window to the front door, so that Matilda could show off what was euphemistically called her "walking." She lurched unsteadily on plump dimpled legs, supported by the reins that Lydia held, and crinkled her face up at Lettice in a friendly smile.

"She honestly does walk," said Lydia. "There's no weight at all on the reins. They just help her balance, that's all."

Her pretence of ignoring Matilda's existence had worn very threadbare. She remembered occasionally to act the part, but did it now without much conviction.

"She's just picked it up herself," she added carelessly. "No one taught her. She talks quite a lot, too."

"Dad – dad – dad – dad – dad," said Matilda proudly.

"You can say more than that, you idiot," said Lydia.

"Dad – dad – dad – dad," repeated Matilda firmly.

"Look," said Lydia. "I'm not really holding the reins at all now. She's walking quite by herself."

Matilda took two or three unsteady steps then fell forward and was jerked back to safety. She chuckled and said " 'Gain!"

"Lots of children don't start walking till they're well over twelve months," said Lydia. She glanced at her watch. "Time I was putting her to bed."

She threw away the cigarette-end and picked up Matilda, who patted her cheeks with soft little palms. Lydia moved her head aside.

"The way she mauls me about!" she groaned.

Lettice hesitated. It was Bella's afternoon out and she felt reluctant somehow to enter the empty cottage, where the memory of Harvey still seemed to be lying in wait, ready to spring out at her in her first unguarded moment.

"May I come and help you put Matilda to bed?" she said. "I love seeing her in her bath."

"I think it's a disgusting spectacle," said Lydia aloofly. "I've never seen such a paunch on anyone. ... She's almost as bad as I am and I've got an excuse, which is more than she has." She looked down at her woollen dress. She had given up wearing trousers as her pregnancy showed more plainly. "I can't think why I've let myself in for the whole revolting process again. I must have been crazy. You've never had children, have you?"

"No. ..."

"It's awful when they start waking you up in the night playing football inside you. Matilda had a kick like a giraffe's. ... Well, let's get this beastly business of the bath over."

"I must just go and see Frank first," said Lettice. "He says I ought to order my vegetable seeds this week."

"Don't let him do it for you," Lydia warned her.

"No, Mrs. Turnberry called last week and told me not to. One feels a bit mean letting him go every time without paying him."

"Yes ... and there's something too pathetic about the way the poor old thing trudges round each day to collect his money. Clifford's watching them both like a cat. He is rather like a cat, too. A handsome worried tom-cat. ... I suppose the trouble will come when things start growing in the gardens, and Frank starts carting them off to market on his own."

"He works well."

"I know. ... I made him take up all those awful crosses that Miss Pendleton had put over the cats' graves and burn them. I couldn't bear the sight of them any longer. I expect she'll come round and make the hell of a scene. ... I don't know why I kept them up so long."

"She was very prim and proper," said Lettice dreamily, "and she brought up a half-sister young enough to be her daughter."

"Poor kid! I wonder she didn't die of it."

"She did die . . ." said Lettice.

Lydia groaned again as Matilda took a strand of her hair in one hand and her nose in the other and pulled both as hard as she could.

"I shall get no peace till this creature's out of the way. ... Come along as soon as you can."

Lettice went round to the back garden, where Frank Turnberry was digging in the vegetable patch, turning over the hard earth with easy rhythmic movements. When he saw Lettice he raised himself upright, and stood looking down at her, his hands resting on his spade handle, a beaming smile on his red perspiring face. His enormous size and powerful physique always made her feel ridiculously small and puny.

"About the seeds, Frank," she began.

"Shall I see to that, Mrs. Helston?" he said hopefully.

"No, I'll get them," said Lettice, "if you'll tell me what to get."

Unabashed, he gave his whole attention to the making of the list: one pound of peas, half a pound of French beans, half a pound of runner beans, half an ounce of purple sprouting broccoli, half an ounce of cabbage, half an ounce of cauliflower, half an ounce of lettuce. He told her the best sort of each to get – Little Marvel, Nonsuch, Flower of Spring, Early Snowball, All the Year Round, Sunrise, Early Giant ... the names vaguely satisfied and soothed her. They were ridiculous, but somehow just right.

"And now you'd better go," she said, closing her notebook. "It's after your time."

Frank never knew the time and would work several hours after the regulation five o'clock if not sent home by his employer. He was almost embarrassingly eager to please. The weather-beaten face would light up like a child's at a word of praise, and not even the studied insolence of Mrs. Webb's manner to him could damp his amiability. He reminded Lettice of a large mongrel, deprecating and friendly, wagging its tail in wild delight at a kind word. He was even ingenuously proud that Clifford should see him there working in the gardens, keeping his job, and never lost hope that one day Clifford would become fond of him again as he had been when they were boys.

Lettice watched his clumsy figure lumbering across the green to the "Fox and Grapes." His mother always gave him the price of a glass of beer when she saw him off in the morning.

Then she went in to watch Matilda being put to bed.

When she returned she sat down at her writing-desk to make out the list of seeds for the post . . . 2 oz. Cress, Fine White Curled; 1/2 oz. Lettuce, Tom Thumb and Trocadero; 1 oz. Beet, Blood Red. . . .

Suddenly there was a knock at the front door – a loud imperious knock that made her start. She put down her pen and waited for Bella to answer it, then remembered that she was out. Impatient at the interruption, she pushed back her chair and went to the door. . . . Harvey stood there. For a moment the shock was so great that she could only stare at him. He smiled, his usual charming smile, wholly at his ease.

"May I come in?" he said.

She stood aside for him to enter. She was trembling so violently that she could hardly stand. Her heart fluttered in her chest like an imprisoned bird. He walked into the little sitting-room and looked around, still with that easy charming smile – interested, faintly amused.

"May I sit down?" he said, and, without waiting for her answer, took the arm-chair that had always been his favourite.

She sat down, too, because her knees were too unsteady to uphold her any longer. If only her heart would stop beating like this. She could hardly hear what he was saying.

"Well, old girl, how are you getting on? You seem quite, comfortable."

She moistened her dry lips and tried to say something, but no words would come.

"Sensible of you to take a holiday," he went on. "Bit of a strain, the whole thing. I felt it myself. Olga was quite knocked up. She's all right now."

She found her voice at last.

"Harvey, what have you come for?" she said.

He threw her a quick glance, and she saw that he wasn't quite as much at his ease as he was trying to appear.

"Well, my dear girl," he said, throwing out his hands, "why not be friends? You've always meant a lot to me, and I flatter myself that I've always meant a lot to you. Nothing's happened that should prevent our still being, good friends."

"Hasn't it?"

The shock of his sudden appearance was fading, and, though she still trembled, she was beginning to feel more mistress of herself. The smile he turned on her was just a little too easy.

"Come, darling—"

That cut through her guard.

"Don't call me that," she said sharply.

He shrugged. She could tell that he was annoyed by the rebuff, but determined not to let her see his annoyance.

"Just as you like. You were always a little unreasonable, weren't you? If you hadn't been—"

He left the sentence unfinished. Having administered her punishment, he smiled at her again – the smile that used to thrill every nerve in her body but that now seemed curiously artificial. He was as good-looking as ever, but – had that charming manner of his always been so deliberate, or was it that he was nervous?

"Will you please tell me why you've come, Harvey?" she said again.

"It's just a friendly call," he said. "I heard that you'd come down to this part of the world, and I happened to be passing, so I thought I'd look you up." His eyes smiled at her. "I just couldn't pass without dropping in to see if there was anything I could do for you. Business," gaily, "knocking a shelf up, filling in an income-tax form, looking out a train, putting a tradesman in his place? Our marriage hit the rocks, Letty, but I'm still fond of you, and I still want to do all I can for you."

Her body was rigid, her hands clenched till the nails dug into her palms.

"There's nothing you can do for me," she said, "except leave me alone. Please go, Harvey. And I don't want ever to see you again."

To her horror her voice quivered hysterically on the last word. He leant towards her, all tender concern.

"You're not yourself, dear," he said. "I thought you were ill as soon as I saw you. Now you must let me look after you. You—"

He put a hand out to hers. She snatched hers away and rose to her feet with a quick, jerky movement.

"Will you *go*, Harvey?" she said in a strangled voice. "If you won't I'll go myself. . . . I—"

He rose, too, and stood looking at her as if considering his next move. His smile had faded. He looked thoughtful and a little – shifty, was the word that came into her mind. Then he smiled again suddenly – a disarmingly boyish smile.

"All right. I'll make a clean breast of it. I came because I'm in a hole and I want you to lend a hand."

She gazed at him helplessly, fighting against his power over her. That boyish appeal touched something deeper than the bonds of sex that had united them.

"What do you want?"

He sat down again, resting his elbows on his knees and speaking in a low confidential voice.

"It's about Susan," he said. "Olga and I want to go to the south of France for a month or two, and they say they can't keep Susan at her school for the holidays. . . . Naturally, Olga doesn't want the child with her. Well, you know what a beastly fag it is having a child about. She's old enough to look after herself in some ways, but still she'd be a responsibility and a tie – not to speak of the expense. Olga's people have been absolutely rotten about it. You'd have thought one of them would have taken the kid, wouldn't you? It's only for a month, and she's no trouble. Poor Olga's been round to every single one, and they've all raked up some futile excuse or other not to have the kid. I wouldn't have believed people could be so mean. There are places that take kids for the holidays, of course, but they're absolutely extortionate. Charge as much as an hotel. Olga says she simply won't pay it, and I don't blame her. A kid that eats hardly anything and isn't any trouble. . . . She found a cheap place last year, but the kid was ill when she came back, and the doctor said she mustn't go there again. . . . We were at our wits' end when I thought of you. I thought 'Old Letty's never let me down yet and she won't now.' You'll have the kid, won't you, Letty? It's only for a month. . . . We've always meant a lot to each other, you and I. . . ."

He fixed his eyes on her in his most compelling, male-conqueror fashion, with the smile that seemed suddenly a little shop-soiled – as if it had been put to too frequent and too dubious uses.

Every vestige of colour had faded from her face as she listened. Anger such as she had never known in her life swept over her. For a moment she could not speak. Then :

"How dare you?" she said in a low passionate voice. He stared at her, open-mouthed.

"What on earth do you mean?" he spluttered.

"How *dare* you ask me to take your mistress's brat?"

"Draw it mild, Lettice," he blustered. "Olga will be my wife as soon as the decree's made absolute."

"She's been your mistress for long enough, hasn't she?" she said, still in that low furious voice. "I shouldn't have thought that even you would have had the impudence. . . . Please go at once. And if you come here again I shan't see you."

She went to the front door and opened it. He followed her, sulky and glowering. At the door he turned.

"But look here, Lettice——"

"Please go," she repeated.

He shrugged. His handsome mouth was set in a tight snarling line, but she realised, with dull surprise, that he was afraid of her.

"All right," he said, and added with a faint attempt at dignity, "I'm sorry you've taken it in this way. It isn't like you."

She was silent. He walked down the little path to the gate. He didn't seem to be alone. A child was with him – solemn, dark-eyed, resigned but not disappointed, because she was accustomed to be turned away from people's doors.

"Harvey," she said. Her voice was faint but he heard it and swung round. "I'll take her. . . ."

She didn't know that she was going to say the words till she heard them. He looked at her, eager and surprised.

"That's decent of you." He started back towards the door.

"Don't . . ." she said breathlessly.

"All right." He was obviously no more anxious to prolong the interview than she was. "I'll write about dates. It's – decent of you."

He turned and walked away. Though she couldn't see his face, she could imagine his lips curved into a gratified smirk. He thought that his charm had won the day, after all. . . .

She went back to the drawing-room and stood at the window watching him. He walked to a car that had been parked by the side of the green. There was a woman in it. As she turned her head at his approach, Lettice saw that it was Olga. . . . He assumed his best swagger as he got in, and his smile was nauseating in its complacency. She could almost hear the words he was saying. "It's all right. She'll have the kid. Poor old Lettice! I knew she wouldn't refuse. She's still crazy about me. . . ." They grinned at each other like two successful conspirators as he drove off. Anger choked her at the sight. What a fool she'd been! Making things easy for them! Removing the very obstacle over which she had been gloating – Harvey saddled with the responsibility of a child. The thought had afforded her comfort and delight times innumerable, and now, on a crazy impulse, she had taken the responsibility from his shoulders. She thought of the arnused interest with which her friends would hear the news ("My dear! *Have* you heard the latest? She's taking

Olga's kid for the holidays! Can you beat it! Olga says she'd do anything he asked her to. She's still crazy about him"), and humiliation swept through her like a wave of fire. And they'd be right to laugh at her. . . . Well, it was soon enough undone. She only had to write to him. . . . If she wrote now to say that she'd changed her mind, he would get it tomorrow morning. It would wipe the smirk off his face, and he'd have to set to work again to find a parking-place for the kid. Probably end by sending her back to the cheap place where the doctor said she hadn't to go. She shrugged. . . . It wasn't her business. Olga's brat was nothing to her. . . . She sat down at the writing-table and took up her pen.

"Dear Harvey," she began, but her hand was trembling so violently that the letters sprawled about as if she were drunk.

She tore up the paper and threw it into the waste-paper basket, then stopped, her heart racing wildly. . . . There was another knock at the door. Could it be Harvey back again? She went slowly into the hall and opened it. Mrs. Fanshaw stood there.

"Oh . . . come in," she said. She gave a laugh that was almost hysterical with relief. "I thought . . ."

Mrs. Fanshaw followed her into the drawing-room then stood and looked at her with quizzical blue eyes.

"What's the matter?" she said shortly. "Been seeing ghosts?"

"Yes," said Lettice. "Sit down and have a cigarette. I need one badly myself." She drew a deep breath and handed the cigarette-box to her visitor. Suddenly everything seemed sane and normal again. "My husband – my late husband—" She stopped. Her voice was still unsteady. She tried again. "My late husband's been here. He came to ask me to take charge of my supplanter's little girl." She tried to speak in a tone of light amusement. "Did you ever hear of anything more brazen?"

"Are you going to?"

The voice sounded casual and uninterested, but the blue eyes watched her closely.

"Of course not," said Lettice. "Why should I make things easy for that bitch? You don't mind language, do you?"

"Not at all."

"I – I rather stupidly didn't make it quite clear, I'm afraid. At least I – I said I wouldn't, and then I gave him to understand that I might. I can't think why. It was just – well, one does have moments of complete madness sometimes, and I was upset. I'm writing to him now to make it quite clear that I won't have her."

"Why write now? You don't look up to writing letters."

"I want to jerk him out of his fool's paradise," said Lettice with a shaky laugh. "I want him to get it tomorrow."

"I think one puts oneself at a disadvantage, writing an important letter when one's in what I might call a wrought-up state," smiled Mrs. Fanshaw.

"I'm not wrought-up," protested Lettice.

"My rule for all really important letters," went on Mrs. Fanshaw cheerfully, "is never to write them till the day after I've decided to write them. Letters one writes under the influence of emotion are generally undignified and ridiculous, and it's a mistake to give people an excuse to make fun of one."

Lettice flushed. Harvey and Olga making fun of her, laughing over her letter. . . . Then her lips tightened. They wouldn't laugh over this one. It would put too much of a spoke in their wheel.

"Your cigarette's gone out," said Mrs. Fanshaw, striking a match. "Nice to think Thea's getting away from her grandmother, isn't it?"

"Yes," said Lettice.

She spoke a little sulkily. She felt piqued by Mrs. Fanshaw's lack of interest in her news. Any other woman would have been wildly curious, bombarding her with questions (What had he said? . . . What had she said?. . .), wanting to know all about Olga and the child.

"I'm a bit worried about Lavvy," went on Mrs. Fanshaw. "She looks so strung-up. I wish her mother could have managed the two of them. She'll miss Thea horribly."

"I suppose so," said Lettice.

Really, the woman might have made at least a pretence of sympathy, she thought resentfully. She must see that she was desperately unhappy. Tears of self-pity welled up suddenly into her eyes . . . but the visitor didn't seem to notice them.

"It's so unfortunate, that Sylvia's away just now," she went on. "She'd have helped Lavvy. Lavvy needs someone of her own generation. We're no good." She didn't seem to notice her hostess's lack of response. "You'll have her to tea again, won't you? She's devoted to you. She's really only a child, and you seem to have a knack with children."

"I haven't," muttered Lettice ungraciously.

"But what I really came for," went on Mrs. Fanshaw, "was to ask your help."

"Do you want me to get you out of a hole?" said Lettice hysterically. "That's what Harvey said. . . ."

She knew that she was behaving outrageously, but her nerves were in shreds, and she longed for the help and sympathy that this woman seemed to be deliberately withholding.

"In a way. . . . I told you about Miss Maple, didn't I? Well, she's going to make my life a misery about the organ. She'll come round after every service to say that we never had that setting in her uncle's day, and what was good enough for him ought to be good enough for us and so on, but if you were to play it I'd be able to say that it had nothing to do with me, and she wouldn't dare to attack you, or, if she did, I'm sure you'd be equal to it. You didn't know her uncle, anyway. She could hardly expect his crotchets to mean anything to you. . . . Just for matins. I'll still do evensong. And anyway it'll be only for a few weeks. She never stays anywhere for more than a few weeks."

"Certainly not," said Lettice coldly. "I told you from the beginning that I shouldn't."

"Oh, very well," said Mrs. Fanshaw, with the air of one making a graceful surrender. "Very well. . . . But you won't refuse to come and help me practise now, will you? Sandy's in bed with a cold, and I can't get anyone else to blow for me."

Lettice hesitated. She didn't want to be left alone in the house that was now full of Harvey's disturbing personality, its peace shattered, its harmony jarred. She could hear his voice . . . see his complacent smile. . . . She couldn't bear to stay here alone without the comfort of this woman's presence. And that thought surprised her, for she hadn't realised till this moment that there had been any comfort in it.

"Very well," she said. "I'll come. . . ."

Chapter Twelve

"BUT why not, Ivy?" said George persuasively. "I can afford it now I've had a rise. We'll manage fine."

She tossed her head.

"I'm not in such a hurry as all that," she said pouting.

He looked at her, his handsome face darkening.

"It wasn't so long ago as you said you'd marry me soon as I could fix it up," he said. "You said you didn't want to wait. You've changed a good bit lately, haven't you?"

"Oh, have I?" said Ivy affectedly. "I don't remember that I was ever so keen as all that, Mr. George Harker."

"Well, you was," he said shortly. "Remember it or not as you like."

They walked on in silence for some yards. A slight mist hung over the wood, and through it the rosy glow of the birch saplings told of rising sap. Overhead, birds chattered excitedly in the bare branches as if discussing their plans for nesting. Their notes blended with the sound of the little stream that burbled clamorously along its channel, swollen by last night's rain.

Ivy stole a glance at her companion from beneath her long lashes. His body was virile and muscular and finely proportioned, vibrant with youth and youth's confidence in its strength. His face and neck were burnt red by exposure to all weathers, making his eyes – now narrowed and moody – vividly blue. His fair hair was untidy. He had sleeked it back with water before he came out, but it rose now thick and wiry from his bronzed forehead. He had his muscles under perfect control, but he walked clumsily, with the lumbering gait of the farm worker.

Something of her old pride in his good looks and strong body stirred in her heart, then died away. He was "common." He wasn't like the men on the pictures or the men she'd seen in London that day she went there with Miss Lennare. She had always known, of course, that those men existed, but she had looked on them till now as outside her orbit. Last week, however, she had been to London again with Miss Lennare, and they had met one or two men whom Miss Lennare knew. She had introduced them to Ivy, and they had been delightfully, flatteringly kind. The memory still thrilled her. Just as if she'd been a lady. Well, she would be a lady. Anyone could be a lady. It was just a question of speaking and behaving in a certain way. Just a trick. . . . Miss Lennare had told her yesterday that her table manners were improving, and she was correcting the way she talked, too, making her put her aitches in. George was always dropping his aitches. He spoke downright common. She wouldn't meet men like George when she went abroad with Miss Lennare as her companion-secretary. She'd meet men like the men on the pictures. Miss Lennare stayed at grand hotels and met grand people. She knew the sort of places. She'd seen them on the pictures. Big doors and enormous rooms and miles and miles of passages and waiters in evening dress. Posh. No telling who you might meet in a place like that. No telling who you might marry. Day-dreams often swam before her eyes, of which in her saner moments she was ashamed. She sat at little tables in palatial dining-rooms with handsome men. The most handsome of the lot turned out to be a duke. He was passionately in love with her. They were married at a posh church, with people standing in crowds to watch them come out. Men with cameras. Photos in the newspapers. . . . A house as big as Beverton Public Library, with footmen and chauffeurs and lots of "company," who formed an admiring crowd around her, while the duke hovered attentively in the background. She'd come down here, of course, occasionally to see Mum and the others. It would be a proper thrill for them all. . . . A duchess. She wouldn't be a bit proud. Quite kind and pleasant . . . wearing clothes like people on the pictures. . . . She'd hunt and dance and do all the posh things. One could probably pick them up quite easy. Easily. Miss Lennare had been telling her about that last night.

"An' I know who's changed you, too," George was saying. "It's that Miss Lennare."

"Oh, is it?" said Ivy, with another affected toss of the head. "You know a lot, don't you?"

"I know that much, all right," he said sullenly. "You're a fool to be took in by her, Ivy. Oh yes, she's making a fuss of you now, all right, but – don't you see? – she's the sort that'll drop you like a hot brick soon as she gets tired of you. An' she's the sort that'll get tired of you pretty quick."

"Oh, reelly?" said Ivy, with high-pitched elaborate sarcasm. "It may interest you to know that she's takin' me abroad with her. That doesn't sound like gettin' tired of me, does it?"

"Yes, it'll be nice for you stranded somewhere abroad, won't it?" he said. "I wouldn't trust that woman 'alf an inch. No one in the village can stick her, an' everyone says she's doin' you no good."

Ivy gave an elaborate shrug of her thin shoulders.

"I'm not interested what common people like you an' the village think," she said. "She's a lady, is Miss Lennare."

He looked down at the weak pretty face and felt a sudden desire to take her by the shoulders and shake her till she couldn't breathe. . . . Instead he said:

"An' I suppose you think she's goin' to make you one."

She flushed at the sneer in his voice.

"Oh yes," she flamed. "You'd like to keep me down. I know that, all right. I've got the chance of gettin' on in the world. She's learning me typin'– teachin', I mean, – an' I'm going to be her secretary, an' go abroad with her, an' all you can think of is of tryin' to keep me down. She says that's men all over. Rotten with selfishness, all of them, she says, an' she ought to know. She's been all over the world. . . . You don't think of nothing but yourselves. I'd be mad, throwin' myself away on a farm labourer like you, she says. . . ."

His face darkened with anger. It was as if he shared suddenly her vision of herself surrounded by handsome admirers against a background of opulent splendour. He looked down at her small white throat and thought how easy it would be to press the life out of it with one hand. . . . She was so tiny. She'd hardly struggle at all. . . . In a lurid flash of understanding he knew why men killed women rather than let someone else have them. Then his brain cleared, leaving him faint and dizzy.

"Oh, so you an' her have been talkin' me over, have you?" he said in a strained unsteady voice.

"Well, why not?" she said, quickly on the defensive. "She takes an interest in me. A girl's got a duty to herself, hasn't she? All you want is someone to look after you and sleep with you—"

Her voice trailed away uneasily as if she were suddenly afraid of what she had said. The hot wave of anger flooded him again.

"So that's the sort of muck she talks to you."

She flushed and turned her head away.

"Well, it's true, isn't it?" she said in a voice that was both aggressive and uncertain. "It's true. . . . There's no reason why a woman should be a man's slave. . . . Why should I give up a chance of seein' a bit of life? She says that if I'd take trouble with my accent an' table manners I'd soon be a lady. When I go abroad with her I'll wear evening dress in the evening same as her an'—"

She caught her high heel in a root that ran across the path and clung to him for support. The small slight body in his arms turned his anger to an aching tenderness. He held her closely to him.

"Ivy . . . little Ivy," he murmured.

She surrendered for a moment to the old happiness, to the feeling of peace and security that his arms about her had always given her. His lips pressed against hers, his hard virile body against her soft fragility, the harshness of his skin against hers, sent the old thrill of delight through her. Then there seemed to come between them the picture of Miss Lennare, her lips curved into a contemptuous smile, as she said, "How a woman can give up her freedom just to be mauled about by a man—." She stirred restlessly. He held her more tightly and she began to struggle away from his embrace. Reluctantly he released her, and they walked on slowly.

He could feel her trembling against the arm he still kept about her waist.

"You do love me, Ivy," he said with sudden confidence.

"I don't know as I do . . ." she muttered. "I've never been anywhere, nor seen anyone."

"I s'pose that's what *she* says," he said, keeping a tight grip on his patience. It didn't help matters to quarrel, and the tenderness their embrace had raised in him filled mind and body with a glowing aftermath.

She turned her face away and made no answer.

"Won't you trust me, Ivy?" he pleaded. "I'll make you happy, I promise you. I've loved you since you was a little one. . . . I'd never hurt you. I'll cherish you and look after you. . . ."

"Oh, I know what it'd be like," she burst out pettishly. His arms around her had made her dreams of glamour seem remote and unreal, and she was fighting desperately to recover them. "Housework from morning to night and kids. . . . My mother and yours over again. . . ."

His anger flared out despite himself.

"Well, what's wrong with my mother an' yours?" he said. "They've made their husbands happy an' kept their homes nice and brought up their families."

She pushed his arm away.

"What sort of a life is that?" she demanded.

He set his lips.

"It's a life that should satisfy any decent woman," he said.

She gave her affected little laugh.

"I suppose I'm not decent then," she said pertly. "It doesn't satisfy me."

"Why not?" he demanded.

"Look at your mother," she said. "D'you think I want to grow up to that? You're only young once. You've got to take your fun while you can get it."

"I've heard that talk before," he said contemptuously.

"I know the sort you want for a wife," she flung at him. "Well, there's plenty of them about. Why don't you get one and leave me alone?"

"Maybe I shall," he said sullenly.

She threw him a quick glance of mingled resentment and fear. The feeling of cold loneliness his words brought to her took her by surprise. He was striding along, his handsome young face dark and lowering. . . . She could see the fair hairs glistening on his cheek bones above the line where he had shaved. His thick muscular neck was brick red where it joined the blue collar of his shirt. Tears suddenly pricked her eyelids.

"All right, do!" she said. "I shan't care."

He said nothing and she continued:

"If you loved me you'd be glad for me to have a chance to better myself."

"Better yourself!" he echoed scornfully. "You're a little fool or you wouldn't be took in by a woman like that. Your own mother says so."

She stood still and stared at him, her blue eyes blazing.

"Oh, so you've been talking about me to her, have you?"

"Yes I have, an' she says it's a pity you're too old to have the nonsense spanked out of you."

She stumbled on, her heart racing with anger.

"Go away!" she gulped. "I never want to see you again."

Beneath his anger he was bewildered and uncertain. He couldn't make out this maddening inconsequent creature, this bundle of affectation and insincerity, and yet, because she was still Ivy, he still loved her. He had looked forward all day to this walk with her through the woods. He had been upheld by a firm unreasoning conviction that he would win back her love, and find again the Ivy who had been his childhood's sweetheart, his "little love." And apparently he had only made things worse. He had been stupid and clumsy. . . . He had lost his temper and made her lose hers.

"Let's not quarrel, Ivy," he said humbly. "I didn't mean—. You were so different once."

She plunged on without answering, trying to outdistance him in the absurd little high-heeled shoes that she couldn't resist wearing, though Miss Lennare had told her that they weren't suitable for the country.

He put his arm tentatively about her waist, but she flung away from him.

"Leave me alone," she said. "I hate you."

They had reached the stile that led from the wood onto the main road. He put out a hand to help her over, but she pushed it away, caught her high heel on the top rung of the stile, and fell forward into the road. She scrambled to her feet, the ridiculous little hat on one side, the pretty, common little face pink with anger and humiliation.

"Ivy . . ." he pleaded.

She turned and ran from him in the direction of the green, down the road that stretched like a white tunnel between the shadowy woods. Above the leafless trees, the setting sun hung like a great red ball in a sky of lavender grey. George watched her uncertainly, wondering whether to run after her, and finally decided not to. She ran ungracefully and jerkily on the unfamiliar high heels. She had snatched off the disarranged hat and carried it in her hand. . . . He waited a few moments then walked down the road with his slow lumbering gait.

"The little fool!" he muttered. "The darn little fool!"

But he spoke softly, tenderly, as one speaks of a beloved child. . . .

Ivy ran into the kitchen of Honeysuckle Cottage, slammed the door to, and bolted it in case George might be following her. She stood listening with wildly beating heart then turned away, glad that he wasn't coming and at the same time hurt and disappointed. *That* was all he cared for her. Well, she knew now. Good thing she'd found out in time. . . . That was just what Miss Lennare had said, that hundreds of girls married men just because they flattered them, and then found out too late what beasts they were. Well, she'd found out this afternoon what a beast George was and no mistake. . . .

She turned to look at her reflection in the mirror that hung on the wall between the two windows, and humiliation overwhelmed her again as she saw that her fall had turned one of the carefully wound curls into a lank strand of loose hair, and that there was dust all down one side of her coat. She'd taken such trouble to prepare herself for this walk with George. The elegance of her appearance was meant to impress on him the gulf that lay between them. She wasn't just an ordinary country girl any longer. She was going to be a lady. . . . She dressed like a lady. All the time that she walked with him in the wood, she had seen herself, as it were, through his eyes – the halo hat perched on the erection of curls, the smart new suit, the thin stockings, the high-heeled shoes. . . . Why, he'd only got to look at her to realise that she wasn't likely to marry the likes of him. Of course, she didn't actually want him to stop wanting to marry her. His devotion had formed the background of her life for so long that she couldn't really imagine herself without it. . . . She'd always be fond of him in a way, too. She'd be very kind to poor old George on those flying visits she meant to pay to Steffan Green in the large motor-car with the adoring ducal husband in attendance. George, of course, mustn't marry anyone else. George married to someone else would spoil the picture. . . .

And now his last impression of her was this – floundering in the road, scrambling ungracefully to her feet, her hair coming down, her suit covered with dust. . . . Her eyes filled with tears of hurt pride as she turned from the mirror. . . . She shrugged her shoulders petulantly. . . . Oh, well, what did it matter? She didn't care what George Harker thought. Why should she? She wasn't sure that she would come down here when she was married, after all. Better make a clean break. . . . It would be annoying to have people remembering things like that about her. No, she certainly wasn't going to worry about what George Harker thought of her. Probably when once she got abroad with Miss Lennare she'd have forgotten even that he existed. . . .

She went upstairs to her bedroom to take off her coat and skirt. A murmur of voices came from the room below. She remembered that Miss Lennare had told her that Miss Pendleton was coming to visit her. What on earth did Miss Lennare see in that old hag? She was always asking her round, and she generally let Ivy go for a walk on the afternoon when she was expecting her. They talked and talked – heaven knew what about. . . . To restore her self-respect, she rearranged her curls, put the halo hat on again at the right angle, brushed her coat, and postured a little before the glass, smiling sweetly and with gracious condescension, being herself both actor and audience, seeing herself through the eyes of George, the duke, and an admiring throng of onlookers. Then she took off hat and costume and slipped on the red woollen dress. She was trying to imagine the duke, but he kept turning into George. It was annoying just when she wanted to forget George. . . .

She'd make herself a cup of tea now. Miss Lennare had told her not to bring tea in for Miss Pendleton when she came. Well, everyone knew it wasn't tea Miss Pendleton wanted. And, though she'd never said so, Miss Lennare gave her a bit of what she wanted, all right. Miss Lennare washed up the glass herself, so that she shouldn't know, but she knew, all right. She'd seen the difference in the bottle of brandy that was kept in the sitting-room cupboard before and after Miss Pendleton's visits. Didn't seem quite fair, priming the old thing up, when everyone knew she couldn't stand it, and it only meant she went about making a nuisance of herself to everyone, especially to Mrs. Morrice. Going and bawling over the hedge at her. . . . The Morrices must be sorry they'd ever taken the old creature's house. Funny to think of Miss Pendleton like Mum said she'd been when she was a girl, teaching in Sunday School and running the Band of Hope and never a hair out of place and keeping the house spotless. Fussy, she was, Mum said. Must have everything just so. Fussed the life out of that young sister of hers – the one that died. Mum said that if anyone had told her then that she'd turn into a dirty drunken old woman like what she was now she'd never have believed them. Mum's mother had been in her "district," and Mum said she used to lecture them if there was a speck of dirt anywhere when she came visiting. She'd got eyes that could see right through things. The children had to mind their manners, too, when she was by. A vague terror of life seized Ivy.

. . . It could do dreadful things. . . . It could turn the Miss Pendleton Mum had known into the dirty old hag whose shrill quavering voice rose from the room below. What would it do to her? Would she ever turn into a creature like that? Instinctively her thoughts fled to George for protection, but she jerked them back resentfully. She could manage without *him*, thanks, she told herself with a toss of her head. Time she was going abroad with Miss Lennare. Getting in a proper rut, she was. . . .

She went down to the kitchen, put on the kettle, and set out the loaf of bread, the jam jar, and the butter on the table. When they were alone she often had tea with Miss Lennare in the sitting-room. Miss Lennare said it was silly, two people in the same house having meals in different rooms. She taught her table manners and told her how pretty she was and called her "childie." Ivy enjoyed it, but felt vaguely uncomfortable. She knew that her mother wouldn't have approved. Mum had silly old-fashioned ideas about people "keeping their places." Oh, well, she'd get a shock one of these days when she came home married to a toff. . . .

The voices from the sitting-room below still continued – Miss Lennare's deep booming voice, curiously softened, then Miss Pendleton's wavering cackle. What on earth did they find to talk about? The kettle wasn't boiling yet. In idle curiosity she went out and put her ear to the keyhole. Miss Pendleton seemed to be doing most of the talking. Miss Lennare put in something occasionally on a low note – something that always seemed to set the old girl off again. Isolated sentences reached her.

"In the place her father was churchwarden for forty years. . . . I'll never be able to hold up my head again. . . . Talk . . . talk . . . there's bound to be talk. . . . They'll guess. . . . If they don't guess already, they're blind. . . . There she was in the garden this afternoon, showing herself off for everybody to see. . . . Brazen . . . I'm shamed before them all – me that's always held up my head so high . . . shamed before them all. . . . She'd have been flogged at the cart's-tail in the old days, and serve her right. Flogging's too good for the likes of her. . . . 'Out you go, you trollop', I said. 'Out you go. You

don't have your brat here. I've kept myself respectable all my life.
... I won't be shamed by you ...' " her voice trailed into inaudibility.

Ivy, listening with renewed interest, thought that she heard the faint click of a glass. Miss Lennare's voice was so low that Ivy couldn't hear what she said. Miss Pendleton began to speak again. Her thin voice rose shrilly.

"I'd turn her out, bag and baggage, but they'd talk. ... They'd talk. ... They're whispering already. ... They *know*. ... Me that's kept myself respectable all my life. ... If her father'd been alive he'd have killed her, the brazen huzzy." Her voice sank to a vicious undertone, and Ivy caught only a word here and there. "The sly little vixen. ... So shy and timid, wasn't you? ... butter wouldn't melt in your mouth, would it? Oh, the shamelessness of it ... the shamelessness."

Miss Lennare put in something that Ivy couldn't catch.

"Down at the chalet by the lake," shrilled the old woman. "Night after night. ... It was her caught them at it. ... Pretty morsel for her to stomach, wasn't it. Her precious Simon. ... Sent for me the next day and told me. Cold as ice, she was. ... I turned sick. 'Make him marry her,' I sez to her. 'I'll die of shame if he don't.' She looked at me with eyes like daggers. 'I'll die of shame if he does,' she sez. If he'd been a man he'd have married her, spite of the old woman, but he wasn't. He was her favourite, but he'd always been afraid of her. She'd kept him under. ... They had a row, and he went, and I was left to bear it alone. ..."

Ivy strained her ears to hear the mutterings that followed "... hundred pounds through her lawyer without a word ... I sent it back. ... I've that much pride left. ..."

The kettle began to boil, and Ivy left the door to make her tea. What on earth was the old thing maundering about? Crackers, that's what she was. ... She drank a cup of tea and ate a piece of bread and butter, then the irresistible fascination of eavesdropping drew her back. ... There was the clink of glass against glass again. ... "What am I going to do?" moaned Miss Pendleton. There was maudlin tearfulness in her voice. "I can't face it ... the disgrace ... the shame ... and me that brought her up as if she was my

own child ... I wish I'd killed her the day her mother died. ...
To see her there in the home my mother slaved over ... in the
garden my father made with his own hands ... the shameless
creature! ... the harlot! ..."

The mixture of past and present bewildered Ivy.

"What's it all about?" she muttered as she went back to finish
her tea. "Somethin' that happened or somethin' that's happenin'
now? ... Crackers," she disposed of it finally with youthful contempt.

She took out *Peg's Paper* from the drawer of the kitchen table
and began to read it as she drank her third cup of tea. She kept
the drawer of the table half open, ready to slip it in, if she heard
Miss Lennare's footsteps, and take out *Pride and Prejudice*, which
Miss Lennare had given her to read and which she couldn't make
head or tail of.

At last she heard sounds of departure and went to the kitchen
window. Miss Lennare was piloting Miss Pendleton down to the
garden gate. They made an odd contrast – Miss Lennare's neat
compact thick-set figure by that of her tatterdemalion visitor. Miss
Lennare stood at the gate, watching her as she went down the
road, lurching from side to side, the grey hair straggling from under
the battered hat. ... Miss Lennare must have filled her up, all right,
thought Ivy wonderingly. Proper pickled, she was.

Miss Lennare went back to the study, and Ivy glanced curiously
through the half-open door to see what she was doing.

She was scribbling away like mad in a little note-book.

Chapter Thirteen

THE congregation streamed out of the little church into the crisp cold air.

The pessimists had been justified, and the warm days of early February had been followed by the sharpest frost of the winter. Plumbers were besieged by householders with stories of water dripping through ceilings or pouring downstairs. Methods of precaution were discussed on all sides – wrapping exposed pipes in sacking, leaving taps running, keeping oil-lamps at special danger points.

Among the congregation gathered in groups outside the church, however, this topic of conversation yielded place to the more exciting one of Miss Maple's ceremonial exit just before the second hymn. As soon as Mrs. Helston at the organ had played the opening bars of "Fight the Good Fight," Miss Maple had gathered her things together and walked out of church. She always sat in the front seat, which she had once occupied as the vicar's niece, and the "walking out" was a formidable, almost ritualistic affair. She had perfected her technique to such a point that it might have been a dozen people walking out instead of one. Even though the service went on during the process, it gave the impression of being suspended.

The groups round the church door were discussing the question of whether she had stayed at the church on this occasion longer than on the previous one, and to which other local place of worship she was now due. They stamped their feet to keep warm, and the frost turned their breath to little tongues of mist as they talked.

"She's only bin here three Sundays. She was eight last time she tried it."

"No, she was seven. Don't you remember? She came at Easter, and it was the anthem at Whitsun that upset her. She said they'd never had it in her uncle's time."

"She always says that. I suppose she'll go to St. Chad's down in Beverton now."

"Surely not. She was there only in December. She stayed till the vicar started having the collectors stand waiting till he'd held up the offertory."

"She's not been to St. Mary-at-Friars Church for some time. Bet you sixpence she tries that next."

"She's stopped going out there. She says it's too far."

"All the parsons in the place'll be shaking in their shoes now they know she's given us the go-by. . . . Old Mr. Peterson said they were talking about it at the last ruridecanal meeting. They hoped she was good for all the summer here."

"Well, she isn't now. . . ."

"I knew she'd never stand for Hatton's tune to 'Fight the Good Fight.' We always had Boyd's in her uncle's day."

"D'you remember that time when she walked out because—?"

They moved on one side respectfully to allow old Mrs. Ferring and her granddaughter to pass. Old Mrs. Ferring walked slowly and as if with difficulty. Lavinia had offered her arm, but her grandmother had refused it with a curt gesture. The bitter cold had brought on the old lady's rheumatism, but she would not admit it or allow anyone to mention it. She carried her small slight figure as rigidly upright as ever. Her face was as white as the frost that sparkled in the grass around her, her mouth was tightly set, but the keen eyes raked the groups as she came out, missing no detail. She gave greetings here and there to members of the old village families in her clear precise voice. They murmured respectful answers. "Yes, thank you, Mrs. Ferring." . . . "Good morning, Mrs. Ferring." The old women who had known her as the young squire's bride made little half-furtive bobs as they replied.

"She's a good plucked 'un," they murmured in unwilling admiration when she had passed.

"Proud as the devil. Always has been. . . ."

"Do you remember . . .?"

And they slid back into the stories that had once set the whole village agog and that even now held something of the old magic.

Mrs. Webb and Colin came out, Colin carrying his mother's prayer-book. She slipped her arm into his as they reached the porch. She liked to parade his devotion before the village. She looked like a sleek Persian cat in her thick fur coat. Beneath the veil of her elaborate feathered hat her hair looked very golden, her eyes very blue, her cheeks very pink. She had been keeping a tight hand on Colin lately. She couldn't forget how odd he'd been that night when Mrs. Turnberry had come to ask her to let Frank do her garden. She'd given in about that for the present (after all, one only had to give Frank Turnberry rope enough and he'd hang himself), but it had put her on her guard. She was haunted by the fear that he had begun to meet that Dorking girl again. She had been watching him closely ever since, and she felt more or less reassured now. He came back so punctually from his work that he could not have wasted any time on the way. She had gone into Beverton one evening to make quite sure and had watched him, from the cover of a shop opposite, go straight from the bank to the 'bus stop and catch a Steffan Green 'bus. She had caught the next one, explaining that she had been to meet him but must have missed him on the way . . . She had even spied on him in his lunch hour to make sure that he lunched alone or with another clerk. No, he hadn't taken up with that Dorking girl again. He still didn't seem quite himself, but she had to be content with buying a bottle of tonic for him and trying to persuade him to give up the walk that he now took every evening. She sometimes idly thought of accompanying him (she was jealous of every moment he spent out of her sight), but walking made her so breathless after a heavy meal. . . .

She stole a glance at him as they stepped out into the winter sunshine from the darkness of the church. He *did* look tired . . . his young face lined and strained. She'd ask the chemist for a stronger tonic and try again to make him give up that evening walk. She never had believed in exercise, and she resented his going off like that when he might be sitting cosily in front of the fire with her. It wasn't fair after all the sacrifices she'd made for him. She would put it to him like that. . . . Neglecting her, that was what it was. . . . Her tight little mouth tightened still further. She'd never allowed his father to neglect her and she wasn't going to start allowing him. (Give them an inch and they'd take an ell. . . . She knew them. . . .) Yes, there were dark shadows round his eyes. Perhaps he was going to be ill. Her spirits rose at the thought, and a wave of tenderness swept over her. Her little Colin . . . her little boy. She only felt really happy and secure when he was ill. He was all hers then . . . no rival claims or interests to separate him from her. And he'd always been so grateful to her for nursing him. She would be very firm about that evening walk. . . .

Colin walked slowly by her side, accommodating his usual long stride to her tottering little steps, responding absently to greetings, hardly knowing who had spoken, seeing nothing but Lavinia's face as he had seen it across the aisle in church. . . . At the thought of those stolen nightly meetings in the wood his heart-beats quickened. She came in such desperate terror – of herself, of him, of her grandmother, of the iniquity of coming at all. It was so sweet to hold her in his arms, to soothe and calm and comfort her, to hear her shy passionate protestations of love. . . . Such a child . . . but staunch and tender and true. In the protection of his presence, she would gradually lose her terror, becoming happy and carefree, building up a dream picture of their life together, ignoring every practical obstacle to its fulfilment.

"It doesn't matter waiting a few years, does it?" she would say. "Gran can't stop me when I'm twenty-one, and you'll be making enough to marry on then, won't you?" Or, "When Mother comes she'll understand. She'll help us. I'm sure she'll help us. . . . I daren't write and tell her. It's so difficult to explain properly in a letter. It would be so dreadful if she didn't understand, if she wrote to Gran. . . ." She paled at the thought. "But – when she comes over, she's so sweet, I'm sure she'll understand. Colin, are you sure your mother wouldn't help us if she knew? She looks so kind."

She was always returning to his mother, trying to persuade him to take her into his confidence, so starved for kindness that she fancied she saw it even in his mother's small pursed mouth and rosy plumpness.

"She looks kind, Colin," she pleaded. "Wouldn't she help? It would be so different if I could go to your house and meet you there properly. I couldn't bear not to meet you, but there's something so horrible in meeting like this. It – frightens me. Sometimes I wake up in the night and feel *sick* with fright. It seems – wicked. I'm sure I could manage to get Gran to let me go and see your mother about something. Colin, won't you tell her?"

Colin set his lips and shook his head.

"She's kind," he said with uneasy loyalty, "but she wouldn't understand."

Some instinct had warned him from the start that to tell his mother of his love for Lavinia would mean the end of it. His mother would be sweet and sympathetic, but – it would be the end of it. He shrank from even trying to understand why this was so, but he knew it as surely as if he'd seen it happen. And he had seen it happen a hundred times in less important matters. He wouldn't yield to her about this, he assured himself, but he felt convinced that even if he didn't she would manage somehow to spoil it, and he didn't want to give her the chance. Already she was growing restive about the evening walk that gave him his opportunity for meeting Lavinia, lamenting that she was dull and lonely by herself, inventing a hundred little things that she wanted him to do for her indoors.

It was difficult to explain this to Lavinia without saying more than he wanted to say, more than he wanted to understand. . . .

She would sometimes be gay and happy with a delicious childish gaiety, making him laugh at her description of old Albert's clumsiness, old Hannah's dourness, her grandmother's magnificent ignoring of the poverty and straitened circumstances of her life, but always her fear returned as the end of the meeting drew near. She was terrified lest her grandmother or Hannah might have discovered her absence, that she might find one of them waiting to confront her in her empty bedroom.

"They can't kill you," said Colin, trying to sound braver than he felt, for he too dreaded the conflagration that would follow discovery.

"That isn't any comfort," said Lavinia. "I'd almost rather they could. . . ."

He always took her to the edge of the park and stood in the shadow of the trees till he received the signal from her bedroom that she had returned safe and undiscovered – a lighted candle passed slowly across the window and then back.

Last night she had clung to him convulsively when the time for parting came.

"Colin, why must we go on like this? I can't bear it. . . ."

"It won't be for long, dearest," he had reassured her, tortured by his love for her, weighed down by as black a hopelessness as hers that he was trying to dispel. "It won't be for long."

"It wasn't so bad when Thea was there. She made things – fun. We could laugh at them."

"Does she write to you?" he asked, resentful of the ease with which Thea had escaped, leaving Lavinia to bear her burden alone.

"Sometimes," said Lavinia. "It's lovely to hear what she's doing, and she can make things sound so exciting even in a letter, but she seems to have – forgotten what it's like here. I know it's selfish of me to mind."

"It's not you who's selfish," he said hotly.

He held her tightly against him, as if to shield her from Thea and everyone else who could hurt her. She clung to him for a moment with thin childish arms, then released herself.

"If it weren't for you I'd run away," she said. "Thea was going to run away, but she'd have been better at it than me."

"Try not to be frightened of them," he counselled anxiously.

She gave a quick little sigh.

"Oh, it's not only that. It's the – dullness. All day and every day. No one but Gran and old Hannah. And the awful food and never being warm and never seeing anyone young. Sylvia was the only young person we were allowed to know and she's away now. And I get those beastly headaches and I daren't tell Gran and she says I'm stupid and not trying." She smiled tremulously. "I'm sorry. I didn't mean to grumble like this. I'm so lucky to have you and I do love you so."

He looked down at the shadowed eyes, the pale thin face, the hollow temples ... and anxiety stabbed his heart. She looked like a lost child.

"I'm only happy when I'm with you," she added.

A wave of shivering shook her as she spoke, and her teeth chattered uncontrollably. He could feel her shoulder-blades through the threadbare serge of her coat.

"I oughtn't to keep you here in the cold," he said.

"I'm not cold. Oh, Colin, it will be all right some day, won't it?"

"Of course it will," he assured her. "You mustn't let yourself ever think it won't."

"I don't generally," she said, "but just sometimes I think, 'Suppose it isn't,' and everything goes black. It's like when you think, 'Suppose there isn't a God.'"

"You little idiot!" he laughed, trying to conquer the depression that hung over them both.

He kissed her hands tenderly. The fingers were red and swollen with chilblains.

"I'm ashamed of them," she said, drawing them away. "It's only in the winter that they're like this. ... I ought to go now, oughtn't I? Oh, Colin, I do love you so. ...."

At the edge of the park they clung to each other for a moment, his mouth pressed against hers, before she tore herself away and ran off into the darkness. ... He waited in sick suspense till he saw the signal at her window, then set off homewards, steeling himself for his mother's cross-examination ("How far did you go, dear? ... Did you meet anyone you knew? ... Was there a light in Honeysuckle Cottage? I heard that Miss Lennare had gone to London for the night and taken Ivy. ...").

This morning, stealing furtive glances at her across the aisle, he had been shocked by the look of exhaustion on the small wan face, and in the dark-circled eyes. The short, dry, strangled cough that shook her shoulders and drew a quick glance of disapproval from her grandmother cut through him like the stab of a sword. Despair swept over him. What were they to do? They couldn't go on indefinitely snatching stolen meetings like this. It was criminal of him to have let her come to him through the fog and frost and rain of the winter nights. But he couldn't live without seeing her. What was to come of it? He felt like something hunted. The whole world seemed to be against them. . . .

"Penny for your thoughts, darling," said Mrs. Webb, as they went through the lych-gate into the cobbled courtyard.

Her tone was bright and casual, her lips curved into a pleasant rallying smile, but her small blue eyes watched him narrowly, ready to detect any sign that she had been excluded from his thoughts.

"Oh, just nothing," he said, his slight flush deepening because he knew that she had noticed it. She made no comment on his flush or sudden look of constraint.

"I've got pork for lunch, dear," she said in a light conversational tone. "You do like it better than mutton, don't you?"

Mrs. Fanshaw came out of church, smiling a greeting at the people who still stood about, despite the cold, gossiping desultorily. Her blue eyes wore a look of faintly ironic amusement. By persuading Lettice to take over the organ and play Hatton's tune for "Fight the Good Fight" she had got rid of Miss Maple and escaped the scene that generally accompanied the process of getting rid of her. Lettice had played well, too. She was losing her nervousness. She must manage somehow to persuade her to play again next Sunday.

A small anxious-looking elderly woman, wearing a worn black coat and neatly darned black gloves, stepped forward.

"May I have a word with you please, Mrs. Fanshaw?" she said respectfully.

"Of course, Miss Calder."

They walked down the path that wound among moss-grown tombstones to the gate.

"It's about Sarah," said Miss Pendleton's cousin. "She's gettin' queerer an' queerer. I don't think I can keep on with her much longer."

"I'm so sorry," said Mrs. Fanshaw, her brows coming together in a quick frown. "I'd hoped that she was getting better."

"Oh, as to her health . . ." said Miss Calder, with a shrug, "she eats quite hearty now. It's her mind that's worse."

"How?"

"She talks that wild. Stuff I can't make head nor tail of. All about—" she shrugged again helplessly.

"About what?" persisted Mrs. Fanshaw.

"I don't know. I said I couldn't make head nor tail of it. Seems to have got that Mrs. Morrice and her sister all muddled up in her mind with some bad woman. Gives you the creeps to hear her. You don't know whether she's talking about somethin' that went on years ago or somethin' that's goin' on today. Come to that, she don't seem to know herself."

Mrs. Fanshaw considered this.

"But surely it does no harm," she said at last. "Just take no notice of her."

"If it stopped at talk . . ." said Miss Calder.

"Doesn't it?"

"So far. But I tell you straight, Mrs. Fanshaw, she frightens me. I don't know where it's going to stop. You've always been good to me, an' I'd try to keep her for your sake, but – well, she's not responsible. She'll do some hurt to herself or someone else before she's finished."

"Shall I ask the doctor to come and see her again?" Miss Calder shook her head.

"No, she's cunning. She acts sane as you or me when he's there. . . . I woke up in the middle of last night, Mrs. Fanshaw, an' heard her ravin' away in her bedroom. It made my blood run cold, the words she said. Where she ever heard them beats me. Her sister's name kept comin' in, then Mrs. Morrice's. She can't get over Mrs.

Morrice livin in her old home, of course, an' it's been worse since Mrs. Morrice pulled up those cats' crosses. . . . But the things she said fair turned my stomach. I tell you straight I was frightened. I locked my door and covered my ears with the bed-clothes, and I said to myself, 'I'll speak to Mrs. Fanshaw tomorrow after service.' "

"I'm so glad you did, Miss Calder," said Mrs. Fanshaw soothingly. "It's very unpleasant for you. But you've been so good. . . . Can't you just put up with it a little longer while I look round and see what we can do about it? It would break her heart to have to go into the workhouse."

"I couldn't think of that," said Miss Calder with a quick access of family pride. "We've always kept ourselves respectable."

"I'll try to get someone to help you."

"Oh, people are kind enough," said Miss Calder. "They all try to help, but Sarah's that bad-tempered she won't have no truck with them. Seems to think they're all lookin' down on her about somethin'. As I said, I can't make head nor tail of her. She's took a fancy to Miss Lennare an' that gives me a bit of a rest. Miss Lennare's had her to tea once or twice. Real kind of her, it was."

"Miss Lennare?" said Mrs. Fanshaw uneasily.

"Yes, but—?" Miss Calder sighed. "I can't go everywhere with her an' she gets the stuff somehow. She got it on the way home last time she'd been to Miss Lennare's. She was in a shocking state when she got home. Shocking. I had to put her straight to bed."

"Poor old thing!"

"I know," sighed Miss Calder. "And when you think what she used to be! So respectable and looked up to. Everything just so. Couldn't bear anything out of place. If she could've seen then what she'd come to, it'd've killed her. I'm sorry for her, Mrs. Fanshaw, but I'm not as young as I was, and – well, I'm findin' it too much."

"I'll speak to the vicar," said Mrs. Fanshaw, "and I'll ask him to come and have a talk with her. And we'll look round and see what we can do. . . ."

"Thank you, Mrs. Fanshaw," said Miss Calder. "It's very good of you to bother with her, really. I knew you'd understand. I'd better be gettin' back to her. I left her in bed. . . . Good mornin', Mrs. Fanshaw."

She set off down the road with a scurrying stooping gait that seemed to express her whole, anxious, conscientious, worried little personality.

Mrs. Fanshaw stood where she had left her, gazing thoughtfully in the direction of Honeysuckle Cottage. What was Clare up to? She'd tackle her about it, but she was afraid she wouldn't get any satisfaction. The last time she had spoken to her about Ivy, Clare had chosen to take offence and was now avoiding her.

She came back slowly to the church door. Most of the groups had dispersed. Lettice was just coming out of the porch.

"Thanks so much," said Mrs. Fanshaw. "You played her out magnificently."

"You've got odd gloves on," said Lettice.

Mrs. Fanshaw looked down quickly.

"I know. I was in a hurry. I thought they were so much alike that no one would notice."

"You thought wrong, then," said Lettice. "And they aren't a bit alike."

"I still think they are," said Mrs. Fanshaw. "Anyway, Sylvia's not here so it doesn't matter. I shouldn't have done it if Sylvia had been here. . . . You saw her go out, didn't you? It was her most impressive yet. She somehow made it into real procession. If my senses hadn't told me that she'd gone out alone, I'd have thought that half the church had gone out, wouldn't you?"

"How's your hand?" said Lettice coldly.

Mrs. Fanshaw flushed slightly.

"Oh, well . . . it *is* rheumatic. These cold mornings do catch it, you know."

"How long has it been like that?"

"Several years."

"Was it worse than usual this morning?"

"N-no. Not really. I didn't say it was. I just said, would you play as I'd got a bad hand."

"Yes, you sent the message at the very last minute," said Lettice, "leaving me no time to ask any questions about it." She burst out laughing. "I knew you'd get me sooner or later, but you shan't do it again. You can't play the same trick on the same person twice."

"I know," said Mrs. Fanshaw calmly. "I shan't try, but you enjoyed it and you'll enjoy it more next time. Shall I walk home with you? Paul won't be out for ages."

They walked out of the cobbled courtyard into the road. The last of the small procession of soberly dressed village people were just crossing the green. The sun had come out, melting the surface of the frozen ground, so that it was treacherous to walk on. The Barton children were running across, laughing as they blew the frosty air in clouds from their mouths. One of them slipped and fell, raising, a howl of pain and fright. Mrs. Turnberry, who was just vanishing down Crewe Lane, came back and popped something into his mouth. The howls ceased. Frank, his large face scrubbed clean and wearing a neat dark suit that his mother kept locked up during the week, watched with an amiable grin.

As they reached Pear Tree Cottages, Philip Morrice came trotting round the side of No. 2, pipe in mouth, Matilda on his back.

"Just look what Lydia's done," he said, trying to sound as if he weren't enjoying it. "Clamped the brat onto me and I can't get it off."

Matilda gave an imperious yell and he turned obediently and trotted back.

A pleasant smell of Sunday joint met them as they opened the front door of No. 1. Mrs. Fanshaw breathed it in with a half smile.

"I love to think of thousands and thousands of people opening their doors at just this moment and meeting just this smell," she said. "Beef, isn't it? We're having beef, too. Cook says it 'eats up' cold better than any other joint. Paul never knows what it is even when he's eating it – it's just meat to him. I've known him eat a whole dinner, most carefully thought out and beautifully cooked, and not have the foggiest idea at the end what he's eaten."

Lettice laughed.

"Come and look at the garden," she said. "Frank's been planting wallflowers and forget-me-nots and polyanthus all along the fence.

He's a born gardener, isn't he? I love to see his great fingers handle the seedlings. He talks to them, too. 'Come on, my beauty, in you go. . . .' "

"I know," smiled Mrs. Fanshaw. "I've heard him make love to a rose bush he was spraying. He said, 'There, my pretty, my little beauty. Let Frank make you nice and clean.' "

They walked slowly down the path.

"He says I ought to have that branch of the pear tree cut off," said Lettice. "He says it keeps the light out."

"I should leave that," said Mrs. Fanshaw casually. "It will do for Susan's swing."

Lettice stopped short. Her face looked suddenly white in the winter sunshine.

"Susan?" she said.

"Yes," said Mrs. Fanshaw absently. Her whole attention was apparently absorbed by a drift of scillas that showed bravely blue beneath an old apple tree. "Aren't they beautiful! We had some in the vicarage garden, but they don't seem to be flowering this year. I must get some new bulbs in the autumn."

"Did you say Susan?" said Lettice again.

"Yes," said Mrs. Fanshaw innocently. "I thought she was coming to you for the holidays."

"You know quite well that she isn't," said Lettice. To her surprise she was trembling with anger. "I told you so definitely."

"Have you written about it?"

"Not yet. I haven't felt calm enough. But I'm going to. I've never even considered not doing."

Mrs. Fanshaw looked round.

"She'd have a wonderful time here. It's an ideal garden for a child."

"Why should I care whether she has a wonderful time or not?" said Lettice. She was ashamed of the cheap vindictiveness of her tone, but somehow she couldn't help it. "And why should you?"

"I don't," said Mrs. Fanshaw. "I wasn't thinking of Susan at all. I was thinking of myself. I was thinking what fun it would be to have a six-year-old about the place. That was the only stage in Sylvia that I'd have liked to keep for ever."

"Have her yourself, then," snapped Lettice, miserably angry and ashamed of her anger.

"Oh no," said Mrs. Fanshaw calmly. "I'd like you to have all the trouble and responsibility of her and me all the fun. She could come and play in the vicarage garden and make little loaves in the kitchen on baking days and have a 'house' under the weeping willow and help Frank make the garden fires. ... I can see her lying in the wheelbarrow munching apples ... romping about the lawn with the puppy. We'd take her up to the Zoo and the pantomime——"

"Who would?" said Lettice stonily.

"You and I would," said Mrs. Fanshaw.

"In any case I think pantomimes are stupid," said Lettice.

"So do I, but I love to hear a child laugh at the funny man. I used to take Sylvia just to hear her laugh at the funny man."

"I'm sorry to be rude," said Lettice, "but I have several letters to write before lunch."

"That's quite all right," said Mrs. Fanshaw, sweetly obtuse to Lettice's rudeness. "I've got quite a lot to do myself. Don't bother to see me out."

She went before Lettice, grudgingly ashamed, could apologise.

"It's her own fault," she muttered as she went slowly indoors. "She's intolerable. I shall never speak to her again. I wish I hadn't played her wretched organ. ..."

She went into the drawing-room and sat down at her writing-table, staring unseeingly in front of her. Her heart was racing. ... The impertinence of the woman. ... Susan, Olga's brat. ... Harvey, Harvey, Harvey. The thought brought a black despair but no longer the old heartache. When she thought of him now she saw him stripped of his glamour, a little shifty, a little second-rate, saw his lips curved into that foolish complacent smile, saw him as he'd hurried away from that last interview, craven but still swaggering, still with that foolish smile. And, perversely, she missed the heartache, resented the disillusionment, felt aggrieved against the child as if it were her fault, as if, had he not come on that fateful afternoon to ask her to have Susan, she could still have kept her illusions, still remembered him as the lover she had adored. The loss left her life emptier than ever. . . .

She had been a fool not to write before to Harvey to tell him quite definitely that she couldn't have the child. She had kept putting it off, telling herself that there was plenty of time, shirking the pain that the letter would give her, trying to forget both the Harvey she had adored and the Harvey of their last meeting. She wouldn't put it off any longer. She'd write at once. She pulled a sheet of note-paper towards her and wrote the date. "Dear Harvey. . . ." No, she couldn't write now. She felt too angry. The letter would sound peevish and spiteful. She would wait till she was more mistress of herself. . . . She got up and went to the window, looking out at the pleasant old-fashioned garden. Yes, Frank had been right. That branch ought to come down. It wasn't strong enough for a swing, anyway. Or was it? She shook her head angrily. How absurd even to consider the question! She'd ask Frank to cut it down the next time he came. . . . She stood at the window, looking out dreamily. Making little loaves in the kitchen on baking days . . . playing "house" under the weeping willow . . . helping with the garden bonfire . . . lying in the wheelbarrow munching apples. . . . The words called up vivid pictures of a child – not Susan, Olga's brat, but the child she had longed for before she knew that Harvey did not want a child, pictures that she had admitted shyly into her mind when first she was engaged to him and that she had never dared to confess to him. Her thoughts went back to her own childhood, and half-dead memories sprang suddenly to life. . . . Curled up in the old apple tree with the Red Fairy Book . . . riding her pony round the paddock . . . marshalling a fleet of acorns on the stream in the wood, guiding them with tiny sticks, making them shoot the rapids . . . nursery tea after a brisk walk on a winter afternoon with toast and dripping, damp leggings drying on the tall fire-guard. . . . Hide-and-Seek in the shrubbery with Ponto, the fox terrier, who seemed to understand the game as well as she did . . . making a snowman . . . the almost unbearable excitement of birthdays and Christmas . . . hay-making . . . blackberrying . . . walks in the wood in autumn . . . dragging one's toes in newly fallen leaves . . . bringing home treasures – pine cones, chestnuts, little bunches of wild flowers. And behind it all the gentle kindly presence of her parents, guarding and protecting her, filling her childhood with happy memories. . . . She had never considered the question before, but she realised now that she had had an unusually happy childhood, and that she owed them gratitude for it. She felt dully ashamed of never having realised it before, of having, when they were alive, rather resented the restraints of the home life thay had striven to make carefree and sheltered for her. One never seemed to realise that one was happy till the happiness had passed. . . . Perhaps the very happiness of those far-off days had unfitted her for bearing the unhappiness that Harvey had brought into her life. . . .

She had been a spoilt child, was perhaps a spoilt child still. . . . She felt ashamed – but more than ever determined to write that letter to Harvey before she went to bed tonight.

Chapter Fourteen

EVERY time the door of the Village Hall was opened, a warm wave of human essence met a cold blast of east wind. March was coming in like a lion. Branches of trees had been blown down across the roads, whole elm trees uprooted, while yesterday all traffic had been suspended beyond Beverton because of a telegraph pole that had crashed across the main road.

For days now the east wind had howled and moaned and whistled, rattling doors and windows, bringing down chimney pots and slates, cutting through the warmest clothing and finding out weak spots in chests, lungs, and joints.

It took more than this, however, to deter the inhabitants of Steffan Green from coming to the Women's Institute annual Sale of Work, which was one of the chief events of the year and was attended not only by Steffan Green but by people from all the neighbouring villages. They arrived red-nosed from the cold, and became still more red-nosed from the atmosphere of crowded humanity in its warmest clothes. The hall was notoriously badly ventilated, but Steffan Green on the whole considered ventilation a fad of the idle rich and got on very well without it. Most of them earned their living by working in the open air, and they liked to get home to a good fug and roaring fire when their work was done.

The Village Hall stove was a small noisy contraption, with a tin chimney going out through the roof, which smoked incessantly and gave out very little heat, but Steffan Green was proud of it as representing the result of three Sales of Work and a whole season's whist drives and would have resented the suggestion of anything more up to date.

Stalls and platform were hung with bunting – a little worn and faded, as it had been used on all festive occasions for the last six or seven years, but still preserving something of its pristine gaiety. At the back of the platform hung a large Union Jack, and at the side, covered by another Union Jack, the harmonium that had been turned out of the church when the organ was installed. It required a certain amount of ingenuity to play it, as a good many of the notes were dead and the pedals were unreliable, but it served to give an occasional note for "Land of Hope and Glory" and "God Save the King." On special occasions Miss Fordyce, the village schoolmistress, had her upright piano brought over from her cottage. It had belonged to her mother, and most of the pleated silk behind the fretwork front had rotted away, but it had a gay tinkly sound and was tuned religiously every three months. It had been brought over to the Village Hall this afternoon, decorated by strips of red, white and blue bunting and by a fern in a purple pot next door to the large handbell that was rung for silence before notices were given out.

Just beneath the platform, in the place of honour, stood the Fancy Stall, under the nominal charge of Mrs. Ferring, President of the Women's Institute. Mrs. Fanshaw, as Vice-President, took her place at the monthly meetings, but on this occasion Mrs. Ferring generally put in an appearance. She also supplied the main contents of the fancy stall, sending them down by Andrew in the morning. They consisted chiefly of pieces of expensive glass, presented once for the occasion by a visitor staying at the Castle, and some pieces of elaborate embroidery sent to Mrs. Ferring many years ago by a relative who was wintering in Madeira. The prices were not unduly high for the quality of the goods, but they were far beyond the purses of Steffan Green, who looked on them as old friends and were apt to resent any alteration in the arrangement of them on the stall. People who bought fresh contributions slipped them furtively and a little guiltily onto the front of the stall, feeling like poachers.

There had been considerable speculation this year as to whether Mrs. Ferring would brave the biting east wind and come, to the Sale as usual. Somehow the departure of Thea, with her unquenchable vitality and high spirits, had made Mrs. Ferring seem much older and Lavinia much younger than they had seemed before. A new indefinable suggestion of pathos seemed to hang over the pair of them on the rare appearances they made in public.

There was a stir as the door opened to admit them, Mrs. Ferring leaning on her stick, Lavinia bent sideways over a case that contained the things Andrew had been unable to bring down that morning. The women drew aside respectfully to let them pass. Their approach to the stall had something of the effect of a royal progress. Mrs. Ferring gave faint unsmiling inclinations of her head as she recognised old retainers or acquaintances.

She took her place in the chair behind the stall, watching Lavinia with keen eyes as she unpacked the goods' and put them in their accustomed places. Then Lavinia took her seat at a small table at the end of the stall with a cash-box in front of her, ready to give change. She was thinking of last year, when Thea had sat there with her and they had giggled together all the time. Thea had made fun of everything and everyone, defying her grandmother's quelling glances. Later, in their bedroom, she had imitated the performers at the concert that always formed part of the proceedings, till Lavinia choked with laughter. Things had been so different then. ... Her eyes searched the room for Colin's mother and finally found her with Mrs. Helston at the Provision Stall on the other side of the room. She *did* look kind. She couldn't think why Colin wouldn't tell her. ... How lovely it would be to be able to go to her house – such a warm, cosy, comfortable little house (she looked at it with special interest whenever she went into the village) and meet Colin there! Like ordinary people. ... Yes, she *did* look kind – kind and soft and gentle. Surely she'd understand, if only one had the courage to tell her. She tried to imagine herself telling her. "May I come and see you sometimes? Colin and I are friends. ..." No, of course, she wouldn't be able to. ... A weary resignation of despair weighed down on her. There was nothing one could do.

One must just go on. . . . But one *couldn't* go on. . . . The fear, the uncertainty, the suspense. . . . Somehow loving Colin made things both better and worse at the same time. She couldn't have endured it without Colin's love, and yet it was Colin's love that filled the world with terror. . . . If only Mother would come. . . . Lavinia had written to her last night – an unhappy fearful little letter, trying to tell her how much she needed her help, and yet not to say anything that could get her into trouble with her grandmother. . . . Her cough seized her again though she strove to repress it, and Mrs. Ferring threw her the familiar glance of disapproval.

"Doing anything for that cough, Lavvy?" said Mrs. Fanshaw.

"It's nothing," said Lavinia, suddenly terrified lest Mrs. Fanshaw should persuade her grandmother to send her to bed and so prevent her meeting Colin tonight.

"I'll send you round some cough mixture that did Sylvia good last winter," said Mrs. Fanshaw.

"Oh, thanks," said Lavinia, relieved.

Mrs. Fanshaw officially "helped" Mrs. Ferring with the fancy stall. Actually Mrs. Ferring served the old inhabitants of the village, leaving the new-comers to Mrs. Fanshaw.

"One and six from ten shillings, Lavinia," said Mrs. Fanshaw, who had just sold a tray-cloth from the front of the stall.

Mrs. Webb came across from the Provision Stall. She wore the feathered hat, beige georgette dress, and fur coat, and walked with a little mincing step.

"*Good* afternoon, Mrs. Ferring," she said effusively.

"Good afternoon," said Mrs. Ferring, giving her a fleeting ice-cold glance before she turned to gaze detachedly round the room again. Mrs. Webb stood for a moment digesting the snub. Her pink cheeks became a little pinker, her foolish smile a little more foolish than usual. Then she went back across the room to her provision stall, her small mouth set tightly.

Mrs. Ferring turned to Mrs. Fanshaw.

"Who is that extremely vulgar little woman?" she said in her quiet precise voice.

Mrs. Fanshaw smiled wryly, aware that Mrs. Ferring knew who

Mrs. Webb was and all about her. Ever since Mrs. Webb came to Steffan Green she had made ceaseless efforts to ingratiate herself with Mrs. Ferring and be treated by her as an equal. Last year, on the occasion of the Sale of Work, she had even bought one of the most expensive pieces of glass, but Mrs. Ferring had merely given her the glass and taken her money with no further exchange of courtesies. Mrs. Ferring never forgave what she considered an impertinence, and she considered Mrs. Webb's assumption of equality with her an unpardonable impertinence. Her response to it was to pretend that she did not know who Mrs. Webb was.

Her glance went round the room again. It rested finally on Lydia Morrice who stood behind the tins of polish and piles of home-knitted dusters that represented the Household Stall. She wore a rather tight dress that revealed her pregnancy without disguise and had painted her lips an unusually vivid shade of red. Mrs. Ferring's eyes narrowed.

"Who is that woman?" she said.

"Mrs. Morrice," sighed Mrs. Fanshaw.

The old lady seemed determined to be trying today. It was more than likely that Mrs. Webb would resign after her public snub, and, though Mrs. Fanshaw was pretty sure that she could finally be persuaded to withdraw her resignation, the whole thing would be a nuisance. And now she was starting on Lydia. . . .

"The woman who wears trousers ?" said Mrs. Ferring.

"Yes," said Mrs. Fanshaw, knowing that the old lady had recognised Mrs. Morrice from the beginning. (There wasn't much those sharp black eyes missed.)

"I didn't realise that we had women of that type as members of the Institute."

"She isn't 'that type,' " said Mrs. Fanshaw patiently.

"She uses lipstick and she's going to have a baby. Is she married?"

"I understand so. Lavinia went to her little girl's christening."

"I remember. I didn't approve of it but you over-persuaded me. . . . Couldn't she dress so as to conceal her condition to a certain extent? My generation used to."

"It was easier in the days of frills and furbelows," said Mrs. Fanshaw, "and people aren't ashamed of it nowadays."

"It's not a question of being 'ashamed of it,'" said Mrs. Ferring, "it's a question of ordinary decency. . . . Is that Mrs. Helston at the Provision Stall?"

She smiled graciously across the room at Lettice, who stood next Mrs. Webb behind the Provision Stall. Lettice smiled back rather nervously, hoping not to be summoned for an interview, and pretended to be busied in the contents of her stall. Mrs. Ferring's eyes passed on to the end of the room by the door, where Mrs. Turnberry, together with Mrs. Skelton and Ivy, stood before a long trestle-table piled high with a jumble of old clothes.

Mrs. Turnberry always presided over the Rummage Stall, which did not open till five o'clock, when the women who went out to work might be supposed to be free. Mrs. Turnberry thoroughly enjoyed the occasion. She knew each one of her customers – what they wanted and why they wanted it. She had spent the last three or four weeks collecting her stock, begging persistently and indefatigably from every possible and impossible quarter. She had persuaded Mrs. Fanshaw to give her a coat and skirt that she had meant to keep till the end of the spring, because Mrs. Barton needed one so badly. She had put it on one side for Mrs. Barton and had seen that she had the necessary 2s. 6d. for it. She had been as far afield as Beverton, begging from everyone she knew there. . . . On one occasion Clifford had met her trudging along the road from Beverton to Steffan Green, her arms full of old clothes, her sallow face beaming with childlike satisfaction. Even his cold anger had failed to damp her delight. She had put aside a little selection for the bedridden and would take it round afterwards, collecting their coppers. Her whole heart was in the task, and she enjoyed every minute of it. The women, aware of her interest in them and her eager desire to help them, were docile and accommodating. She ordered them about and they obeyed her meekly. There were none of the "scenes" that generally took place when, for some reason or other, she could not preside over the stall. She had an eagle eye for pilfering, and few dared attempt it when she was in charge.

"Put back those stockings, Mrs. Grimling," she would call out sternly, and Mrs. Grimling would at once put them back. She knew all the local "dealers," too, and gave them short shift. "Off with you!" she would say brusquely. "This isn't your show."

She was laughing and joking with the group of women who stood around the stall waiting for five o'clock, when it would officially open, ready to pounce on their purchases as soon as the signal was given. She felt unusually happy today. Things were going well. Frank was keeping his jobs and not getting drunk. As Mrs. Ferring's eye fell on her, she was opening her mouth in a roar of laughter that showed the large gaps between her yellow teeth.

"That's Mrs. Turnberry, isn't it?" said Mrs. Ferring.

Mrs. Ferring had always liked Mrs. Turnberry. There was a bond of sympathy between them that neither quite understood. Both had come to Steffan Green as young brides. Mrs. Ferring had seen Clifford and Frank grow up, had watched Mrs. Turnberry change from a harum-scarum young woman to what she was now. She enjoyed her flashes of mordant wit and the local gossip she brought with her when she came up to the Castle to beg for her protégés in the village.

In her dealings with the lady of the Castle, Mrs. Turnberry, on her side, was utterly unself-conscious. She accorded Mrs. Ferring's superior social position its due, without compromising her own independence in the slightest degree. She had been brought up in the country, where social differences are rigidly preserved without loss of dignity on either side.

"Ask her to come over and see me," said Mrs. Ferring.

On receiving the message Mrs. Turnberry laid aside the straw hat that she had been trying to bend into some recognisable shape, occasionally putting it on her own head to amuse the onlookers (she could never resist clowning to a suitable audience) and crossed the room to the Fancy Stall. Her long sallow face wore a look of ingenuous pleasure and kindly solicitude. Nice to have a word with the old lady again. She'd looked smaller somehow lately, the white face more drawn and lined, the proud lips tighter. Different from what she'd been when Mrs. Turnberry first came to Steffan Green.

Well ... a lot of things were different. She took the empty seat next her and turned on her the wide smile that showed her inadequately furnished gums. Mrs. Ferring read the solicitude and loyalty behind the smile, and the harsh lines of her face softened.

"Well, Mrs. Turnberry," she said kindly, "how are you?"

"Quite well, thank you, Mrs. Ferring," said Mrs. Turnberry. "And you?"

Mrs. Ferring shrugged.

"I'm an old woman, and sometimes I feel an old woman ..." (she wouldn't have admitted that to many people). "How's Frank going on?"

That was another bond of sympathy. Frank wasn't "satisfactory." Simon hadn't been "satisfactory" either. ...

"All right so far," said Mrs. Turnberry. "He's fond of gardening, you know. He's being a good boy now."

"I'm glad. And his brother?"

"Oh, Clifford always does well ... but – it's funny, isn't it?—" dreamily, "Clifford's never given me any trouble and yet Frank's always been my favourite."

"I know," sighed Mrs. Ferring. Simon had been her favourite, too.

Mrs. Webb watched them with smouldering eyes, the memory of her own snub still rankling. Oh, she knew what had happened. They couldn't deceive her. It was Mrs. Turnberry who had set Mrs. Ferring against her, making fun of her in her wicked spiteful way, running her down, telling lies about her. They were probably talking about her now. ... Her mental picture of the contrast between her own smartness and Mrs. Turnberry's shabbiness added fuel to her anger. Fancy a lady like Mrs. Ferring was supposed to be, making a fuss of a shabby old thing like that (why, that navy-blue coat hadn't any shape and was almost *pink* with age). And it wasn't only Mrs. Ferring. All the village people made a fuss of her, crowding round her, talking to her, laughing with her, while she, Mrs. Webb, was left severely alone. She knew that she was unpopular in the village, and she decided now that Mrs. Turnberry was solely responsible for this. A wicked woman ... as bad as that wicked son of hers. She'd be doing a good deed, showing up the pair of them.

Mrs. Ferring was gathering her things together. She had spent the regulation hour there and was, as usual, taking her departure before tea was served and the village children burst in noisily from school.

"Wake up, child," she said to Lavinia, and Lavinia woke with a start from her dream. She had been dreaming that she and Colin had ordinary families like ordinary people and were properly engaged. ... Looking round, she saw Mrs. Webb's eyes fixed on her grandmother across the room. No, she decided suddenly, she didn't look kind, after all. Perhaps Colin had been right. ... She felt as if another door of escape had closed on her. ... She put the cash-box on the stall and prepared to follow her grandmother, who was going to the door, accompanied by Mrs. Turnberry.

Mrs. Webb watched them, her lips curled into a slow unpleasant smile. She'd laid several little traps for Master Frank lately without catching him, but somehow she thought that the one she'd laid just before she came out this afternoon would be successful.

It was late that night when Mrs. Turnberry came round to see Lettice. Lettice had enjoyed the afternoon but found it unexpectedly tiring. Mrs. Ferring's departure had been the signal for a general relaxation of tension, and, with the influx of the school children – red nosed, rosy cheeked, mufflers wound round their throats, across their chests, and pinned behind their backs – the noise became almost unbearable. They besieged the bran tub with their pennies, and raced up and down the floor between the stalls till quelled by their mothers or Miss Fordyce, who had come in after them.

Tea was served in the tiny room behind the platform, the little tables packed so closely together that there was barely room to move between them. Cake's and scones had been made by the members of the Institute, and they shouted good-natured comments and criticisms to one another across the room.

After tea the battle of the Rummage Stall began in earnest. Mrs.

Tumberry's voice rang out above the uproar, calling customers to order, crying her wares. . . .

When Lettice went, the handbell was just being rung for silence, and Miss Fordyce was mounting the platform steps to give the "pianoforte solo" that she gave every year on this occasion, accompanied by the favourite pupil of the moment, whose duty was to stand by her and turn over the pages of the music book at a nod of the brisk grey head.

Lettice was stretched comfortably on the sofa by the fire with her tapestry work when Bella announced Mrs. Turnberry. She groaned inwardly as she rose to her feet, but her annoyance vanished as soon as Mrs. Turnberry entered and she saw the stricken look on the long sallow face. Gone was the sparkle of kindly humour, the hint almost of mischief in the dark eyes.

"Mrs. Helston," said Mrs. Turnberry, taking the chair that Lettice drew forward for her, "I'll come straight to the point. Can you lend me five pounds? . . . Wait a minute" (as Lettice began to speak), "I don't know when I'll be able to pay you back."

"Of course I will," said Lettice, "and you mustn't think of paying me back."

Mrs. Turnberry relaxed in her chair and closed her eyes. Her face had whitened beneath its sallowness.

"Let me get you some water," said Lettice solicitously.

"No, no," said Mrs. Turnberry. She sat up, mastering herself with an effort. "It's just the – relief. You were the only person I could think of, and if you hadn't been able to—" she stopped.

Lettice sat down on the chair next her visitor's.

"What happened?" she said.

"It's Mrs. Webb," said Mrs. Turnberry, speaking slowly and carefully as if her voice were not quite under her control. "She told Frank to cut back that bush that grows by the dining-room window because it made the room dark, and she left the window open at the bottom and her note-case with five pounds in on the table just by the window. She must have done it on purpose. She must have known he'd take it."

"Where is he?"

"I don't know," said Mrs. Turnberry helplessly. "He's gone off. I don't suppose he'll come back tonight. When he does he won't have a penny of it left. He'll have got drunk and had it stolen. Or spent it. You wouldn't think he could spend the money he does. He never has anything to show for it. He doesn't know himself what he's spent it on. . . . He can't resist money, but once he's got it a child could take it from him. He's not quite – normal, you know."

"But Mrs. Webb shouldn't have left the money there."

"Oh, she knew what she was doing," said Mrs. Turnberry with a twisted smile. "She's always disliked me. I ought to have been prepared for it, but somehow I never thought she'd do that. It's partly my own fault. . . . I've always been a bit of a tease, and I suppose I've let my tongue run away with me sometimes. She's not one to forget. She never wanted to have Frank working for her. Colin made her. . . ."

"And what does Colin think about this?"

"He doesn't know. She waited till he'd gone out for his walk – he always goes out for a walk after supper – and then she came in to me. I saw her walking up to the front door with a little smile on her face – pleased as Punch. She said she was going straight to the police. I begged and prayed – I nearly went down on my knees – and in the end she said she'd give me half an hour. If I haven't paid her back in half an hour she's going there."

"Well, it's all right," said Lettice. "I'll let you have it at once, and I'll go with you if you like."

Mrs. Turnberry shook her head.

"No . . . it's kind of you but it'd only put her back up. You see . . . even if she didn't go to the police she might go to Clifford, and then he'd turn Frank out and make me go to live with him. He said he would the next time Frank disgraced him. I'm terrified of that. I couldn't bear it."

Lettice considered this in silence, then said gently:

"It sounds unsympathetic, but – don't you think it might be the best thing that could happen? You're not as young as you were. All this is too much for you."

"No," said Mrs. Turnberry breathlessly, "you don't understand. I'd rather die than let them take Frank from me. . . . Oh, it isn't anything wonderful – mother love or anything like that. I don't know that I even like him. Sometimes I'm almost sure that I don't like him, but – he's all I've got, and I'm all he's got. He'll never marry. He doesn't care for women. He never goes with them even when he's drunk. I don't know what he'd do without me, and I don't know what I'd do without him. We're company for each other. And he's fond of me. He often does funny foolish little things that show he's fond of me. He bought me a handkerchief last week out of a tip someone gave him – pink silk with yellow imitation lace round. He's no taste, of course, but it showed he was thinking of me. He's never been unkind to me. He couldn't be unkind to anyone. . . . They'd make me leave my home, too, and I couldn't bear that. I've lived in it since I was married, and I want to finish in it. And, after all, Frank's as much my son as Clifford is. He needs me and Clifford doesn't. I'd just be a nuisance to Clifford. . . . When I think of going to live with him and Marcia——"

"Well, don't worry," said Lettice. "I'm sure they won't make you."

She took her bag from the bureau and opened her notecase.

"There you are," she said, counting five one-pound notes, "and you're not to think of it again."

Mrs. Turnberry suddenly dropped her head on to her dirt-ingrained hands and began to cry.

"I'm sorry . . ." she said in a choking voice. "It's so kind of you. . . . I'm so grateful . . . and so ashamed."

"There's nothing for you to be ashamed of," said Lettice firmly.

Mrs. Turnberry raised her face. Her eyes were swimming in tears, her face twisted and defeated.

"There is," she said. "I try to forget it, but sometimes I could die of the shame of it. I've no pride left. I've dragged it in the mud so long. I've borrowed from people I thought I'd rather have died than borrow from and I've borrowed from other people to pay them back. I've lied to Clifford till he takes for granted now that I'm always lying. . . . Clifford's a good son, really, and I'm proud of him, but he doesn't understand about Frank. Sometimes I feel I can't go on with it ... wondering very moment of every day where he is and what he's up to, never knowing what I'll hear of him before the day's out. .... Sometimes," dreamily, "I feel it'd be a relief if I never saw him again, and then he's late home and I go nearly mad in case he's had an accident or something, and I know I couldn't bear it if they took him from me. ...." Her lips twisted into a faint smile. "I used to be ashamed of the sort of work he had to do, and his going about in workman's clothes, but I'm past caring about that now. If I can just keep him with me ..." Her voice trailed off and she sat staring into space. She looked so old and tired that Lettice's heart ached for her.

"Let me give you a cup of tea," she said.

Mrs. Turnberry roused herself and dragged her gaunt figure from the chair.

"No, thank you. ... I must go to her."

She took out a handkerchief and wiped the traces of tears away from her lined gipsy face.

"You've been so good. I'm so grateful. I'll pay it back if ever I get the chance. Goodbye."

On an impulse Lettice kissed her and stood at the window watching her as she went out of the gate of Pear Tree Cottage, along the green, and in at the gate of Eastnor.

Chapter Fifteen

MRS. FANSHAW ushered out the Sunday School teachers, who had been holding their weekly meeting round the table in the Vicarage dining-room under her presidency, took up a pile of letters from the hall chest, and went into her husband's study. He was seated in an arm-chair by the fire, smoking a pipe and reading. They exchanged the intimate half smile that was their usual greeting.

"Meeting go off all right?" he said.

"Yes," she answered, "but I find the undiluted society of Sunday School teachers rather depressing. They're so heart-rendingly earnest."

"I know," he agreed. "Contact with the young frequently has that effect. It's a pity." He looked at the letters she was sorting out on the writing-desk. "Anything from Sylvia?"

"No, I don't think the mail gets in till tomorrow. It's mostly circulars."

She glanced through the letters and put them in a neat pile on the table. "Nothing that need be answered before tomorrow. They want you to speak to the Men's Temperance Society at Beverton again. Why can't they leave you alone?"

"I'm not here to be left alone," he reminded her.

"I suppose you're not," she replied with her faint smile. "Anyway, it's nice to find you in at this time of day. I thought you had to go over to Basset's farm."

"I went over, but the old man has been taken worse and been sent to hospital. I'm going to see him there tomorrow afternoon. So I came home and snatched a lazy hour."

"I'm glad. You don't often get the chance of that."

She went over to the window and stood there looking out. The east wind had died down during the day, and the trees stood motionless, outlined against a primrose sky. Westwards, banks of purple clouds were flushed rose by the setting sun. Dark tussocks in the elms at the bottom of the garden showed where the rooks were beginning to build. Their notes – sleepy and monotonous – floated down through the still air.

"I woke up last night," she said dreamily," and looked at the sky – it was deep blue covered with stars – and I thought: Thank God there's one thing we can't spoil. We can spoil the earth and we can spoil ourselves and we can spoil each other, but we can't spoil that."

"I don't know . . ." said her husband reflectively. "*Is* it any comfort to know that when we've made the earth a shambles the stars will still look down on it?"

"It is to me." She crossed the room again and sat on the arm of his chair. "What are you reading?"

He showed her the title of his book.

"I was torn between *St. Thomas Aquinas* and *The Serial Universe*, and *The Serial Universe* won."

She slipped her hand into his.

"I'm glad I married someone who can be torn between *St. Thomas Aquinas* and *The Serial Universe*."

"So am I," he said with a twinkle. "I have been for some time."

"I know," she said. "You were sure from the beginning, weren't you? I wasn't. I knew I was in love with you, but I couldn't be sure it would last. . . . I used to wake up in the night and go cold with terror thinking of people I knew who'd once been in love with each other. . . . Be honest after all these years. Didn't you have any qualms at all?"

"Not a shadow of a qualm."

"You were rash. Militant suffragettes weren't supposed to make good wives. . . . And I was stupid over Sylvia for years, trying to make her a different sort of person from the person she really was. When one looks back over one's life and sees all the mistakes one's made one can hardly bear to think what might have come of it.

It's as if a sort of power went behind one, straightening up the mess."

He nodded.

"That's what He does, of course."

"It must break His heart ... and make Him smile at the same time. I remember a conversation Clare and I had when first she came here about Christ's sense of humour. ..." She was silent for a few moments, then went on, "I wish Clare hadn't come. Ivy's broken it off finally with George. And she's playing some game with poor old Miss Pendleton that I can't quite make out. ... I told you about last night, didn't I?"

He nodded.

Last night Lydia Morrice had been roused from sleep in the middle of the night by some sound outside and, going to the window, had seen Miss Pendleton in the back garden digging frenziedly on the spot where her cats' graves had been.

"She must have been at it for some time," said Lydia, describing the scene to Mrs. Fanshaw, "because there was a pile of little bones on the path near where she was digging. The moon was full, you know, and it was too grisly for words. Her face looked so white and – evil, somehow, and her dirty white hair was straggling about her shoulders, and she was gibbering to herself. ... Fortunately Philip was at home, so he went down to her. As soon as she saw him coming, she gathered up the horrible little pile of bones and held it in her arms as if it were a baby and scuttled away. ... It was the most gruesome thing I've ever seen. Thank heaven it was one of Philip's nights at home or I'd have been scared to death."

"Did you get in touch with Beverton Cloisters?" said Mr. Fanshaw.

"Yes, I rang them up this morning. They say that they'll have a vacancy for her next week, as one of their old ladies is going to live with a married daughter. She has to be proposed and seconded and have a majority of votes, so I was on the telephone all morning, pulling strings. I think it's all fixed up now. Pulling strings is another thing I've learnt from being a parson's wife. It didn't come easy at first. ... By the way, what did you make of her when you went to see her yesterday?"

"Nothing at all," said her husband. "She was very quiet and respectful. 'Yes, Mr. Fanshaw,' and 'No, Mr. Fanshaw,' as if, somehow, she were determined not to give herself away."

"I suppose that was it. I've told Miss Calder to be careful not to let her go out alone. I shall be glad to get her safely out of Steffan Green. I'm going round to see Clare about her after tea. Someone told me that Clare's been giving her drink. I can't believe it."

"I can," said her husband grimly.

"You don't like her, do you?"

"I never did."

"I know. You disliked her in the old days. You were prejudiced. There was something fine about her then. She's gone to seed since. ... Isn't it strange what a lot's happened here since Sylvia went away – Clare's coming, Thea's going to Paris, Lettice Helston's coming to live here?"

"She seems happier, I think," said Mr. Fanshaw thoughtfully.

"She is, but she doesn't know it yet," said his wife. "She thinks she's still as unhappy as ever. ... She'll get quite a shock one day when she realises that she's happier than she's ever been in her life. That's where Susan's going to help."

Her husband looked at her with his grave twinkle.

"Does she know that Susan's coming?"

"Not yet," admitted his wife. "She only suspects it. She knows that she keeps putting off writing the letter, and she knows that she's stopped Frank sawing off that pear tree branch, but that's all."

The smile in his grey eyes deepened.

"She does know now, I presume, that she plays the organ for matins."

"Oh yes," said Mrs. Fanshaw. "She quite realises that. I think she realised it when she agreed to do it just till the end of the month. She's beginning to realise that she enjoys it, too, but she's fighting against the knowledge. She's a darling. ... She and Susan are going to be a great help with Lydia's new baby."

He burst out laughing.

"What a woman you are!" he said. "Any other schemes?"

"Plenty. I must get rid of Clare. I don't think Steffan Green's good for her and I don't think she's good for Steffan Green. Then there's Mrs. Turnberry—" Her quick eyes caught a change in her husband's expression. "Yes – what is it?"

"Well . . ." he hesitated. "I hadn't meant to tell you till later."

The smile faded from her face.

"Has something happened?"

"Nothing really more than usual," he reassured her, "but I'm afraid it's final this time. I met Clifford as I was coming home. Evidently Frank got roaring drunk yesterday and was arrested in Beverton. His mother was at the Women's Institute sale, I suppose, and he took advantage of being left on his own. He'd had a pretty good run for his money from all accounts – climbed up Gladstone's statue in the Market Place and smashed several windows. It took half the police force to get him to the station. Someone went to tell Clifford, and Clifford bailed him out and paid his fine, but, as far as he's concerned, it's the end. He's put The Moorings into a house-agent's hands, and he's taking his mother to live with him. He's given her to the end of the week to get her things ready. Then he's turning Frank out, storing the furniture, and fetching his mother. He won't even discuss it – with her or anyone."

"Poor old woman!" sighed Mrs. Fanshaw.

"I must say that I have a certain amount of sympathy with Clifford," said the vicar. "The whole thing will come out in the local paper on Friday, and it's not a pleasant pill for a man of that type to swallow."

"I don't like men of that type," said Mrs. Fanshaw firmly. "He's got a wrong sense of values."

"That may be," said the vicar, "but he's had a lot to put up with, all the same. It would have tried the patience of a saint, and he's no saint."

"Was he very angry?"

"Very. He never lets himself go, you know, and he's bottled things up for a long time."

"I'll go and see him about it," said Mrs. Fanshaw.

The vicar knocked out his pipe.

"I knew you'd want to do that," he said. "That's why I didn't want to tell you till it was too late for you to go. I shouldn't go and see him if I were you."

"Why not?"

"Because it wouldn't be any use. He's made up his mind, and he's the sort of man who never unmakes it."

"He's narrow-minded and pigheaded and intolerant and conceited and without a spark of humanity or human kindness," she said.

"Maybe," said her husband, "but you'd be wasting your time telling him so. It wouldn't make things easier for the old lady, either."

"I'll go and see her, anyway," she said. "Poor old thing! She must be desperate. . . . Paul," thoughtfully, "isn't there *anything* we could do?"

"I'm afraid not. It was bound to come sooner or later."

"What on earth will happen to Frank?"

He shrugged his shoulders without answering.

She went into the hall and took her hat and coat from the hatstand, putting them on characteristically without consulting the mirror.

As she crossed the green, Clare came out from her cottage. She was smiling to herself. She greeted Mrs. Fanshaw pleasantly.

"Hello, Helen. Where are you off to?"

Mrs. Fanshaw felt vaguely surprised. Lately Clare had been avoiding her, pretending not to see her when they met and ignoring her greetings. This smiling affability was something quite new.

"I'm going to Mrs. Turnberry's," she said.

"Oh, she's not in," said Clare carelessly. "She just went down the road towards Beverton. I think she was going to see Clifford. Come in for a moment. It's a long time since you paid me a visit. You can see from the window when she comes back."

Mrs. Fanshaw hesitated.

"Very well," she said at last and followed Clare into the little sitting-room.

"I was just going to have a late tea," said Clare. "Won't you join me?"

"No, thanks," said Mrs. Fanshaw.

She stood by the window, looking anxiously down the road.

"When did Mrs. Turnberry go out?" she said.

"Quarter of an hour ago, or it might have been a half an hour," said Clare. "I really can't remember. Do sit down. . . . Ah, here's tea."

The door opened, and Ivy came in with the tea-tray. She looked pale and sullen, her eyes red-rimmed as if she had been crying. She set the tray down and went from the room without looking at either Clare or her visitor.

"What's the matter with her?" said Mrs. Fanshaw.

Clare threw back her head and laughed.

"She's a priceless little idiot," she said. "The whole thing's too amusing for words. . . . You know that I have to work from models, don't you?"

"You've often told me so," said Mrs. Fanshaw dryly.

She wasn't interested in Clare's work, anyway, and certainly didn't want to discuss it at this moment. Her eyes were still fixed on the point where the road from Beverton appeared between the woods.

"Sure you won't have some tea?"

Clare had seated herself at the table, massive and foursquare in the inevitable tweeds, and was beginning to attack the meal with obvious enjoyment.

"I got these scones at Jordan's in Beverton. They're delicious. Once you start eating them you can't stop. Won't you have one?"

"What's happened about Ivy?"

"Oh. . . ." Still smiling amusedly, Clare munched half a scone before she answered. "Well, I really *am* getting going with my book at last. I've had the most marvellous piece of luck about that. I'll tell you later. I've finished making notes for it, and I wrote the first chapter last night and began the second one this morning."

"I'm not interested in your book, Clare. What's happened about Ivy?"

Clare reached out for the jam-pot and spooned a liberal helping onto her plate.

"I'm coming to that. Have you tried Hepple's blackberry jelly? It's good. ... Well, in the second chapter I had to describe the heroine naked, and so I made Ivy take off her clothes and sit—? or rather stand – to me for it. The *fuss* she made! You'd have thought I was committing some indecent assault on her. She said it was 'rude.' If it weren't so ludicrous it would be heartrending. Helen, why don't you educate these yokels not to be ashamed of their bodies? 'Rude'!" Grinning, she thrust her large white teeth into another scone. "I held forth on the subject of false shame for about ten minutes, but the little idiot wouldn't listen. She's been crying off and on ever since. I don't know that I will take her abroad, after all. She makes me tired sometimes, and her typing's still atrocious."

Mrs. Fanshaw gave her a long direct look without speaking. Then she said slowly:

"What a fool you are, Clare!"

"Why?" said Clare, cutting herself a large piece of plum-cake. "You've never understood me, Helen. You've never even tried to. I sometimes think you've never wanted to."

"Don't you realise that you'll have set the whole village by the ears? You don't suppose Ivy will keep it to herself, do you? These people have a sort of desperate personal fastidiousness."

Clare interrupted with a chuckle.

"Desperate false modesty, I call it. Ivy's got a lovely little body ... I told her it was wicked to be ashamed of it. ... I got a pretty good description of it, too. Let me read it to you——"

"I don't want to hear it," said Mrs. Fanshaw, turning to the window again. "I was going to try to make you leave Steffan Green, but I don't think I need trouble to do that. You'll have made the place too hot to hold you, in any case."

"How?" jeered Clare. "By making that blasted little fool take her clothes off?" She laughed again. "And isn't she a blasted little fool! Just crouched in a corner of the room and wouldn't let me even touch her. ..."

"Oh, be quiet!" said Mrs. Fanshaw impatiently. "You make me sick. Why couldn't you have left the child alone? You know that she's broken off with George Harker because of you, I suppose?"

"I'm glad she had so much sense. . . . Have a cigarette?"

Mrs. Fansnaw shook her head.

"Any other grievances against me?" went on Clare, taking a cigarette from a box on the desk and opening her lighter.

"Yes," said Mrs. Fanshaw, wheeling round from the window. "Have you been giving Miss Pendleton drink?"

Clare lit her cigarette before answering.

"She's given me the plot for my new novel," she said, "and that was the only way I could get it out of her."

"Get what out of her?"

"The plot." Clare blew a series of "rings" into the air. "Did you know that her sister and Simon Ferring were lovers?"

"No."

"She's never told anyone but me, and I had enough trouble digging it out. At first I thought she was just a marvellous bit of atmosphere, then she let out a hint and I dug it out of her bit by bit. It cost me endless patience and several bottles of brandy."

"I don't believe a word of it," said Mrs. Fanshaw. "A thing like that could never happen without anyone's knowing about it, and I've never heard even a whisper."

"It *did* happen," said Clare. "The sister was a sort of sewing-maid at the Castle, and she and Simon Ferring fell in love with each other. They used to meet in that chalet by the lake every night, and one night the old woman found them there. She was livid and packed Simon out of the country. The girl was going to have a baby, and – well, in those days Miss Pendleton was evidently a pillar of respectability and it shocked her so much that she never got over it. Oddly enough no one suspected it, and she took the girl away when her time came near, ostensibly for a holiday. The child was born dead and the girl died a few days later. And the old bird managed everything so cleverly that not even a whisper of it followed her back here."

Mrs. Fanshaw stared at her incredulously.

"And do you expect me to believe," she said, "that after keeping that secret all these years she'd blurt it out to a comparative stranger like you?"

Clare stubbed her cigarette on her saucer and smiled to herself before replying.

"Well, there's a bit more to it than that," she said. "Wait a moment," as the door opened. "I'll tell you later. . . ."

Ivy came in to clear away the tea things. Clare sat slumped over the table, watching her with an amused smile. Ivy kept her eyes sullenly downcast as she put the crockery on the tray. Turning at the door, she caught Mrs. Fanshaw's grave searching gaze fixed on her. Her cheeks flamed, and she plunged from the room with a gulping sob. Clare laughed softly as the door closed on her.

"The priceless little fool," she said. "It's enough to make a cat laugh."

Mrs. Fanshaw was silent. She was thinking of the poor pretty child who had been Miss Pendleton's sister, torn from her lover, hounded to her death. . . .

"Clare," she said at last, "are you sure this is true?"

"Yes," said Clare. "Everyone knew at the time that her sister died when they were away on a holiday and that the old woman packed Simon off out of the country."

"You haven't explained how she came to tell you about it. Was it just – the brandy?"

"N-no," said Clare. "I wish you'd sit down and have a cigarette and look human, Helen. You worry me standing there staring at me like an avenging angel."

"In a way I feel responsible for these people," said Mrs. Fanshaw slowly, "though I can't expect you to understand that."

"No, I don't, thank heaven!" said Clare, "and if anyone had told me in the old days that I'd live to see you turn into the worst type of officious interfering parson's wife I shouldn't have believed them."

"Never mind that," said Mrs. Fanshaw quietly. "It's Miss Pendleton we're discussing, not me."

"Well—" Clare knocked the ash from the end of her cigarette. "You know that she used to live at Pear Tree Cottages?"

Mrs. Fanshaw nodded.

"It was there, of course, that she found out about her sister, watched her growing nearer her time, scared stiff that the village would notice. Fortunately for the old devil, the girl was one of those people who don't show babies much. Anyway, no one guessed. The old devil only didn't turn her out of doors because that would have given the show away. She knew that Mrs. Ferring would hold her tongue, and Simon had been kicked out in double quick time. However – she spent three months brooding over the disgrace to herself and her parents and her home, and wondering what on earth she was going to do with the kid when it came. ... As it happened, of course, she didn't have to worry. ... But when Mrs. Morrice came to live in the house, it somehow touched the old chord. Mrs. Morrice has, perhaps, a look of the sister about her, and the trousers and lipstick stood for the abandoned character that Sarah connected her with. Then there was the kid in the pram in the garden that seemed like the old nightmare come true, and, to crown everything, it was pretty plain that Mrs. Morrice was going to have a baby. ... Anyway, the past and present all got gloriously jumbled up in the poor old thing's mind and she didn't know which was which."

"And you encouraged it," said Mrs. Fanshaw.

Clare looked at her quickly.

"My dear Helen, I have my art to think of. It's given me a marvellous plot. Those meetings in the chalet ... the old woman finding them ... those months of waiting when Sarah wouldn't let the girl out of her sight ... the sudden flight ... think of the drama of it all. ... No writer could resist it. I'm not quite sure how to end it – whether to make the old devil repent and beg the girl to live, and break her heart when she dies, or to make her put both the girl and the kid out of the way. My own belief is that, directly or indirectly, that's what she actually did, but I think that my public would like the other ending better. I'm not a bit ashamed of it, Helen. I did encourage it, as you say. I pretended that the whole thing was happening today. I pretended that I'd found out by accident and swore that I wouldn't tell a soul. She was relieved to have someone to talk to about it. Gosh, the language she used, too! Trust your really respectable woman for that. The foulest words I ever heard in my life! It beats me where she could have heard them. Anyway, I got every detail of the story out of her——"

"With the help of a few bottles of brandy," put in Mrs. Fanshaw contemptuously.

Clare leaned back in her chair, and crossed her legs.

"Yes, with the help of a few bottles of brandy. The old fool used to go home not knowing whether it was today or forty years ago, but I don't see what harm that did her or anyone else. You know I'm not really inventive. I have to get my story from outside and I got it from her. With that – and the notes on scenery and country life I've made here – my next year's novel's as good as written. In fact, as I told you, I'm well away with it already. That was what I wanted Ivy for this morning."

Mrs. Fanshaw sat down and looked at her without speaking. Clare drummed her fingers on the table.

"Quite frankly, Helen," she said at last, "I resent your attitude. You may be the parson's wife, but you don't own the place."

"I suppose you've never considered the annoyance and – mental suffering you've caused Lydia Morrice by all this," said Mrs. Fanshaw, "just when she's going to have a baby. You've behaved like a conceited fool. Just for the sake of one of your rotten books that hardly anyone reads anyway, you come down here and poke your clumsy fingers into people's affairs."

Clare rose slowly and lumberingly to her feet. Her face was a dull brick red.

"Shut up and get out," she said thickly. "I'm sick of your sermonising, you blasted little parsoness! You—"

She stopped abruptly. There was the sound of voices outside. . . . Then Ivy opened the door.

"It's Miss Calder," she said.

Miss Calder appeared in the doorway. She looked pale and anxious.

"Is Sarah here?" she said.

"No," answered Clare abruptly.

"I don't know where she is," said Miss Calder. "She's been so strange all day that I went round to ask Dr. Mercer to see her and when I got back she'd gone. She isn't fit to be out alone. . . . I've looked everywhere."

"Well, she's not here," said Clare curtly. "Why don't you get the old fool locked up?"

A sudden fear stabbed Mrs. Fanshaw's heart. Without a word she went out of the front door and crossed the green to Pear Tree Cottages. Lydia answered her knock, staring at her in surprise.

"Whatever's the matter?" she said.

Mrs. Fanshaw gave a gasp of relief.

"I'm sorry. . . . I suddenly thought . . . Is Matilda all right?"

"Right as rain," said Lydia cheerfully. "Come and look at her. She's in the pram in the garden. I was just going to fetch her in."

Mrs. Fanshaw followed her down the little passage to the garden door. There Lydia stood and looked round, her face freezing slowly into lines of horror.

The garden was empty. The little gate at the bottom hung open on its hinges. . . .

Chapter Sixteen

LAVINIA sat at the schoolroom table, laboriously translating a page of Macaulay's essay on History into French. She had used up the small schoolroom allowance of coal and had put her out-door coat over her shoulders cape-fashion, so that she could throw it off quickly if she heard her grandmother's step outside. Mrs. Ferring considered that to wear an overcoat in the house showed a lack of both breeding and self-control.

"A perfect historian must possess an imagination sufficiently powerful to make his narrative affecting and picturesque. Yet he must control it so absolutely as to content himself with the materials which he finds and to refrain from supplying deficiencies by additions of his own. He must be a profound and ingenious reasoner."

She put the book aside and rested her chin on her hand, gazing unseeingly into the distance. Her thoughts had gone back to the day when Thea had broken up her pencil-box to kindle the dying fire and they had laughed together over the photographs in the old album. So much had happened since then that it seemed to belong to another life. Thea dressing up in the old-fashioned dresses they had found in the attic trunk ... smiling at the imaginary "royal personage" from behind a tattered fan ... racing up and down the stairs ... imitating Hannah and old Andrew ... flinging veiled impertinences at their grandmother with demurely dancing eyes.
. . .

Her thoughts came back to the present. There had been a letter in her mother's handwriting among her grandmother's post that morning. Lavinia had trembled so much at sight of it that she had hardly been able to hold her knife. Her grandmother had read it in silence, then put it back into the envelope without comment. At the end of the meal she had turned to Lavinia, and for a breathless moment Lavinia had thought that she was going to refer to it, but all she had said was, "We will begin with European history this morning, Lavinia."

The morning dragged interminably. The lessons were dreary (of late, the old lady seemed to have lost interest in them), and the short curt reproofs more frequent than usual. "Sit straight, Lavinia ... don't fidget ... don't mumble, child." Whenever her grandmother looked at her, Lavinia thought that she was going to mention the letter, and her heart would beat unevenly, but the morning passed without any reference to it. In a way, Lavinia was not surprised by this, for it had never been part of Mrs. Ferring's system to take her young charges into her confidence. She knew, of course, that Lavinia had seen the letter, but she did not intend to divulge its contents till it seemed fit to her. Suspense was a salutary discipline. Her silence swung Lavinia from the heights of hope down to the depths of despair. It must be something important or her grandmother would have mentioned it by now. . . . It couldn't be anything important or her grandmother would have mentioned it by now. . . . Her mother had told her grandmother about the letter she had written and her grandmother was angry. . . . Her mother hadn't mentioned her letter but had just sent for her as she had sent for Thea. She would go out to her – next week, perhaps – and tell her all about Colin, and her mother would understand, and – Oh, the details didn't matter, but soon she and Colin would be married and living in a little house of their own – somewhere near Beverton, of course, because his work was there. She would have Thea to stay with her ... and her mother. . . . The picture dissolved in a rosy mist of happiness.

Luncheon was eaten in silence. The old lady seemed lost in her own thoughts and unaware of Lavinia's presence – so much so that Lavinia, who was feeling slightly sick, managed to leave a piece of meat on her plate without her grandmother's noticing it. It seemed the longest day she had ever known. . . .

She drew Macaulay's *Essays* nearer and took up her pen again.

No use making things worse by getting into trouble over her work. If that happened, her grandmother was quite capable of withholding any news there was in the letter for several days.

As she moved the book across the scored ink-stained table, the straggling uneven carving of the name "Simon" came into view. . . . She thought again of the time when Simon and her father had done their lessons at this table as little boys and wondered idly what they had been like. All the old stories of boyish pranks and mischief handed down by the servants were of Simon, not her father. She wished she had known him. . . . She shook her head as if to shake the daydreams out of it and began to write in the old-fashioned "copper plate" hand that her grandmother always insisted on.

"Le parfait historien est celui qui possède une imagination assez puissante pour rendre son récit attachant et coloré. Il lui faut, néanmoins, la tenir en bride de façon à se contenter des matériaux qu'il découvre et se refuser à combler les lacunes par ses additions à lui. Son raisonnement doit être profond et—"

She wasn't quite sure about "ingenious." She'd better look it out and underline it. Gran always made you underline all the words you'd looked out. She got up to fetch the dictionary from the bookshelves and paused for a moment at the window on the way back. She could see the spot at the end of the wood where Colin waited for her signal after their meetings, and the little chalet by the edge of the lake. The trees were already in bud, and soon you wouldn't be able to see either from the window. She imagined Colin standing there watching . . . and love for him welled up in her, filling her whole body with sudden sweetness and delight.

As soon as she was back in her seat, she heard her grandmother's footsteps at the door and, slipping the coat from her shoulders, threw it under the table.

Mrs. Ferring's keen glance travelled round the room, to rest finally on her granddaughter.

"What are you doing, Lavinia?"

"The French exercise, Gran."

The old lady came to the table and looked down at the exercise book.

"Is that all you've done?"

"Yes."

The old lady read the paragraph and put her pencil through the words "ses additions à lui."

" 'Additions de son cru' would be better," she said.

"Oh yes," said Lavinia, making the correction.

"You should take more pains with your handwriting, Lavinia. A careful handwriting is the mark of a lady," she said, but she spoke with comparative mildness and as if she were thinking of something else.

Then she went over to the fireplace and stood for some moments in silence, looking down at the dead fire.

"Lavinia," she said at last. "I heard from your mother this morning."

Lavinia's heart leapt, then began to beat with loud suffocating throbs.

"It will be as much a surprise to you as it is to me," went on the old lady. "She has married again." She paused, and went on, "Her husband is a Monsieur d'Assonville, an old friend of the family."

Lavinia sat very still. A fly was walking across her exercise book. She watched it, noticing how it stopped and seemed to draw its front legs over its tiny head before it resumed its progress. At last she said:

"Does she want me to go to her?"

"No," said Mrs. Ferring.

Again there was a long silence. At the end of it Lavinia said:

"Has she sent any message for me?"

Again Mrs. Ferring shook her head.

"No," she said slowly. "There is no message for you." Then she seemed to rouse herself with an effort and went on in her usual brisk voice, "You have been wasting your time, Lavinia. You could have done more than that first paragraph if you had really given your mind to your work. You must learn to do whatever you have to do thoroughly. Lack of concentration means lack of self-control."

Long pent-up forces in Lavinia suddenly burst their bonds. She sprang to her feet and flung the exercise book across the room.

"I'm sick of it," she sobbed. "I can't go on. ... I won't. ... I hate it. ... I—"

The black eyes flashed fire at her.

"Control yourself at once or go to your room," said Mrs. Ferring. She spoke in the voice of cold biting anger that had quelled Lavinia from her childhood. She stood there trembling, catching her breath in dry gasping sobs.

"You will come and apologise to me before you go down to dinner," said the old lady, and went abruptly from the room.

Lavinia stood staring at the closed door for a moment, then sat down again at the table and covered her face with her hands, fighting back her tears. At the sound of the opening of the door, she bent her head down and pretended to be busy with her work. Hannah entered and drew the curtains across the windows.

"What call had you got to go upsetting her?" she muttered. "I thought we'd got shot of that sort of thing when your sister went. Can't you let her be in peace?"

Lavinia dug her teeth into her lips and said nothing.

Hannah bent down, straightening the worn hearthrug in front of the fireplace.

"She told you about your mother?" she said.

Lavinia wheeled round, showing her white tear-stained face.

"I'm going out to her," she said. "I won't stay here—"

Hannah looked at her.

"You don't flatter yourself she wants you, do you?"

"Of course, she wants me," panted Lavinia. "She's my mother."

Hannah shrugged her shoulders.

"She wants to start clear with this marriage," she said. "He's had to take on Thea, but he's not taking on you. He wants a wife, but he doesn't want a couple of great girls. No man would. It's only natural. No, she's washing her hands of you from now on, and you'll have to make the best of it. So shall we all," she added grimly.

"I don't believe it . . . it's not true."

"Didn't she show you the letter?"

Lavinia shook her head. Black waves of despair engulfed her.

"Well, she put it plain enough there," said Hannah, "and you'll have to stomach it whether you like it or not. And I'll thank you to mind your manners and not to go upsetting your grandmother any more."

"Go away," said Lavinia in a strangled voice.

"I'm going," said the old woman. "I've work to do if you haven't."

She went out, slamming the door after her.

Lavinia's one thought was to reach the refuge of her bedroom before she surrendered to the sobs that filled her body like some irresistible force invading it from without. She groped her way blindly along the passage, then, closing the door, flung herself on her bed. The sobs seemed to rise up from the depths of her, choking her, tearing her thin frame. . . . She gave herself up to them, surrendering with youth's ready despair, seeing no ray of hope through her misery. . . . She felt as if she had received a sentence of lifelong imprisonment. . . . She'd never get away from this hateful place now. Never. Even Colin's love became part of the black hopelessness that enveloped her. It held only terror and unhappiness. It showed her no way of escape. . . . Her mother had failed her and there was nothing left. Life was unbearable, unlivable. Suddenly she felt something moving in her hair and raised her head just in time to see a grey form glide down from the pillow to the floor. She stared after it, her eyes dilated in her tear-stained face, while waves of nausea swept over her. She staggered to the hand-basin and retched over it. . . . Then she wiped the tears from her cheeks and stood looking round the room. Her face was set and stony. It was as though some unbearable tension had broken. She didn't feel unhappy or afraid any more. She didn't feel anything at all. Only, she knew that this was the end. She didn't care where she went, but she couldn't stay here any longer. . . . She had no suit-case, but there was an old Gladstone bag on the top of the wardrobe, which had been there ever since she could remember. She stood on a chair to get it down and slowly and methodically packed her night things into it. She felt as if it were happening in a dream, as if she were not herself at all but a stranger whom she was watching. She put on her hat, then remembered that her coat was under the schoolroom table and went back along the passage to get it. Slipping it on, still clutching the Gladstone bag, she made her way down the small side staircase. I'll never come back, she was saying to herself. I don't care what happens to me, I'll never come back. I'd rather die. ... It seemed at first as if she were going to escape without being seen, but suddenly, in the little passage at the foot of the stairs, old Hannah appeared and stood blocking her way.

"Where are you going?" she said.

Lavinia looked at her in silence, and as she looked the old woman seemed to shrink before her eyes. The physical fear that Lavinia had felt for her ever since the days when she had been the – none too kindly – despot of the nursery, faded. I'm not frightened of her any more, she thought with dull surprise. She's only an old woman. I could knock her down if I wanted to.

"I don't know," she said, "but I'm never coming back. You can't stop me. No one can stop me. ...."

The old woman looked at her in silence, then stepped aside with a little gesture of defeat.

"I'm tired of it all," she muttered. "Tired to death. I can't go on much longer. Neither can she. ...."

It wasn't till she'd reached the end of the park that Lavinia remembered it was the time that Colin usually came home from the bank. She decided to go along the main road and meet him. ... She still felt numbed and as though she were moving in a dream. She closed her eyes instinctively as familiar flickering pains stabbed her temples, but she was not really aware of them. Only the thought of Colin seemed to force its way through the ice round her heart like a warm radiance. She had a strange conviction that, once she got to him, everything would be all right. But, when she reached the wood, sudden panic came over her, and she began to run, stumbling over hillocks and roots. ... She fell once and dropped

217

her bag but scrambled to her feet and ran on. . . . At the stile leading into the road she stopped and looked up and down the road. And there, as she had known she would, she saw him. He was walking along briskly, bareheaded, his raincoat over his arm. She ran down the road to him and found to her surprise that she was crying again. He caught her in his arms, and she, sobbed against his shoulder, clinging to him convulsively.

"Darling, what's the matter?" he said aghast.

She poured out a confused story between her sobs. He listened anxiously, trying to piece it together – her mother's letter, the rat, the sudden anguish of despair that had assailed her young spirit. He had realised for some time that something exquisite and delicate in her was being worn to breaking point, but he had never even considered what he should do when the breaking point came.

"I'll never go back," she ended. "I don't care what happens to me, I'll never go back. Oh, Colin, can't we go away somewhere together?"

He looked up and down the road, afraid that someone might see them and take the news to the old lady. . . .

"Come into the wood," he said, "and let's talk it over. . . ."

He took the shabby Gladstone bag and helped her over the stile, then put his arm round her and led her gently to the fallen tree that had been the scene of so many of their meetings. She drew out a handkerchief and dried her eyes and cheeks.

"I'm sorry, Colin," she said in a stifled voice. "I didn't mean to cry. I won't cry any more. . . . But – I'm not going back. Please don't try to make me. Really and truly, I'd rather die. I wouldn't mind dying at all. . . . I just can't face going on and on there alone with Gran and old Hannah . . . never knowing when I shall see you again. It wasn't so bad when I thought that things would come right, but now I don't see how they can. Unless we just go away together. . . . Colin, let's do that. Why not? We'd manage somehow. We'd be so happy. . . ."

She looked at him appealingly, and, meeting her eyes, desire for her welled up in him in an overmastering flood. He turned his face away.

"We can't. . . ."

"Why not?" she persisted.

"You don't understand what it would mean to you."

"You mean because we couldn't be married? I shouldn't mind anything as long as I was with you. . . . Couldn't we get married?"

"You're only seventeen. We couldn't be married without your mother's consent."

"That means Gran's. . . . She'd never give it."

"And I'd lose my job. I shouldn't have any money."

"You'd get another, Colin. I shouldn't mind how poor we were. We couldn't be poorer than I've been ever since I can remember. I'm used to old clothes and not enough to eat. I shouldn't mind at all. Couldn't I get some work, too? Oh, Colin, just to be together . . . to have each other. . . ."

For a moment he was tempted to agree. He loved her so desperately. What did anything else matter? Then:

"We couldn't, Lavvy," he said. "I'd never forgive myself for the rest of my life if I did."

She dropped her head into her hands. At first he thought she was crying again, but when she raised it she was dry-eyed.

"What am I to do then?" she said stonily. "I won't go back. . . ."

He tried to feel experienced and capable, but he could only feel young and helpless and afraid. He didn't know what to do. He would gladly have let himself be torn in pieces for her, but – he didn't know what to do. And he *must* know what to do. Already it was dusk. Night would soon be on them. Already his mother would be standing at the window wondering why he hadn't come home. The old lady at the Castle would probably have discovered Lavinia's flight even if Hannah hadn't told her. He cursed himself for his helplessness and stupidity. Any other man in the world, he thought despairingly, would have known what to do.

"Your mother . . .?" said Lavinia suddenly.

He shook his head.

"That wouldn't do," he said. "What about the Fanshaws or Mrs. Helston? Just for tonight. Just till we've thought things out."

"No one here would be any use," she said. "They wouldn't dare stand out against Gran. You don't know Gran. No one dare stand out against her. . . . She'd make me go back. She'd be – dreadful. You don't know how dreadful she can be. And now there isn't Mother. . . ." She rose to her feet. "I haven't any money, but I must go. . . . It's getting late, isn't it? If you don't want to come, Colin, will you lend me some money? I'll pay you back. . . ."

"Lavvy . . ."

He caught her to him, and they clung to each other, strained in a desperate embrace. She pressed her lips upon his.

"Colin, I do love you so," she whispered. "Come with me. . . ."

"I'll go to the ends of the earth with you," he said hoarsely, and wished that the words did not sound so banal and unreal. He meant them so utterly. . . .

Suddenly he remembered a sister of his mother's who lived in Hampstead. She and his mother had quarrelled many years ago, but she had frequently made overtures of friendship to him, to which his mother had not allowed him to respond. Lavinia listened almost absently to the suggestion.

"Yes, yes. . . . Anywhere, anywhere."

"I ought to go back for some things."

"Don't, Colin."

"I swear you'll never regret it. . . . I swear I'll make you happy."

They kissed again, not passionately this time, but with a grave earnestness of purpose, as if sealing some solemn pact.

"I shall die if you leave me," she said, and was seized suddenly by a fit of coughing that made her gasp for breath.

"Isn't your cough any better?" he said anxiously.

She smiled at him reassuringly through the tears that had come into her eyes.

"I'm all right, really," she whispered. "Perhaps it's with crying so much. . . . I'm so afraid that Gran will find out and stop me – even now. Let's go at once. We can take the 'bus to Beverton Station and get a train to London from there, can't we?"

"Yes. . . ."

He was remembering his aunt more clearly – not unlike his

mother, complacent, self-indulgent, conventional. He tried to stifle his misgivings.

Just before they reached the stile she stopped and turned to him.

"Colin, if your aunt won't have me, you won't leave me, will you?"

"No. ... I swear it."

He was almost relieved to have thrown prudence to the winds, to have made up his mind at last, whatever it might lead to. There came to him a sudden intoxicating vision of a life in which miraculously all their troubles and problems were at an end, and she was well and happy, surrounded by his love. ... It faded, and he faced the darkening night, his helplessness, and Lavinia looking at him with anxious trusting eyes.

"There's the 'bus," she said suddenly. "We mustn't miss it."

He stopped the 'bus at the stile and helped her into it. She leant back wearily in her seat. ... The sudden light emphasised the shadows round her eyes, the dead pallor of the oval face, and the faint lines of exhaustion round the delicate mouth. She looked pathetically young and defenceless. Terror at what he was going to do seized him, but he fought it down. He couldn't give her up now.

She started suddenly and seized his arm, staring out at the gathering darkness.

"*Colin!* Who was that?" she said sharply.

"What?" he said.

She was still staring out.

"We've passed her. ... It was an old woman. I think it was Miss Pendleton."

"Well, what of it?" he said.

Her hand tightened on his arm.

"She had a pram with her."

"What of it?" he said again.

"I think it was Mrs. Morrice's pram. ... Colin, we must get out and see."

Now that he had made up his mind to take her away, he was impatient of delay or interruption.

"Darling, what does it matter if it was Mrs. Morrice's pram?" She had risen to her feet.

"We can't go on without knowing. I thought there was a baby in it. It – couldn't be Matilda. . . ."

"Of course, it couldn't," he reassured her. "Why, you aren't even sure that it was Miss Pendleton, are you?"

"No, but – I must make sure. It won't take long." She went to the door. "May we get off here?" she said to the conductor.

Colin followed her reluctantly. They stepped down into the road, and the 'bus went on towards Beverton.

"It was down there I saw her," said Lavinia, "just round the bend."

She ran down to the bend of the road and stood looking about her. There was no one in sight.

"There!" said Colin. "It's all right. There probably wasn't anyone there at all. Shadows look like anything in this light, and you're overwrought."

"It was someone," said Lavinia doggedly. "I'm almost sure it was Miss Pendleton. . . ."

"Darling, would it matter if it was?" he pleaded.

He was wildly impatient to get her away before their flight was discovered. Unreasoning optimism had again seized him. He was sure that his aunt would take her in, and be good to her, and that he would find work in London. They would be married and live happy ever after. He didn't want to waste a moment. . . .

"No, but it would matter if it was Matilda she'd got in the pram."

"Why should it be?"

"I don't know, but it might be. . . . Colin, darling, I *must* make sure. . . . I'll just run along to Pear Tree Cottages and see. I won't let anyone know I'm there. I'll just peep through the nursery window and come straight back. . . ."

"I'll go with you," he said jealously.

"All right – we'll run. It won't take long."

They ran back along the wood-bordered road to the green. There was a little group at the gate of Pear Tree Cottages. Among them were Mrs. Morrice, a policeman, and Pete, the brawny potman of the "Fox and Grapes," who had come across the green to see what was happening.

"I'd seen her only a moment ago," Mrs. Morrice was saying, "and she was fast asleep in her pram, and I went indoors to get things ready for her bath. Then Mrs. Fanshaw came and we went out into the garden and she'd gone."

Lavinia pushed her way through the group.

"Is it Miss Pendleton?" she panted.

"Yes," said Mrs. Fanshaw, "we're afraid that she's taken Matilda."

"I saw her, then. She was going down the Beverton Road. She had the pram with her. She's not there now."

Lydia started off without a word. The others followed her.

"It was here I saw her," said Lavinia. "I saw her from the 'bus."

It did not occur to them to wonder what Lavinia was doing on a 'bus at this time of the day, or indeed at any time. Colin hovered anxiously in the background, his mind more on Lavinia than on the missing child.

Suddenly Lydia gave a cry and pointed to the overgrown ditch that ran by the side of the road. Through the thick rank grass two pram wheels projected. She dived down in sudden frenzy and dragged out the empty pram. The only trace of Matilda was the white shawl that had been wrapped round her.

"Oh, my God," she said on a quick intake of breath.

At the point where the pram had been found, the wooden railing that separated the road from the wood was broken, and the spot was regularly used by the village boys as an unofficial entrance to the wood.

"She must have gone into the wood," said Lavinia.

She scrambled across the ditch and into the wood. The footpath led to the Castle park. She ran along it, forgetting her fear of her grandmother in her desire to rescue the child.

Even Lydia Morrice could not keep up with her.

Suddenly they heard her voice, upraised on a note of terror.

"The chalet! ... It's on fire."

Chapter Seventeen

FRANK TURNBERRY sat in the bar of the "Fox and Grapes" and ordered another beer. He had finished the previous One as slowly as possible because he didn't want to get drunk and disgrace Clifford again. He didn't remember at all clearly what had happened yesterday, but he knew that he'd got drunk and disgraced Clifford. That had started the trouble – that and the five pounds he'd taken from Mrs. Webb's table. One part of him realised that it had been wrong to take the money, but the other part couldn't understand it. . . . It had been there and he'd taken it. Even the part that realised it had been wrong knew that he couldn't have helped taking it. It was money, and he liked money. . . . He had been distressed by his mother's anger when he pawned his father's clothes after his death, but while he had protested his penitence he had known all the time in a despairing bewildered fashion that he couldn't have helped doing it, that he'd have done it again. . . . You could get things you wanted for money, you could buy drinks for yourself and other people, you could make foolish little bets and pay up when you lost, as you invariably did, you could give it away to people and be treated like a king. He didn't quite know what had happened to the five pounds. It had just gone, as money always did, but it had been grand while it lasted. It had made him lose that bewildering sense of being different from other people. . . .

An unusually thick haze of depression lay over his spirit, and he ordered another half-pint of beer in the hopes of clearing it away. He'd disgraced old Cliff, and old Cliff was turning him out. It wasn't just a threat this time. He really had to go. His mother was to live with old Cliff and he was being turned out. He felt no indignation or resentment – only a sort of dull hurt that old Cliff should do this to him. They'd been such pals once – he and old Cliff. They'd slept in the same bed and had pillow-fights and a secret password. He had once knocked a boy down and given him a black-eye for tripping up Cliff in the school playground. Cliff had cried all night when he (Frank) had cut his head open falling out of a swing. Once, when Miss Pendleton had asked Cliff to tea alone, he had said stoutly, "I'm not going if Frank can't go, too." He couldn't understand what had changed things. . . . He was still as fond of old Cliff as ever. He'd have done anything for him. . . .

His mother had gone to Beverton in a last attempt to persuade old Cliff not to turn them out, but he knew it was no good. He could tell that by the look on her face. She'd stood out against Cliff always before, but this time she'd given in. She realised that it wasn't any good standing out. . . . Cliff was furious. It was natural, of course, for Cliff to be furious. Nobody liked being disgraced. Remorse overwhelmed him. It was dreadful to think that it was he who had disgraced Cliff. He wouldn't have hurt him for the world – not old Cliff. He tried to face the thought of his own future. He knew that he'd never keep his gardening jobs without his mother to wake him in the morning and get him off to them in time. She even saw to it that he washed properly. . . . Sometimes on Sunday she would say, "I'm going to wash you myself and see that you're clean, you great baby," and she would wash his neck and ears and hair at the kitchen sink while he spluttered and gasped. It would generally end in their horse-playing about the kitchen together. . . . She was over sixty but she loved a romp. She would often play tricks on him, putting an empty egg-shell in his egg-cup, a clothes-brush at the foot of his bed, hiding his things. . . . She could take people off, too, so that you'd hardly know it wasn't the real person. She was fun . . . and she stood between him and a sort of abyss of which he was always half unconsciously aware. He didn't know how he'd get on without her, but he'd have to, of course. What could he do? He'd go North, he thought vaguely. He might get work here and there on the way. If he didn't, he'd sleep in ditches or in barns. And one could do a little poaching for food – or get a chicken from a farm at night. He knew he'd never keep a settled job without his mother. It didn't really matter what happened to him, though. He'd be all right. . . . He'd get on somehow. . . .

A man came in and sat down next him.

"They say that summer-house thing by the lake up at the Castle's on fire," he said. "Everyone's trecking up there to see it. . . . Take more than a fire to make me miss my drink. I've seen enough of 'em in my time."

Frank rose and went outside. The evening air struck sharply cold on his flushed face. Above the trees showed a faint red glow. He made his way through the woods to the lake, guided by the glow in the sky and, as he got nearer, by the sound of voices.

When he reached the end of the wood he stood motionless for some moments looking at the scene before him. Flames leapt and danced over the crazy little wooden chalet, throwing lurid lights and shadows on the faces of the watching crowd. He recognised Mrs. Fanshaw . . . Mrs. Helston . . . Lavinia Ferring . . . Colin Webb . . . Ivy Skelton . . . George Harker. . . . Some men were fetching pails of water from the lake and throwing them ineffectively onto the flames.

"Ain't the engine come yet?" shouted one.

"No, an' no signs on it," shouted another.

In a sudden burst of flame, Frank saw Miss Pendleton. She was struggling in the grasp of a policeman not far away from him. Her eyes gleamed wildly in her blackened face, her lips were flecked with spittle and her grey hair hung in disorder over her shoulders. Part of her bodice was torn away, showing a bare bony shoulder. The policeman seemed disconcerted by his position. He was used to a peaceful patrolling of country lanes, and this situation was beyond him. He had somehow to control this mad-woman and keep an eye on the fire and crowd till the fire-engine arrived. He looked round uncertainly . . . and, as he did so, his prisoner freed herself by a sudden violent twitch of her arms and ran towards the blazing doorway of the chalet. They saw her for a moment lit up by the flames, her mouth open in a grimace of triumph, her torn garments flying out behind her ... then smoke and flame seemed to swallow her up. The policeman started after her but staggered back, his hands to his eyes, choking. Frank took in the situation. She'd gone into the burning house and had to be got out of it. He was fuddled enough, but he saw that quite clearly. She had to be got out of it. ... The policeman tried to catch hold of him as he passed, someone shouted, "Come back, you fool," and a woman screamed.

It was the passing of the 'bus that had made Miss Pendleton snatch Matilda from the pram, overturn the pram in the ditch, and escape into the wood. It seemed to be watching her with its great eyes, spying on her, pursuing her. ... And she'd been so clever up to now. ... She wouldn't let herself be caught. ... Already the reasons that had made her take Matilda and the pram from the garden were fading from her confused brain, but the thought of her cleverness sent a thrill of delight through her. Oh, she was too clever for them, too clever for them all. ...

The child had at first been Ellen's child, the child of sin that must be hidden from all eyes. Finding it there in the garden of their old home for everyone to see had nearly killed her. ... People would guess. ... People would know. ... It had been the work of a moment to snatch the child away, pram and all, before anyone discovered Ellen's shame. She'd known quite well what must be done with it, too. It must be destroyed, as all evil things must be destroyed, as that place of sin where Ellen had met her lover must be destroyed, the very sight of which through the trees had turned her sick with horror all these years – ever since she knew what had happened there. She had the key of it in her bag. She had forced Ellen to give it her, to make sure that she never met him again – there, at any rate. They must be destroyed together – so that no one would ever know, no one ever guess.

And then, as soon as she felt the warm weight of the sleeping child in her arms, it became the baby Ellen, given into her charge by Ellen's mother just before she died.

"Little Ellen," she crooned in her cracked quavering voice as she stumbled through the wood. "Sarah's little precious. . . . Sarah's baby girl. . . ."

But, though she was the baby Ellen, the poor muddled brain saw the end that she must come to, saw that it must at all costs be prevented. Better death . . . better death . . . better death.

"It won't hurt, little sweet," she quavered. "It'll be quick. Sarah will be with you. Sarah will go, too. . . ."

At the end of the wood she paused for breath, and looked around. The park lay serene and peaceful before her in the twilight. The lake was a dark shadow, the trees still showed a delicate tracery against the violet sky. The chalet seemed to stand out grotesquely in the fading light.

She took the key from her pocket and fumbled in the lock. Both key and lock were rusty. It was thirty years since that night when Ellen had last unlocked the door, glancing back over her shoulder, her blue eyes wide with fear. It opened with a grating sound, and she entered the little front room, closing the door behind her. The airless musty atmosphere stabbed like a knife. She stood and looked around. The carved wooden furniture was covered with dust and mildew. The carpet was moth-eaten, the once gay cushion-covers and curtains faded to a drab indistinguishable shade. The walls were stained with mould. It smells like a grave, she thought, and then: It is a grave. . . . There was a glass vase on the table, still with the traces of foul dark water at the bottom, and by it what looked like a little heap of brown dust. She had a sudden memory of Ellen on that last evening, picking clusters of the small creamy roses that grew up the wall of Pear Tree Cottages. She had brought them here and put them in that vase. She saw her quite plainly standing on tiptoe to reach one of the higher clusters, her head bent back, showing the lovely line of chin and neck. She had on a dress of pink muslin with a black velvet sash. Her hair caught and held the sunshine in its golden ripples. . . . The love that had turned to hatred flared up again in the old woman's heart, and she clasped the child to her more closely.

"I've got to save you from it, my little love," she crooned. "I've got to save you. . . ."

Matilda woke up with a loud wail. The sound seemed to rouse the old woman to action. She laid her down gently on the small wooden settee and looked round the room. On the walls were some photographs of Switzerland, framed in a complicated pattern of coloured celluloid, cut into strips and fastened together with paperclips. The making of such frames had been a passing craze about forty years ago, and these had been presented by a distant relative after a visit to the Castle. They were covered with dust but had resisted the general dampness of the atmosphere. Swiftly the old woman tore them down, and flung the strips of celluloid onto the floor. Then, taking a box of matches from her pocket (she'd kept one there lately because she had known for some time now that something must be burnt) she crouched down by the heap of celluloid and put a match to the pieces one by one with trembling claw-like fingers. ... The flame leapt up hungrily, and she went about the room, collecting what she thought would feed it best. The sight of the fire excited her and she began to laugh, peal upon peal of thin cracked laughter that blended horribly with the child's cries. The flames crept up the table leg, licked at the flimsy table-cloth with red lapping tongues, then flared up suddenly. ... She heard voices outside. ... Someone tried the door.

"Open the door," cried a man's, voice.

A lamp with a rotted shade of once red silk stood on a table in a corner of the room. She took it up, held it high above her head, and flung it into the fire. The flames sprang to meet it. Her cackle of triumph rang out exultantly above the tumult outside. There came the sound of splintering glass. Someone was breaking the tiny window in order to get in. Blinded by smoke and flames, she groped for the child, found it, and plunged towards the stairs.

"You shan't get us ... you shan't get us," she cried.

She fought like a maniac when they found her. The policeman dragged her downstairs, while Pete put the child under his coat and carried her out to Lydia. Matilda was unhurt, more angry than frightened, and the well-known voice quickly soothed both anger and fear.

White and shaking, Lydia held her baby in her arms.

"Let me hold her," pleaded Lettice. "You aren't fit."

"No, no," said Lydia, clasping Matilda as though she could never let her go.

"The engine'll be too late now," said a woman near them with a certain gloomy satisfaction. "They'll never put it out."

The fire had gained hold, and the efforts of the men who had fetched buckets and were ladling water from the lake were obviously unavailing.

"I hope they won't," said Lydia with a little sobbing gasp in her voice. "Let the hateful place go. . . . I couldn't bear ever to see it again."

Mrs. Fanshaw's eyes looked round the semi-circle of faces lit up fantastically by the flames. Her eyes fell on Miss Pendleton struggling and screaming in the policeman's grasp, the last remnant of her sanity gone.

"I wish he'd take her away," she said, "but I suppose he's got to stay here."

"He's sent to Beverton for help," said someone. "They should be here any minute."

Suddenly she saw Clare, standing at the side of the group, stout and stocky in her tweed suit, making notes in a small note-book.

"I suppose she'll have a fire in the next book," said Lettice. "How I dislike the woman!"

"So do I," said Mrs. Fanshaw grimly.

At that moment Mrs. Skelton arrived, followed by Ivy. Ivy had slipped home as soon as Clare had gone out, to describe with self-pitying snivels what had happened that morning.

"I didn't want to, Mum," she wailed. "She made me."

And Mrs. Skelton was furious. She had brought Ivy up to be a nice girl, and nice girls didn't take their clothes off in the day-time. She felt almost as outraged as if Clare had stripped Ivy naked in Beverton market-place. A nice girl like Ivy. Why, she'd smacked her once when she was a little girl for just tucking her frock and petticoat into her cambric drawers and running round the garden. Nice little girls didn't do rude things like that, she had told her. . . . And Ivy was as nice a girl as even her mother could desire, dressing and undressing under her nightgown if ever she had to share a room with a cousin at Christmas. . . .

"Don't you worry, my girl," she said grimly. "I'll learn her."

And, setting her tweed cap at a more pugnacious angle, girding yet another sacking apron round her waist, she sallied forth like a knight to battle, followed by the still weeping Ivy. She traced her enemy to the fire. It happened that, being busy with her washing, she had not heard about either the fire or the disappearance of the Morrice baby, but just for the moment she wasn't interested in either. She was a woman of one idea, and her one idea just at present was "learning" Miss Lennare. Time enough afterwards for both the fire and the disappearance of the Morrice baby. . . .

She strode down the road, through the wood, into the park, and past the groups of spectators, Ivy trotting at her heels.

"Never you mind, my girl," she kept saying. "I'll learn her. . . ."

She hardly glanced at the fire or at the faces around, lit up by its lurid light. She wiped her hands, still damp and crinkled from the washing, on her apron as she approached Clare, then stood in front of her, arms akimbo on her massive hips.

"I'll thank you," she said, breathing heavily, "to leave my girl alone."

An interested murmur went through the crowd and they gathered round her, greedy of the new sensation.

Clare gave a laugh that was meant to be airily amused but that sounded a little nervous.

"I haven't the faintest idea what you're talking about, my good woman," she said.

"Oh, haven't you?" said Mrs. Skelton threateningly.

She advanced a step nearer and leant forward. Clare took a step backward.

"I've been wantin' a little talk with you for a long time. Dollin' up my Ivy. Takin' her about with you. Makin' a lady of her. I tell you, I don't want my Ivy made a lady of."

"I'm sure you don't," said Clare on a rather high-pitched note. "Quite sure you don't."

Mrs. Skelton took another step forward. Clare again retreated a step.

"Call yourself a lady, do you?" said Mrs. Skelton, her naturally loud voice rising to a bellow. "D'you think any lady'd have served my Ivy like you served her this morning? Take shame to yourself, you loose thing."

"My good woman," said Clare stoutly, "your Ivy's a vulgar little fool."

Mrs. Skelton's large hand shot out and dealt Clare a resounding slap on the cheek. She staggered to one side to receive the full impact of Mrs. Skelton's other hand on the other cheek. She fell down and scrambled to her feet again to receive two more resounding blows one on each side of her head. She turned and, shielding her head with her arms, took ignominiously to flight. Mrs. Skelton's pantomime-dame appearance lent the whole episode an irresistibly comic air, and roars of laughter followed Clare, as she stumbled over the stile and vanished into the shadow of the wood. Mrs. Skelton looked round, her good humour completely restored. She saw George Harker's face as he stood staring at her in amazement. The leaping lights from the fire turned its ruddy tan to a curious pallor. She grinned at him and cocked her thumb in the direction of the sobbing Ivy.

"Now's your chance, lad," she said. "Don't stand there gaping. . . ."

Then, wholly unconscious of the sensation she had caused, she took out the skewer from the back of the tweed cap, ran it violently home again, folded her great arms, and settled down to enjoy the spectacle of the fire.

No one had seen Mrs. Ferring and Hannah approach from the direction of the Castle. It was Andrew who had brought the news.

"They say that summer-house place by the lake's afire, mum," he said.

Sudden tension had come into the old face.

"I'll go . . ." she had said in a voice that was strained and unsteady. "Fetch my cloak, Hannah."

"I shouldn't go, madam," said Hannah. "It'll be too much for you."

"Fetch my cloak," repeated Mrs. Ferring imperiously.

Hannah went to fetch the ancient black cloak that had been one of Mrs. Ferring's wedding presents. It was lined with sable and fastened at the throat by an old silver clasp. It was worn and patched, but the fur lining was as good as new. Every summer Hannah stored it carefully away in moth ball. She put on her own hat and coat and went to slip the cloak over her mistress's shoulders. She had been stubbornly silent about Lavinia's flight, prepared to deny all knowledge of it when it was discovered. . . . Let her go. They'd always been more trouble than they were worth – those brats of Master Gerald's. The old house had never wanted them. Perhaps they would have some peace – she and her mistress – now that the last of them had gone. Not that she'd really gone, supposed Hannah with a shrug. Just a bit of her high-flown nonsense. She'd be back, probably, before her grandmother had discovered her absence – back to apologise and eat her dinner in silence, as usual, trying to stifle her cough and hide her shivering. She'd always been the meek one of the two.

"Don't dawdle, Hannah," said the old woman suddenly, and Hannah quickened her slow footsteps.

A strange excitement had seized Mrs. Ferring at the news of the fire. It seemed, she didn't know how or why, to be a message of reconciliation from Simon. It was to go – the hateful place that had stood like a barrier between them for so long. All these years she had never been able to see it without a twisting of the heart. It had been a perpetual reminder of his treachery to her, her harshness to him. If that were gone, it would be as if the thing had never happened. Her old pride in him would return, his old love for her. . . .

"I could have burnt it myself any time these thirty years," she muttered. "It would have been better if I had done."

"I beg your pardon, madam," said Hannah, seeing the old lips move.

"Nothing, nothing!" said her mistress impatiently. "Come quickly."

As they approached the fire, weariness seized her – a weariness so intense that she felt she could go no further and with it a shrinking from the crowd gathered round the fire. She felt that she could not bear to face them, to hear their comments and questions. There was an old iron seat beneath one of the tall elms, placed there by some former owner of the Castle for the view it afforded of the park and lake.

"I'll stay here, Hannah," she said, sitting down. "Go and find out how it happened."

Hannah set off with her slow dragging step.

Mrs. Ferring relaxed against the hard iron back of the seat and heaved a sigh, partly of relief, partly of exhaustion. Her eyes were fixed on the leaping flames. Nothing could save the crazy little place now. Soon it would be gone and with it the barrier that divided her from Simon. How tired she was – how tired! As the flames leapt up they picked out with fitful lurid gleams the faces of the watching crowd. The old lady's gaze followed the dancing light, recognising faces here and there in the red glow ... Mrs. Fanshaw ... Mrs. Morrice ... Mrs. Helston ... Mrs. Skelton ... Ivy Skelton and George Harker ... and lastly her granddaughter, standing in the shadow of a tree at the end of the semi-circle, her head resting on a man's shoulder, his arm around her waist. ...

"She oughtn't to have come, Hannah," said Mrs. Fanshaw anxiously. "Why did you let her?"

"She would come," said old Hannah grimly. "You know what she's like when she gets an idea in her head. She told me to find out how it happened."

"I'll go to her," said Mrs. Fanshaw.

She made her way across the grass to the seat beneath the tree.

The old lady sat there just as Hannah had left her ... but one side of the face was twisted and awry, and from the corner of the distorted mouth ran a thin dribble of saliva.

"Get the doctor quickly," said Mrs. Fanshaw, but as she spoke there came a murmur of excitement from the crowd, and she turned sharply, just in time to see Miss Pendleton tear herself from the policeman's grasp and vanish into the blazing house. At first no one recognised the figure that darted in after her, then someone called out:

"Frank Turnberry ! . . . It's Frank Turnberry!"

Before anyone could move there came a deafening sound of wrenching and cracking, and the burning house collapsed in a roar of flame and sparks that shot upwards as in a wild dance of triumph.

Chapter Eighteen

LETTICE moved the small white-painted dressing-table from the corner by the wardrobe and put it between the two windows. Then she stepped back to survey the room. Perhaps all this blue and white effect – white-painted bedstead, dressing-table, and wardrobe; blue carpet, bedspread, and eiderdown – was a bit obvious, but it was just the sort of bedroom she had longed for in her own childhood, living among old oak and mahogany, and she felt sure that Susan would love it. . . . She glanced at her watch. There was still plenty of time. . . . She was expecting Susan for tea. Sylvia had pleaded to go and meet her at Beverton Station, and Lettice had been glad to let her. She wanted to be at home to receive her guest. There was an iced cake in the shape of a little cottage for tea and a milk jug in the shape of a cow. . . . For weeks now she had been buying things that she thought would please Susan. She had even got a ginger kitten from Crewe Farm, though she herself rather disliked cats. And Sylvia had that morning brought over her old dolls' house from the Vicarage, with its heterogeneous collection of furniture.

"It wants repapering," she had said. "I'll get some paper in Beverton."

Sylvia had returned from Egypt the week before, and immediately on her return had announced her engagement to Bob Milner.

"It happened the second week," she said, "but I didn't tell you because I thought it might fuss you."

"I suppose that any other parent would have read between the lines," said Mrs. Fanshaw to Lettice. "I'm afraid I've always been particularly inadequate in that relation. . . . He's such a nice stupid boy. . . . I'm sure he'll make her happy."

"But don't think that you can relapse into looking just anyhow when I'm married," Sylvia had warned her sternly. "I shall swoop down on you unexpectedly to make sure that you aren't wearing lisle stockings and odd gloves."

Lettice had taken to Sylvia at once. She was round-faced and rosy-cheeked – kind-hearted, unaffected, and unfailingly good-tempered. Instinctively she took every one around her under her wing, hurrying to Pear Tree Cottages with the ginger kitten for Susan under one arm and a bunch of grapes for Lydia under the other. Lydia's baby, born last week, had been a boy, after all. Lydia was intensely proud of the easy birth and her quick recovery. Her resilient spirits had soon recovered from the ordeal she had undergone on the night of the fire.

"I'm just not going to think about it," she had said afterwards. "It's not the sort of thing that a nice child like Jemima should know anything about."

And later she had said:

"The whole thing was so fantastic that I just can't believe it ever happened."

She and Philip had decided to call the baby James.

"It's a good sound name," she said, "and it doesn't really commit him to anything. If he doesn't turn out a James, there's always Jim or Jimmy to fall back on. Everyone's either a James or a Jim or a Jimmy. And," she added calmly, "I shall have Jemima in two years' time. . . ."

Sylvia and Bob were to be married at Whitsuntide. They had taken a flat in Highgate within easy reach of Bob's work.

"But," said Sylvia, sitting on Lettice's hearthrug and playing with the ginger kitten, "I've got a plan – only you mustn't tell Mummy till it's settled, *if* it's settled – to take Honeysuckle Cottage and keep it just for weekends and the summer holiday. I can't bear the thought of leaving Steffan Green altogether. Then I could go on helping Daddy and Mummy."

"Bossing them, you mean," said Lettice.

"All right," grinned Sylvia, "bossing them. I always thought I'd like to live at Honeysuckle Cottage. I love its thatched roof and green shutters."

"The rooms are rather dark," said Lettice.

"I don't mind. One lives out of doors in the country anyway. I wish I'd seen the Lennare woman before she took to flight. I only just missed her. She took to flight the morning after the fire, didn't she?"

"Yes," said Lettice. "I think she was quite right. She'd never have lived down having her ears boxed by Mrs. Skelton in public. No one would."

"What was she like really?"

"I thought she was hateful."

"Mummy says that she was one of those people who need a Cause. Women getting the vote was the tragedy of her life. She tried Anti-vivisection and Theosophy and Spiritualism, but none of them gave her enough scope, so she ran to seed."

"She'd run to seed all right," said Lettice grimly. "She was horribly out of place in Honeysuckle Cottage. She was definitely fourth-rate Bloomsbury. I'm glad you're going to have it."

"Well, I'm not absolutely sure that we are yet. Ivy and George were going there, you know, but now George has got a chance of one of the lodges at Chart House over at Friars. He would cycle over to his work at Crewe Farm, and Ivy would open the gates and help in the house. He's leaving the decision to Ivy."

Ivy's wedding to George Harker had been one of the great events of the month, though actually Mrs. Skelton, in a large feathered hat and a new coat freely trimmed with imitation leopard skin, had provided a far greater sensation than either bride or bridegroom. Ivy and George were living with her while they looked round for a suitable cottage.

"Which means Mrs. Skelton, I suppose," said Lettice.

"Yes, and I think she'll plump for Chart House. There's nothing of the possessive mother about Mrs. Skelton. She says it's best for Ivy not to live too near her mum."

Lettice straightened the blue coverlet on the white-painted bed and glanced at her watch. No, they wouldn't be here for about half an hour. She imagined Susan arriving at the station alone (officially she was to be in charge of the guard) and stepping down onto the platform, small, grave, shy. . . . Trust Sylvia to see her at once – before that lost bewildered feeling had time to creep over her. She would drive with Sylvia along the wood-bordered road to Steffan Green . . . she would open the little green gate and . . . here she would be, with the blue and white bedroom, the dolls' house, the ginger kitten, and the cake like a tiny house. . . .

She couldn't have told exactly when her decision to put off writing the letter to say she could not have Susan merged into the decision not to write it at all, when the child she might have had merged into the child Susan. . . . She had tried hard to keep them apart, but almost against her will they had gradually become one. The memory of the child she had only seen once had become more and more vivid till it had beaten down all resistance. And Susan had somehow freed her from Harvey. She could see him now as he was – shifty, unreal, a little shop-soiled. The news of the decree absolute and his marriage to Olga had been like news coming from a world in which she had no longer any part. She could even think of him with an exultant sense of freedom.

She had meant to go round to The Moorings this afternoon to see Mrs. Turnberry, but she wouldn't have time now. After Frank's death, Clifford had made no further suggestion of letting The Moorings or taking her to live with him. He had been as tender and considerate as the brusqueness of his manner allowed. And, strangely enough, it was Clifford more than anyone else who had forgotten Frank's faults. From the moment when his charred and blackened body had been found in the ruin of the chalet near to Miss Pendleton's, Frank had become a hero in Clifford's eyes.

"It shows how we all misjudged him," he said, and his memory went back, as Frank's had so often done, to the days of their boyhood when they had been inseparable friends and allies.

"He was always a good chap," he would say. "We all misjudged him. . . ."

Mrs. Turnberry sometimes thought how pleased Frank would

have been if he could have seen Clifford solemnly tending his grave and putting flowers on it. She herself still felt bewildered and shaken. She couldn't believe that Frank had really gone. She missed the constant anxiety that he had caused her, his exasperating presence, his clumsy affection. Rid of the unceasing apprehension as to what trouble he would get into next, she found life empty and meaningless. Even Clifford's sudden cult of his brother's memory seemed to remove Frank further from her, made it impossible that they had ever had those jokes and foolish games together in the kitchen, that she had ever rammed his great rough head into the washing-bowl, laughing at his struggles. But Mrs. Barton at Crewe Cottage was having another baby, and Mrs. Turnberry couldn't resist it. Passing the cottage yesterday, Lettice had heard her hearty laugh ring out – the first time she had heard it since Frank's death.

She went to the window and looked out. The pageant of the year was opening gallantly, with clear skies and brilliant sunshine. Old men sunned themselves on the seat beneath the chestnut on the green. . . . There were drifts of primroses in the hedgerows, and in the woods stout green clusters of leaves guarded the tight-packed bluebell buds.

In the garden outside, the pear tree was covered with blossom like a sea of foam against the blue sky. As she looked at it, her thoughts went back to the first time she had seen it, on that dull October day, its leaves falling drearily through the autumn air. Since then she had seen it leafless, outlined in frost and snow, shrouded in rain and mist, giving heart-stirring flashes of beauty against sunset or moonlit sky . . . but she had not been prepared for this white miracle of loveliness. She tore her eyes away from it and went downstairs to the little garden. The swing hung from a branch beneath the roof of blossom. George had put it up for her yesterday while she was at the Castle. When she came back it was swaying slightly in the breeze as if a ghostly Susan already swung there.

Ever since the night of the fire, Mrs. Ferring had lain there helpless, tended untiringly by old Hannah. She was failing fast, the doctor said, but there was about her a curious atmosphere of quietness and peace, as though her seizure had wiped out the memory of all that had happened before. ... No one knew if she heard what was said to her, and Lettice had wondered whether to tell her of her visit to Lavinia in Paris or not, and had finally decided not to, lest it should break the unearthly calm that seemed to surround her.

It was Mrs. Fanshaw who had urged her to go to Paris.

"She writes cheerful letters, but I want to be *sure*," she said. "I can't go to Paris, but it wouldn't be anything to you. I expect you often went when you lived in London, didn't you?" Lettice nodded. "Well, do go for all our sakes. Just see what sort of a person this stepfather is and if the child's really happy. I shan't have any peace of mind till I know. After all, you're responsible, too, in a way."

It was Lettice who had taken Lavinia back to Pear Tree Cottage after the fire and kept her there till Mrs. Fanshaw received an answer to the letter she had written to Lavinia's mother. The answer was a request that Lavinia should be sent at once to Paris, and Lettice took her to London and saw her off at Croydon aerodrome. She looked lost and unhappy and bewildered, and Lettice was secretly as anxious as was Mrs. Fanshaw to know how she was getting on. And the Lavinia she had met a few weeks later in Paris had done more than calm her fears – a Lavinia whose hollow cheeks were filling out and acquiring a new bloom of health, a Lavinia whose lethargy was changing to a new alertness, a Lavinia happy, lovely, and beloved.

Her stepfather was a tall bearded man with kindly grey eyes and a long humorous mouth. He had obviously taken Lavinia to his heart, and Lavinia already gave him a touchingly shy filial love. Hannah had put her own malicious construction on a sentence of the letter in which Madame d'Assonville asked Mrs. Ferring to keep Lavinia with her for the present. Madame d'Assonville, poised and exquisite, wearing a Worth gown of pale lilac that enhanced her dark beauty and emphasised the long slender lines of her figure, received Lettice in one of the tall spacious houses of the Faubourg St. Germain.

"Lavinia has told me how good you have been to her," she said in her low musical voice. "I am grateful to you. .... I knew that Pierre would learn to love her, of course, but he loved her as soon as he saw her. Already he has been a better father to her than I have ever been a mother. It is not that I have not loved my children, but," she shrugged faintly and threw out her hands in a deprecating little gesture, "things have not been easy for me – till now."

Monsieur d'Assonville, who was a wealthy man, was worried about Lavinia's delicacy and had arranged to take the whole family to Switzerland for the next few months, because the doctor said it would be good for Lavinia's chest.

"Though she is so much better already," said his wife, "that there is no longer need for anxiety. My poor darling!" she sighed. "I am afraid that the régime of my mother-in-law's establishment was too severe for her. Thea is of a different nature."

Thea and her stepfather got on quite well, but she had made so many friends that they fully occupied her spare time. Thea, as ever, took what she wanted with good-humoured carelessness and lived entirely in the present. She was glad to have Lavinia with her.

"Do you remember, Lavvy," she teased her, "how you used to say that if you had a lot of money you'd spend it on coal?"

"Well, I don't care, it *is* lovely to be warm," smiled Lavinia.

For the first time in her life Lavinia was surrounded by an atmosphere of affection and sympathy, and she blossomed in it like a flower in sunshine. She did not mention Colin till she was seeing Lettice off at the Gare du Nord, and then she said suddenly:

"You'll give my love to Colin, won't you?"

Colin came round to Pear Tree Cottages on the night of Lettice's return.

"Did she mention me at all?" he said.

"She sent you her love."

He considered this frowningly.

"She can't bear to hurt people's feelings. .... Was that all?"

"Yes."

He listened to her account of her visit with mingled relief and depression. He was glad to hear that Lavinia was well and happy, but he regretted bitterly not having put things to the test before it was too late – told his mother, bearded the old lady. Better to have made a fight for her than lose her this way. He had told his mother that he meant to marry her if he could, ignoring her reproaches and accusations.

"Going behind my back . . . a stupid chit of a girl . . . what's to happen to me, do you think ? . . . after all I've done for you . . . deceiving and cheating me. . . ."

He had listened in silence, wondering how he could ever have been afraid of her. . . . Then he said shortly:

"Don't talk such nonsense, Mother. I'm my own master. I needn't consult you before marrying."

She checked the stream of reproaches and stared at him, seeing her familiar weapons useless and blunted in her hand. She felt suddenly old and unloved. Tears, of self-pity rose to her eyes.

"It's all right, Mother," he had said awkwardly, "but please don't try to interfere again."

And since then it had been she who had been diffident, propitiatory, anxious to please, terrified of that vision of an unloved old age that had suddenly been opened to her. The boy she had dominated all these years was dead, and she had no rules for dealing with the man who had taken his place. The victory had been so easy that he despised himself for not having joined issues long ago. Suppose he had forced his mother to agree to the engagement . . . suppose he had bearded the old lady and obtained her consent (that was less easy to imagine) . . . he'd have had some claim on her now. As it was there were only a few stolen meetings, a few kisses. . . . She'd probably forgotten all about him. She had been swept away to a world in which he and his like did not exist.

"Monsieur d'Assonville has a house at Juan les Pins," Lettice was saying. "They're going there when they come back from Switzerland."

He continued to stare gloomily in front of him.

"They're grand people," he said at last slowly. "I don't suppose I shall ever see her again. She's probably forgotten all about me by now."

Lettice thought of the steadfastness of Lavinia's dark eyes, of that something untouched and untouchable about her. . . . Any ordinary girl would have forgotten, of course, but Lavinia was not an ordinary girl.

"Well, don't just sit and wait," she said. "Write to her and later on go over and see her. . . . Perhaps she has forgotten, but there's just a chance that she hasn't. Don't make up your mind that she has and sit down under it."

He braced himself, setting his shoulders.

"Thanks," he said. "I will. . . ."

She glanced at her watch again. The train would be in now. Susan would soon be here. . . . She took a vase of polyanthus – salmon, rust red, golden yellow – from the drawing-room and carried it up to the bedroom, trying it first on the dressing-table, then on the chest of drawers, then on the window-sill between the muslin curtains. The window-sill was best, she thought. She remembered that, when she was a child, she had imagined that flowers always liked to be where they could see into the garden. They could talk to their friends and watch everything that went on there. . . . She tried to quell the eager anticipation that filled her heart. It was absurd, she told herself. She had only seen the child once and barely remembered her. But, somehow, she couldn't help feeling as if a new happiness were coming into her life, a happiness deeper and more stable than the old one had ever been.

When she was half-way downstairs, she heard the sound of a taxi drawing up outside, a child's voice, and the ringing of the front door-bell.

She stood still for a few moments, then, with quickly beating heart, went downstairs to open the door.